Courtney
Walt

"In this
Promise and
He will direct "U"
Path."

The Continuing Saga of *The Other Side of Through*...

I
Promise

Cynthia Middlebrooks Harris

T.O.S.O.T. Ministries, LLC
(The Other Side of Through)

Scripture taken from the King James Version of the Bible.

Published by: T.O.S.O.T. The Other Side of Through Ministries, LLC and can be ordered by contacting:

T.O.S.O.T. Ministries, LLC
P.O. Box 565
Waynesville, MO 65583
http://www.tosotministries.org
Email: tosotministries@gmail.com

Available at CreateSpace.com and Amazon.com

Imagery provided by: Cover models Stephanie Harris and 2LT Marvin Ward. Such images are being used for illustrative purposes only. Images are copyrighted and owned by T.O.S.O.T. Ministries, LLC.

ISBN: - 13: 978-1480073036
ISBN: - 10: 978-1480073032

Library of Congress Control Number: 2012919066

T.O.SO.T. Ministries, LLC rev. date: 11/1/2012

Dedicated to:
Caleb Smith and his family.
Ministers Isaac and Tannisha Smith;
Antonio, DeAntre and Aniyah.
You are greatly missed!

Acknowledgments

We are always and forever thankful to our Lord and Savior, Jesus Christ. We thank Him continuously for the gift He has bestowed upon our lives.

Sincere thanks to Dwanda Gossett; for sharing her gracious and excellent gift. I am grateful to her for blessing the ministry with her literary support.

I am sincerely grateful to the cover models. My daughter Stephanie Harris has graced the cover of this work, as well as the first work of the series. And will no doubt, appear on countless others. Special thanks to United States Army 2nd Lieutenant Marvin Ward, for his willingness to accompany Stephanie on the cover by representing the male counterpart.

I would also like to thank Monique Adams; chief editor of *Higher Connection Magazine* for her support of the ministry. She has a most excellent spirit and featured the original work of the series titled, *The Other Side of Through*, in the July/August 2012 issue.

And, to Evangelist Susan Marshall of Still Useable Ministries, who continues to show her support of the work and T.O.S.O.T. Ministries in too many avenues to list. We are forever grateful to her.

The promise is made....

~Chapter One~

No one was more anxious about the reading of the will than Talinda. She had hoped that she would finally get an understanding of exactly what Brandon wanted her to hand deliver to Bernard and why. What could be so important that she, of all people, had to specifically be the one to deliver it to him?

Brandon's parents, her parents and Raymond had all been listed as attendees in the reading. The attorney started out by saying that both sets of grandparents were requested to be in attendance because of the special circumstances of Brandon's request for his family.

To Talinda's surprise Brandon had made major changes to the will they previously had set in place. About six months ago he had taken out a million and a half dollar policy on himself. He left one million dollars to Talinda, which totally floored her and everyone else in the room gasped in disbelief. Upon his death, the insurance paid off the mortgage on the house. He left it up to Talinda as to how she would bless her parents. He also desired that she continue to pursue adopting Raymond. If she were unable to adopt him, Brandon wanted her to continue blessing him as a member of their family and pay for his college education should he choose to attend. Upon completion of college, Raymond would have access to a trust fund in the amount of one hundred fifty thousand dollars.

Before his death, Brandon and Talinda were in the process of trying to convince Raymond's mother to give up her parental rights to make the process easier. Up to that point she had refused. They had considered attempting to prove her an unfit mother; however, Talinda had been reluctant to do that. As much as she wanted to adopt Raymond she had compassion for his mother. She realized that Raymond was everything to her. He was the only thing she had ever accomplished in life, and they were trying to take him away from her. She put herself in his mother's position and convinced both Raymond and Brandon that they should proceed with care and consideration for her feelings. But now the thought of having Raymond permanently warmed her spirit. She and Raymond shared a smile and had a

1

voiceless conversation as the portion of the will that concerned him was disclosed.

She had actually already continued the adoption process with the attorney and had made a consider amount of headway with his mother when she suddenly dropped out of sight.

Brandon left two hundred thousand dollars to his parents, Roger and Helen, and one hundred and fifty thousand to his cousin, Bernard. The package addressed to him contained a personal letter with specific instructions for his eyes only. His inheritance had been transferred directly into his account the day of Brandon's death and had been on hold until the official reading of the will. No one was surprised that Brandon would include Bernard in his will. He was the only brother he had ever known.

"I don't understand," Talinda said as she sits in disbelief. "How could he afford a million and a half dollar insurance policy?"

"That's easy Mrs. Travis," the lawyer answered. "He used his trust fund. Brandon never used his one hundred and fifty thousand dollar trust fund that his grandfather set up for him. It was available to him after graduating college. He invested it, and it has been growing over the last ten years. He used it to pay the premiums on his policy for a year and to set young Raymond's trust fund among, other things, in place."

"So, he knew," Roger managed to say through tears. "He knew something was about to happen to him. Somehow he knew, and he was setting everything in place to take care of Talinda."

Talinda sat in awe as silent tears rolled down her cheeks. Raymond placed his arms around his mother, and she dropped her head on his shoulder. He sat thinking about the conversation he and his father had about six months ago. He wanted so badly to tell everyone, but held true to the promise he had made to his father and remained silent.

At the conclusion of the reading of the will, Talinda was handed an itinerary and a package that said, "To be opened by Bernard Alexander Travis Only". To her surprise her flight would leave Atlanta late in the afternoon the next day. To everyone's disappointment, she would have to reschedule her ultrasound. Despite her size and measurements, her doctor estimated that she was now about three and a half months pregnant. Dr. Harrell didn't note any particular problems, and her pregnancy was developing normally. She ordered an ultrasound simply because her first pregnancy resulted in a stillborn delivery and she was measuring more than average of where she should be considering the timing of her last menstrual cycle.

Talinda already had a passport because she and Brandon were preparing to take the youth on a missionary trip. Brandon included enough traveler's checks to take care of any needs she may have on the trip. She was bewildered as to why the return flight was not scheduled for three weeks let alone the fact that she had been instructed to pack only enough clothes for three days. Bernard is stationed at Ramstein Air Force Base in Kaiserslautern, West Germany. She had hotel reservations at one of the finer hotels in K-town not far from the air base.

The thought of being an instant millionaire had not even registered to Talinda. Her focus was on Bernard and the contents of the package she held in her hands. Her mind raced back to the email she had received from him, and she fought to control her emotions in front of her family. She had to admit she was not only a little confused by everything that had played out today, but she was also excited that she would soon see Bernard again. A thought she instantly felt a twinge of guilt about considering the nature of the reason they were gathered at that point. She was so emotionally cloudy when it came to Bernard. She had a strong attraction to him, but she mostly discounted it to the fact that he was a carbon copy of Brandon.

She also had to admit she was a little frightened about their next encounter as well. She hoped that the contents of the package would bring closure for everyone and let her off the hook emotionally.

"What was Brandon doing?" She thought. There was a gamut of emotions running through her mind as she struggled to stay focused on the present conversations in the room. She thought back to the day of the barbeque when she and Bernard were walking up the driveway to the Travis' house in Athens after seeing the pastor and youth off. She remembers having a very emotional, nostalgic moment about Brandon. But as she looked at Bernard that day as they were walking, she had a sense of future. She felt something she could not put a name or definition to and secretly chastised herself that she had the desire for him to hold her in his arms.

She had to face several things as she sat there in the midst of family conversing. But one thing in particular was that she desired to be in Bernard's presence. She was uncertain as to why because she clearly knew that she was not in love with him. "But....," she thought as her mom tapped her on the shoulder asking if was she okay and letting her know that they were all preparing to leave. She realized she had been totally oblivious to the conversation the family was engaged in. She had been caught up in thoughts of Bernard and had secretly enjoyed them.

On the way home accompanied by her parents, she drove in silence as anticipation riddled inside of her. There was a strange uneasiness about Bernard and the contents of the package Brandon had for him. Raymond had driven his own car to meet them there because he came from an afterschool program.

As she drove she thought one thing was certain: the package would change Bernard's life. But what she didn't realize was that it would change hers as well.

Her father sat beside her in the front seat and pondered all the events of the last few months in his heart. He thought about the love he saw in Bernard's eyes the day he had left to return to Germany after Brandon's funeral. He thought to himself, "Why would Brandon want Talinda to hand deliver the package? Why couldn't it be sent by certified mail with a return receipt? What was Brandon doing, and what was Talinda not saying?"

He turned toward Talinda. "Baby girl, why do you think Brandon changed his will six months ago? I mean don't you think it's strange that you wouldn't know your husband made such major changes to what you and he had previously agreed to? Why would he send you to Bernard and not Helen, Roger or better yet, Bernard's parents themselves? Wouldn't one of them be the more logical choice? I mean, until the viewing before Brandon's funeral, you had never met him face to face. You had spoken with him over the phone a few times, but nothing that would put you in a relationship status enough to hand deliver a letter on Brandon's behalf. Sweetheart is there something that you are not telling mom and dad?"

"Oh honey, leave her alone," Valetta interjected. "Can't you see this was hard for her today? We just left the reading of her husband's will. This was an emotional time for her. Don't badger her about Brandon's demands. She is just as confused about it as everyone else is and..."

"Of course she is," Talinda's father replied. He interrupted her mom in mid-sentence. "I'm sorry princess. How inconsiderate of me."

"That's okay daddy, Talinda replied. I'm sitting here trying desperately to figure out what could by the reasoning behind all this secrecy and strange demands. I guess I'll know tomorrow evening after I get to Germany."

After they arrived at home she decided to call Bernard to inform him of the arrangements that have been made concerning them. He had received the first letter from Brandon's attorney shortly after he had mustered the nerve to email Talinda since he had returned to Germany from the memorial service. He had immediately chastised himself that his timing couldn't have come at a more inappropriate season in both of their lives. But nevertheless, awaited her call with eager anticipation at the notion he would soon hear her voice. He had also already been informed of her flight reservation, and that she would reside at the Lieberitz Hotel.

Talinda asked him if he had any idea what would be so important to Brandon that he would have her to hand deliver it to him all the way to Germany. Bernard assured her that he had no idea, but was told when first contacted by the lawyer a few weeks prior that he was to request a three-week leave while she was in-country.

As he hung up the phone he was somewhat nervous about her upcoming trip because she had not responded to his email as of yet.

4

The anticipation of the contents of the package from Brandon made him extremely nervous, not to mention being un-chaperoned with Talinda for three weeks. "Wow, Brandon certainly had everyone's attention," he thought.

≈

Talinda awoke unusually refreshed the next morning. She could hardly eat because her appetite had all but diminished from the anticipation of the events of the day. She had packed her bag the night before with the three outfits that Brandon had chosen for her to wear. He was very specific with his demands, which had everyone bewildered. She wouldn't have any luggage to check because everything she was instructed to pack fit into a carry-on back pack.

She was instructed not to take her laptop with her, which she had no intentions of doing in the first place. She was also told to take her birth certificate. She was unsure as to why but figured it must have something to do with regulations for international flights.

"Why in the world would he want me to take that old grey sweat suit? It's eighty-five degrees outside," she pondered as she walked into the bathroom. Her flight wasn't scheduled to leave until 4 p.m. and she laughed at herself for being up at 6 a.m. She realized that she was more than eager to see Bernard again. She showered, dressed and was headed downstairs by 8 am.

Talinda had a very uneasy feeling about Raymond's mother's sudden and complete disappearance. Raymond seemed to take it in stride. She often disappeared for an extended amount of time and so this was considered normal behavior for her. Talinda was relieved that he would stay at the house during her trip to Germany. She wouldn't have to worry about him while she was gone. Helen and Roger would also check on him from time to time and have him in Athens with them on the weekends once her parents returned to Virginia. She decided she would drive herself to the airport today and leave her car parked there in case Raymond was unavailable to pick her up when she returned.

Valetta had also risen early to prepare breakfast and addressed Talinda when she entered the kitchen. Her father and Raymond, however, were still in bed. "Okay now, do you have everything dear...your passport, identification and the package for Bernard?"

"Yes," she replied. "I'm so nervous about meeting Bernard again."

"I know you are, dear. I sensed there was something between you two for a while now," Valetta said as she gave her a slight one arm hug.

Talinda looked at her mother in surprise and replied, "But mom last night in the car with dad you..."

"I know dear," Valetta interjected. "I could tell you didn't want to talk about it. I could see the confusion on your face and that your emotions were somewhat aloof."

"I need to show you something mom," Talinda said as she walked over to the computer and opened the email from Bernard.

Valetta read it very slowly and carefully. When she had finished she turned toward Talinda, who sat nervously and watched her mother read the very intimate letter and awaited her response and guidance in the matter.

She cleared her throat and said, "Mmmmm....well I must confess, dear, I am not totally surprised by his letter. Although I wasn't aware of how strong his feelings were for you, I sensed something with him during Brandon's funeral. But with everybody's emotions all over the place I dismissed it. If you don't mind my asking, what does he mean by "the night on the Travis' deck"? Sweetheart if it's too personal you do not have to answer."

"No mom I don't mind at all," Talinda responded. She proceeded to tell her mother of the night she shared with Brandon through Bernard. She also shared some of the other close moments that she and Bernard shared throughout the weekend. She desperately wanted her mother's insight on how she should proceed with this matter.

Valetta placed her hand on Talinda's shoulder and guided her over to sit at the counter so they could eat as they continued the conversation.

As they sat down Talinda asked her mother with tears that now formed in her eyes, "Mom...what is Brandon doing? I'm a little scared because I have no idea what to expect. I mean, Bernard alluded in the latter part of his email that he had gotten his emotions under control concerning me, but I am wondering if that was just a matter of geography. I mean...you know...like...I'm not there with him so..." She sighed and dropped her head in her hands and said through tears, "Mom I have to admit...Bernard wasn't the only one who had struggled with his feelings that weekend."

Valetta sat in silence. She wanted to let Talinda say everything that was on her heart. She had wondered over the last few months what was weighing so heavily on her. She hadn't chalked it all up to grief because she knew what that looked like first hand. She saw something else there but had not been sure exactly what it was. Now the picture was beginning to make more sense.

Talinda continued still teary-eyed, "Mom I wanted...I mean he is so much like Brandon...and my emotions were everywhere when he was close to me...I found myself wanting to be near him. I thought it was because he was so much like Brandon, and I was using him to have a part...any part of Brandon that I could get. But when he held me at the airport before he left there was something different." She paused again, unsure if she should continue. She wondered what her mother would think of her. But despite her apprehension to expose her intimate thoughts, she continued.

"I mean, he offered his hand as he said goodbye, but I insisted on a hug instead. Mom...I found myself wanting him to kiss me, partly because of what God had done on the deck at the Travis'. I thought maybe it would feel like Brandon's kiss. But then I had to be honest with myself and admit I wanted to be loved...I needed to be loved.

Mom, it was just like you said when we were all at the house the night before Brandon's viewing. While we were going through the pictures of George and Daniel, you said you knew you were created to be a wife. That was all you knew how to be. I feel the same way. Mom, I just don't know how to turn it off. I'm a wife...and that's all I have ever wanted to be. The truth is I am afraid to go and spend time with Bernard. I am afraid of where my feelings and desires to be a wife will take me. I'm feeling so guilty that I could even be remotely considering that any man could ever take Brandon's place. Brandon has only been dead a few months, not to mention I am carrying his baby. I should be grieving mom... you know? I had to admit to myself if no one else...that day I wanted him to just kiss me with a passion that a man has for his wife. I scolded myself inside for feeling that way. I'm scared mom. I have to go give him a letter from his cousin that is so serious and intense that he wants it hand delivered to him. Whatever it is, is so sensitive that he didn't want his family there when Bernard read it. Oh mom I just feel so..."

Valetta reached out and touched her arm to get her attention while she reached up with her other hand and wiped the tears that had formed and fell from her baby girls eyes as she responded. "Sweetheart...I know exactly how you feel. Your loyalty to Brandon has your emotions catapulting all over the place. To top it off, your hormones are already at an all-time high because of the pregnancy. But dear listen to me. You don't have to be ashamed of the way God created you. I have always prided myself on being a good loving wife. Some people do well alone after the death of a spouse. Others don't. Some women have a false sense of humility. They say that no man can ever replace their late husbands. They spend an exuberant amount of time trying to prove to everyone that their love with that one particular man was so powerful that no one else could ever measure up to the love they shared. Well that's just a bunch of baloney dear.

When you understand love the way you have been taught you realize it is not limited. And having the desire to be loved and give love doesn't negate the love you had with an ex-spouse. Nor does it say I've forgotten about him or he doesn't matter to me anymore. We have placed a time factor on grieving that makes people feel guilty when they want to move on in life quickly after the death of a loved one. Talinda this is going to be a very challenging time for you. You're going to have to sort through your emotions to see which ones are genuine and which ones are hormonally driven. I believe you know what you were feeling for Bernard, and it scares you because he just happens to be another member of the Travis family. He was very close to your husband and that has you feeling like you are betraying Brandon or cheating on him in some way.

Sweetheart Bernard may be very sincere in his declaration that he has gotten his emotions under control. Then again, he could only be trying to convince himself that there is nothing there. He is probably feeling the same guilt that you are. Not to mention he's wondering what Brandon's parents will think of his feelings toward you. Talinda, take into consideration that the contents of that envelope from Brandon to him could put an end to all your anxiety...or..." she continued as she walked over to the sink and proceeded to rinse their breakfast dishes, "...it could add to it. In fact it could make an already delicate situation even more delicate. But whatever the matter sweetie, you're going to have to put your fears aside and board that plane bound for Frankfurt Germany today. This is an assignment that you are not going to be able to get out of. So just pray, relax, and let God take care of everything."

Talinda was comforted by her mother's words. She seemed to be inside her head and emotions. "Truly," she half smiled as she thought. "Your trials are most definitely for someone else and not about you." Her mother's tragedy had ministered to her on so many levels these last few months. She cherished the closeness that they had formed together and regretted that she had not allowed her mother to be a strong part of her life. "Uhmmm...the things I could have learned from her," she thought as she sat mulling over the words her mother had just spoken.

"Oh my, look at the time", Valetta said as she glanced at the clock. "Talinda, we have been talking for three hours. It's now 11 a.m. You need to get checked in two hours prior to boarding for international flights. You know with the city traffic it just might take you an hour to get to the airport. Now are you sure you don't want us and Raymond to accompany you to the airport? We can..."

Talinda cut her off, "No mom I'll be fine. Besides my flight doesn't start boarding until 3 p.m. and doesn't take off until 4 p.m. By the time I get there, park, take the shuttle to my terminal, and get all checked in I'll still have time for lunch before boarding. Besides, you guys would be stuck in lunch time traffic coming back home. I'm just going to spend a little time with Raymond and dad and then I'll be on my way."

"Okay dear," Valetta agreed. "Hey, make sure you remember the package and keep it in the back pack and with you at all times. Something tells me that envelope holds more than just Bernard's future in it."

"I'm beginning to believe that as well," Talinda said as she rose from the table. "Oh mom...," she said as she gave her an 'I'm going to miss you so much' squeeze, "...I am so grateful for you. Thank you for

8

understanding me better that I understand myself. I am so blessed to have you as my mother. I love you."

"Good morning mom. Good morning grandma," Raymond said as he entered the kitchen. There wasn't any school today so he and grandpa had watched movies well into the wee hours of the morning. He hugged and kissed Talinda and Valetta good morning.

"Well good morning you two sleepy heads," Talinda replied. "I thought I was going to have to come pull you two out of bed to get my good bye hugs and kisses from you."

"Oh, princess you know we wouldn't miss sending off our favorite girl...right Raymond?" Victor said as he descended from upstairs simultaneously as Raymond entered.

Raymond turned toward Talinda and said, "Be sure to tell Bernard we all said hello. Are you leaving right now, mom?"

"Well in about an hour or so. I don't want to be rushing around trying to figure things out at the last minute," she replied. "You have to go through extra security to get checked in when going overseas so I'm going to give myself plenty of time. And before you say it, I'm still driving myself. I'll be fine everyone."

About an hour later they exchange their goodbyes and Raymond walked Talinda out to the car. He gave her another big hug as he expressed how much he loved her and will miss her. She thanked him for taking her parents to the airport the next day as she was getting into the car. He stood waving and watched as the car drove out of sight before returning into the house.

≈

Talinda had time to grab a couple of magazines before she boarded but decided she would read her bible when she wasn't sleeping. Something told her she would need scripture more than entertainment news during her tenure in the old country with Bernard. As she sat on the plane and listened to the preflight instructions she thought of the conversation she had with her mother that morning. She thought of Brandon and all the events that had unfolded thus far.

She then looked at the envelope and realized the warm sensation she usually felt when she thought of Brandon had been solicited by the thought of Bernard just now. She had hoped she would sleep for the majority of the trip so she wouldn't think herself into a frenzy concerning Brandon, Bernard and the contents of the package. Some of her fears turned to excitement as she realized that all her answers were only nine hours away. Soon after the flight took off and some of her jitters had subsided the effects of rising so early took its toll on her, and she drifted off to sleep.

~Chapter Two~

Nevette woke up to Justice propped up on one shoulder and slightly hovered over her. He played in her hair while he stared at her. She smiled as her vision came into focus and she realized that the night before indeed was reality and not a dream. She was really married to an awesome man of God and had spent her wedding night learning from him how to satisfy and share sweet love with him.

"Heeyyy...good morning, what are you doing?" Nevette asked in a daddy's little girl sleepy voice.

Justice replied in a very sexy voice as his fingers glided ever so softly across her face, "Good morning Mrs. Goodfellow. I'm watching you sleep...and thanking God for blessing and loving me so much. You are so beautiful."

She reached up and gently caressed his face and said, "I never imagined it would be possible to be so happy, satisfied and complete. I waited and God blessed me with a man of honor, valor and integrity. I love you so much Justice. I have more love for you than any one woman should be allowed to have for a man. God is so good to grant such and awesome gift between a man and a woman...love. A love that's emotional, physical and spiritual."

"Hmmm," he sighed with a smile as he looked deep into her eyes. "When I first saw you, I prayed to God and asked him if he would give you to me. He answered me and granted my petition. Baby, no words on this side of creation could even remotely describe what I am feeling right now. I love you so much."

She pulled him down to kiss her. She gently began to caress his body and send a subtle but powerful message to him...make love to me.

"Sweetheart," he smiled. He fully understood her non-verbal request but pulled away from her slightly. "I still have a special delivery for you. The service desk is probably waiting for me to call them. Not to mention we have a flight to catch to Miami, which leaves in just a few hours and..."

"And we're going to miss it," she said softly as she kissed him and pulled him back down to her.

"Mmmmm...we most definitely are," he said with a sexy chuckle as he responded to her touch and request for love.

Hours later as she lay in his arms, he kissed her forehead and said, "Well Mrs. Goodfellow, as much as I would love to stay right here forever we have to get the rest of our honeymoon going."

Suddenly in a panic she sat up. "Oh, my God...oh, God please tell me I did not do this. I did not do this! Oh, God, Justice!"

Justice sat up in response to her alarm and said, "What! What is it Naythia?"

She answered still in panic mode, "Oh, God! Derrick I'm sorry. God tell me I did not do this...I did not do this. I FORGOT...I FORGOT!"

"You forgot what baby? Naythia what's wrong? He asked, beginning to get a little panicked himself.

"Oh God...I...I...," she replied almost in tears now.

Derrick turned her toward him and said, "What Naythia?"

"Lindsay told me and I forgot...I never..." Nevette exclaimed.

"What Naythia? What is it baby?" Justice continued to ask.

"I never...ugh...I never got on birth control. I mean I was a virgin...there was never any need. Lindsay reminded me...SHE REMINDED ME...and I still forgot...I was so caught up in getting everything right for the wedding...I meant to, Justice I really did, I just...Justice I'm so sorry..." she said in tears now.

"Baby, is that all?" He chuckled as he coaxed her back on the bed once again hovered over her. "You had me scared that something was wrong."

She looked at him in total surprise of his reaction. "Justice, what do you mean is that all? We made love all night and half the morning...unprotected love Justice."

"Sweetheart," he replied. He smiled as he kissed her again. "There is no such thing as unprotected love in a marriage." He chuckled again and said, "No such thing. Mmmmm...thank you, God."

"Thank you, God?" she responded totally confused. "What do you mean thank you God?"

He continued to give her light kisses as he explained himself. "It's been my prayer since I gave my life to the Lord and He showed me that you would be my wife that on our wedding night you would conceive our first baby."

"What?" She replied with an expression of bewilderment on her face.

"Yeah," he chuckled again. "That's been my prayer. Oh, God, thank you."

"Justice...," she called his name.

"What baby?" he answered.

She responded with a half sigh, half chuckle, "Ahhh, I don't want to be a mommy yet. I want to learn how to be a wife first."

He looked at her and smiled. He shook his head and said, "Oh baby you already know how to be a wife. Look, you already have a job, and I start graduate school. We don't have to wait to start a family. Listen sweetheart. When we get back from our honeymoon we were going to go house hunting anyway."

"Derrick...," she started to say but he cut her off.

"Listen, Naythia. Hear me out baby," he said. He became very serious. "My dad's a lawyer and my mom is a pediatrician. Yogi and I both have trust funds in the amount of $250,000.00 that our parents put in place the day each of us was born. They become ours the day we graduate from college. There are no stipulations on them whatsoever. No strings attached and no catches as long as we graduated from college. We just have to discuss with our parents what our plans are for the funds. But the ultimate choice is ours to do whatever. I talked to my parents already about purchasing a home for my wife and myself. And I guess now for our baby as well. They agreed because even though I haven't started graduate school, I have my undergraduate degree."

"Derrick," she replied.

"What sweetheart," he responded.

"It's amazing how God works. You know when I was younger I was going to get on birth control because I had very irregular cycles. But I remember my mother telling me that if I got an exam the instrument used to retrieve the cells from your cervix would break my hymen and it would be like I wasn't a virgin anymore. I just couldn't do it. I wanted my husband to...I mean...I didn't want keep myself for my husband and then have my virginity stolen by a well-woman exam. I wanted us both to experience the ultimate wedding night consummation. So I never did...I..."

"Oh baby I'm so glad you didn't," he said. He smiled as he continued to shower her with gentle kisses. "Look we're going to enjoy the rest of our honeymoon so relax Naythia okay."

"Lindsay reminded me," she smiled as she thought about the conversation. "She said to make sure I grabbed 'a ton' of condoms. So I wouldn't get pregnant on my wedding night and then I could go for an exam when I got back. You know Lindsay...she is something else. "

"No baby Lindsay is just real," he said humorously. He shook his head as he thought about some of the conversations he had with her about Nevette and the wedding night. "Besides, there is no way that you were going to get me to wear a condom with my virgin wife on my wedding night ....uhnn uhnnnn that was not going to happen baby."

"Justice," she said with a light laugh. "Well I guess we'll know soon enough. I'm due to cycle in about seven days, and I was upset that it was going to put a damper on our honeymoon. Maybe I'm not pregnant."

"Naythia...baby...it only takes one time," he replied with a sexy chuckle.

"Yeah," she said half laughing, "That's what my mom always used to say.

"Ah yeah and we've exceeded the one time barrier," he noted. He still kissed her ever so lightly.

"Oh Justice," she said as she shook her head with a blissful sigh.

"Mmmmm...little junior is probably in there now baby. So relax and enjoy the rest of your honeymoon and your husband because you are probably already pregnant," Justice replied.

She exclaimed as though she has just received some great revelation, "You know Justice, maybe I'm not. We can still go buy some..."

"Naythia I am NOT using a condom with my wife," he said in a joking tone but with conviction. "You know, ideally I would love for you to stay home and not work. You know you don't have to baby. Financially we'll be very stable. My dad's law firm pays very well, and I'll receive income while I'm in grad school working with them as an intern. But, baby, I do understand. You've gone to college and you have a career, and I would never deny you of that. But baby if at any time you get tired and you want to walk away...realize that you can. You don't ever have to work if you don't want to. But if you decide to work, which I get the feeling that you are, we'll have to choose our sitter carefully because I want my wife's and my values instilled in our children. Besides, with grandma being a pediatrician some values will be forced on us so we won't have a choice in that."

She chuckled, "No, we won't."

"You know she's delivered a few babies too," he added.

"Really," Nevette replied.

"Yeah she has. She's a pediatrician and that was not her intention but...uhmm in her internship they got the opportunity to deliver a few babies, so if push comes to shove she is available."

"Oh, Justice I would love for her to deliver our babies. That would be so perfect," Nevette replied. She was elated at the mere thought of it.

"That would be the highlight of my mom's career and life. To deliver and be the pediatrician for all her grandchildren," he said. He chuckled and slightly shook his head with his response.

"Oh Justice this is going to be such a wonderful life," she said as she readjusted herself underneath him.

"It already is baby...it already is," he replied. His light kisses turned into kisses of passion and the room was soon full of the sound of love.

~Chapter Three~

"Okay Mrs. Goodfellow, we have got to move forward here so get your robe on baby because I have something for you before we leave. We missed three flights yesterday. We have to catch this flight today. The rest of your honeymoon is waiting for you, and it starts in Miami. So we are going to catch this flight Mrs. Goodfellow...okay," Justice said as he called the service desk.

"Derrick, what did you do?" She asked with anticipation.

"You'll see in a few minutes," he said with a smile.

"Okay, Justice, what is this," Nevette asked as a wardrobe closet was wheeled into the hotel suite.

He smiled at her anticipation. He then told her, "Go ahead baby open it up."

She approached, almost afraid to see what was behind the closet doors. She opened the closet to a beautiful array of six ball gowns with shoe that matched. There were casual outfits as well. She also had five swimsuits and ten sets of very exotic but elegant lingerie.

"Oh my gosh Justice," she exclaimed.

"Well baby, you have to have something to wear in the Bahamas on the beaches and we have formal dinners to go to on the cruise ship..." he said. "And of course you'll need formal wear when we're having dinner in Paris."

"Oh my God, Justice," she screamed in delight. "The Bahamas...Paris are you serious?!"

"That's not all baby," he said as he walked over to the closet. "You have to have accessories to go with those ball gowns. My mom suggested diamonds and pearls, so I got you one of each." He held the box out for her to open. Inside held one each, beautiful diamond and pearl necklaces, tennis bracelets and earrings to match.

She just started to cry, "Oh Justice."

"Oh baby don't cry," he said as he pulled her into his arms.

14

"I'm okay I'm just overwhelmed," she replied. She wiped her tears and said with a teasing and amused tone, "Ten negligées Justice?"

"Well, yeah. Between Bahamas and Paris that should give you one for each night," he said laughing as he threw her a sexy smile. "My mom helped me pick everything out...well almost everything. She said she thought she had your taste figured out."

"She sure does! I love it," Nevette said, still in tears. "I love everything. This is so awesome! Oh, Justice."

"I love you baby," he declared. He kissed her lightly and stroked her face with the back of his hand.

≈

The two day cruise to the Bahamas was a fun-filled, action packed forty-eight hours. They enjoyed every moment and took advantage of everything the ship had to offer. Nevette was having the time of her life

"Wow, it's so beautiful here," Nevette exclaimed as they checked into their hotel in the Bahamas. "I'm looking forward to the next five days."

"Yeah me too baby," Justice replied. "Why don't we get unpacked and hit the beach?"

They started to unpack everything. Justice held up a swimsuit and gave it to Nevette for her to go change into while he finished unpacking. Still being a little nervous to undress around her husband, she scrambled off to the bathroom to change. Justice simply shook his head and smiled as he continued unpacking. He changed into his swim trunks while he was waiting on her.

"So, what do you think?" Nevette said as she made her grand entrance donning a one-piece bathing suit.

"Beautiful," Justice said as he kissed her and handed her a glass of nonalcoholic wine he had just poured for them while he waited for her to emerge from the bathroom.

"Are you sure that I don't need to wear a t-shirt because this thing you bought to go with it is completely see-through Justice, and everyone will see my swimsuit," she said shyly.

"Baby, it's a one piece," he chuckled. "That's why I didn't even dare get you a bikini. The mesh cover is supposed to be see-through sweetheart. It's just for show."

She sighed and said, "Everybody will be looking at me."

"Yeah they probably will. You're beautiful...but I'm the only one coming home with you," he said with a smile.

"Justice...okay...all right...I can do this," she replied as she took a deep breath.

"You're so innocent," he declared. He shook his head and smiled as he approached her.

"Well, I'm sheltered okay," she said with a school girl laugh. "But I'm learning."

"Yeah you are baby," he said as he pulled her into his arms and kissed her.

"I love you so much Justice," she said as she looked deep into his eyes. "I'm so glad that I have the parents and family that I have. I'm so glad that they instilled the values that they did because this is so awesome. Every girl should experience a wedding, wedding night and honeymoon like this with a husband like you."

"I love you too baby," he replied and kissed her again. "Okay lets head out to the beach."

"Ahhh...you're going with those on. Every woman on the beach won't be able to keep her eyes off you," she said in a jealous but playful tone. He had on brief style swim trunks and a matching male style mesh t-shirt like the one Nevette had on.

"Yeah, but they're not coming back to the room with me you are," he declared.

"Oh Justice," she laughed out.

"Come on baby, the beach is waiting," Justice said. He smiled and grabbed her by the hand and they headed out to the beach for a fun filled day.

$$\approx$$

Even though she had gone way past time for her cycle and the honeymoon drew to a close, the pregnancy test she took in the hotel bathroom that morning was inconclusive. But the fact that she couldn't keep down the dinner from the night before told a different story.

"Are you okay, Naythia?" a very nervous Justice asked her as she emerged from the bathroom. Before she could give him an answer she bolted back toward the bathroom again.

They had enjoyed the Bahamas and Paris was just exquisite. They had toured and experienced every romantic spot that Paris had to offer. Her honeymoon had been all she ever dreamed it would be. They were due to fly back to Atlanta in a few hours and Derrick was beginning to wonder if his wife would be able to tolerate the motion of the plane. Morning sickness hit her hard. Although he felt sorry for his wife in her nauseous state, Derrick couldn't help but be excited that she had experienced morning sickness that day.

They decided to wait until they returned home to schedule an appointment and get a blood test done before they shared the news with the rest of the family.

"Oh baby I'm so happy and so sorry at the same time," Derrick said as he hugged her after her second trip to the bathroom.

"I think I might be okay now Justice," she said as she held her head and her stomach. "I shouldn't have anything left to throw up."

"Oh, sweetheart I'm going to feel bad every day that you're sick," he said very sincerely.

"No you're not, Justice, you're happy that I'm sick and you know it," she said sarcastically. "Because you know this probably means that I'm pregnant."

"Well, not necessarily Naythia. It could be food poisoning," he said I an attempt to encourage her.

"We ate the same thing last night Justice. I'm pregnant and you know it. So don't sit there pretending that you're not excited that I'm heaving my guts out," she said as she once again bolted off to the bathroom. He walked over to the door of the bathroom.

"Well baby, look at the bright side, we'll know exactly when you conceived. That will make it easy for the doctor as far as a due date is concerned," he said and sported that sexy smile of his. He realized by the look on her face that she wasn't the least bit amused by the comment. So, he decided that he would quit while he was ahead.

He walked over to her and said, "Come here, baby. Let me pray for you."

"I don't know, Justice," she said in between throwing up. "I don't know if I want you praying for me. God gives you exactly what you pray for, and you may get the crazy notion to pray for twins or triplets or something."

"Now, there's an idea," he said and laughed. "Wow, two or three boys at one time! Just kidding baby...just kidding. I wouldn't do that to you, although my mom would love it."

He laid his hands on her and began to pray:

Father

> *We come before you in the name of Jesus. We thank you for the many blessings You have bestowed upon our union thus far. Lord, I thank you for blessing my wife in conception. Father I pray that you will shorten her time of morning sickness, ease the nausea and give her a steady system. Father, as I lay my hands upon her stomach I pray for a healthy child that will wax strong in You; a child that will be both a blessing to his parents and all who encounter him Lord. I pray for an uneventful pregnancy filled with joy for the coming addition to the Goodfellow household. Father, give me the wisdom in caring for my pregnant wife. Teach me how to keep her comforted during this stressful time on her body. Truly child bearing is a serious matter for a woman and I pray God that you will protect and preserve the life of my wife and our child. Father, we love You and we trust You with all that we have. Father, as we are about to embark upon an extremely long flight back to the United States, I*

pray that You will strengthen her system Lord; that the nausea she is feeling will dissipate and she will have a pleasant and peaceful flight home God. I love you God, and I thank You for granting my petition concerning my wife. Lord, we thank you for being with us throughout our honeymoon and we look forward to a full and abundantly blessed life with you God. Thank you, Jesus, for being Lord of our life and sacrificing yourself for us. We love you.

In Jesus' name,

Amen

Nevette could feel the nausea easing as her husband prayed for her. Tears rolled down her face as she felt the power of God enter the room and overshadow her husband with authority as he prayed for her and their baby. A new found excitement overtook her, and she began to praise God through tears of joy.

~Chapter Four~

Talinda hadn't taken into consideration the huge differences she would encounter at a foreign airport. As she disembarked the plane, she had no idea where to go so she just followed the crowd out of the terminal area. As she passed through security she realized that she and Bernard had not set up a rendezvous point. So she stood there, a minority in more ways than one, completely lost.

She pulled out her cell phone to call Bernard so they could find each other. But to her surprise and alarm she could not get through to him. She had not considered that she did not have an international plan and her cell phone wouldn't work properly overseas. Just when she was about to burst into tears she felt a tap on her shoulder. She heard a familiar and very sexy voice say, "Excuse me ma'am. You look a little lost. Can I help you find someone?"

She turned around and instinctively jumped into Bernard's arms, relieved that he had found her.

"Hey, are you okay Talinda?" Bernard inquired. He felt her alarm and saw that she was close to tears.

"I'm fine now," she said as they released their embrace. She felt instant relief because of her rescue she talked a mile a minute as she explained to Bernard the origin of her alarm. "MY PHONE DIDN'T WORK AND THEN I REALIZED WE NEVER SAID WHERE WE WHERE GOING TO MEET. THERE WERE SO MANY LANGUAGES GOING ON. AND THE ATMOSPHERE WAS IN SUCH A FRENZY. A MILLION PEOPLE ARE ALL GOING IN A MILLION DIFFERENT DIRECTIONS. AND I WAS GETTING JUST A LITTLE OVERWHELMED. WELL, MAYBE MORE THAN JUST A LITTLE. I WAS JUST ABOUT TO LOSE IT WHEN YOU FOUND ME. HOW DID YOU FIND ME?"

"Whoa, slow down Talinda," he said. He forced himself not to look deep into her eyes and send any confusing or intimate non-verbal communication as he spoke. "I figured you wouldn't wander too far from the security check point. So I thought if I missed you here then I would go to the baggage claim area because you were bound to be at one of the two places. Speaking of which, we better get over there now to secure your luggage."

"Ahhh, there's no need," she smiled as she took her pack back off her shoulder. "This is it."

"What," he inquired with a surprised look as he took the pack from her to carry. "So, I gather you're not staying for three weeks after all?"

She let out a chuckle and a sigh as she replied, "According to the instructions, this is all I was supposed to bring with me."

He looked at her with a somewhat confused expression. She responded with a sigh, "Brandon...need I say more?"

He smiled as he placed his hand in the middle of her back to escort her out to the car. As they reach the car, she took the envelope out of her back pack before he threw it into the back seat and said as she handed it to him, "Here Mr. Travis, this is for you. Now could you please open it? The suspense has been almost too much for me to handle."

"Sorry, I can't," he replied.

Talinda, in total attack mode said, "What! What do you mean you can't? You mean to tell me I came all the way over here to...?"

Bernard interrupted her as he is opened the car door for her, "Excuse me Mrs. Travis...now calm down and let me finish. I can't open it here. My instructions are to get you straight to your hotel so you can relax and open the envelope there."

"Sorry," she replied as she hunched her shoulders with a baby girl apologetic smile that melted his heart completely.

He smiled as he shook his head in amusement and closed her car door. After he got in the driver side he handed her his phone so she could call everyone at home to let them know she had arrived safely. She thanked him and proceeded to make the phone calls. Not wanting to answer a lot of questions she was relieved that she got everyone's answering machines. Bernard reminded her that the time difference was the reason they were probably unreachable.

As they drove along she was very surprised by the German scenery and expressed how she thought it would be like an Old World type country. Bernard assured her that there were areas like that in country, but Frankfurt was very modern.

Ramstein was about 80 miles southwest of Frankfurt. The Lieberitz Hotel wasn't very far from the airbase in Kaiserslautern, commonly known as K-town. It took them about an hour and a half to get there from Frankfurt. They were both somewhat nervous and, to her relief, they enjoyed general conversation. They intentionally stayed away from conversation about the contents of the package. He told her all about Germany. They talked about the sights seen along the way and he began to fill her in on some of the history of the country.

As they pulled into the parking lot the phone rang. It was Helen returning her call. Talinda assured her that she and the baby were fine and she would call back later in the day after she got settled. She said goodbye to Helen because she could Raymond number had appeared on the caller ID. He had returned her call as well.

"Hi Mom, I guess since you called me from Bernard's phone, that means you're there safe and sound huh," Raymond addressed her.

Talinda replied with excitement that surprised her and Bernard as well. "Yes son. My knight in shining armor rescued me from the Frankfurt airport!" She said has she looked at Bernard with a huge flirty smile on her face. "I was about to lose it when he found me...okay don't drive your grandmother crazy...I know, I know...okay sweetie I'll call you later...yes, I'll take lots of pictures...okay I'll tell him...oooh I'm going to miss you too sweetheart...okay no girls...I mean it Raymond...okay sweetie love you too...goodbye."

Bernard laughed as he said to Talinda, "Ahhh, I hate to burst your bubble. But if you just left a seventeen year old boy home by himself, unsupervised for three weeks and told him "no girls" from half way around the world......"

She interrupted, "Oh no, pastor is there. Mom and dad will check in on him from Athens, and he will be with them on the weekends."

"Oh, okay," Bernard replied. "By the way, how is the adoption process going with Raymond?"

She smiled as she replied, "It was actually going pretty good, then Raymond's mom performed another one of her disappearing acts. Although this time it seemed different and I'm a little worried about her. But he doesn't seem to be effected. To him Brandon was dad, I'm mom and Helen, Roger and my parents are grandparents. Believe me when I say, he exercises all his rights as a grandchild with them and they all love it. He has already claimed his dad's room at the Travis' in Athens when he leaves for college in two years."

"Two years..." Bernard said in curiosity.

Talinda slightly cut him off, "He is just going to be a junior this next school year coming up. He spent most of his time on the street when he was fifteen, so he missed almost the entire tenth grade year of school. So when school starts in August he'll be a junior instead of a senior. But he's okay with it. He's not ready to leave home yet and I'm not ready for him to leave me in the house all alone either."

"Oh I see," Bernard responded. "That's the year he ran into Brandon and was all caught up into the Knights. Well," Bernard said with a sly smile, "He definitely is acting like a Travis man. We all had grandparents wrapped and tangled up around our little fingers. There was always a shortage of grandchildren. The Travis men and women all seemed to have a trend of just having one child. I will certainly pray that everything works out with his mother."

"Well I guess Brandon and I broke that trend," Talinda said with a smile. "I have Raymond and little Brandon Jr. on the way."

They laughed as they got out of the car and proceeded into the hotel. As they reached the reception desk the hotel clerk inquired how he could be of assistance to them. "Yes, sir," Bernard replied. "You should have a reservation for Mrs. Talinda Travis."

The clerk spelled out T-A-L-I-N-D-A Travis as he typed it into the computer and quickly found the reservation. "Yes, here we are...Mr. and Mrs. Travis in the penthouse suite. I see you'll be with us for three weeks. Well we hope that you both will find everything to your satisfaction. You are in the family penthouse that features a master suite, and an office that doubles as a second bedroom. There is also a living room and dining area."

Bernard held up a hand to tell the clerk that there must be a mistake in the reservation. It should be for Mrs. Travis only. Talinda put her hand on his shoulder and told the clerk, "Thank you, I'm sure we will be fine...just fine."

Bernard, in full protest mode, said to her, "But Talinda..."

"Shhhh...Bernard," she said again gently as she nudged him. "It doesn't matter. If that is the reservation in the computer, then that is what was arranged for me."

Bernard relinquished his protest as they followed the bellman up to the room. He was so relieved he didn't have a lot of luggage to cart up that he never even inquired as to why they would be in country for three weeks with no luggage.

After the tour of the penthouse, he left them with his card and informed them he would be their personal caregiver should they need anything during their stay at the hotel. Bernard walked over to the living room area and sat down as he proceeded to open the package. As he opened the envelope, the first words threw him somewhat and he was glad that Talinda was attending to the bellman. She thanked, tipped, and assuring him that they were fine for the moment.

She now turned her attention to Bernard, who sat on the living room couch with a puzzled look on his face. He had already begun to read the contents of the envelope.

Talinda sat in the chair adjacent to the couch with her head in her hands and rested her elbows on her thighs as she watched in silence and anticipation for his exposure of what was in the mysterious package. Not to mention her anxiety with all of the secrecy and strange requests Brandon had made of her.

Bernard,

Please read the first paragraph of this letter in silence. I know this will be difficult for you to do. Talinda is no doubt staring at you with a look of anticipation on her face. I'm sure the contents of this package have everyone in an uproar by now.

He paused and smiled. He looked up at Talinda and marveled at how well Brandon knew his wife. He lowered his eyes without saying a word and continued to read.

> *This package contains three envelopes, Bernard. Letter number one is for and addressed to you, and the second is to Talinda. Letter three is for you as well. Do not let Talinda know about the other letter. It is for you to open alone according to the date written on the back of it. It contains very specific instructions for you and Talinda during her stay in Germany. You may read the remainder of the letter out loud now so Talinda can hear it. She will think nothing of it, assuming that you have read it through first and are now reading it again from the beginning.*

Bernard was dumbfounded already by Brandon's strange sequence as to how the events would unfold over the next three weeks. He hoped Talinda couldn't read his expression. He looked at Talinda, cleared his throat and started to read the remainder of the letter

> *Bernard,*
>
> *I know you are a little unnerved that I would make the reservations at the hotel for the both of you. But hear me out. Your next three weeks are so packed that you may want to consider staying there with Talinda for convenience and to save travel time. Considering how conservative a life I led, I know these arrangements have come somewhat a surprise to my loving wife.*

He paused and glanced up at Talinda who was very much unreadable at the moment. He continued:

> *I trust your respect for God and each other. There are two separate bedrooms so you wouldn't be alarmed at the thought of staying in the same room with each other. Of course, I realize that even though there are two bedrooms you both still may be extremely uncomfortable staying in the same hotel suite. If that is the case, then don't do it.*
> *At the closure of this letter you will understand all the secrecy I have held everyone to up to this moment. I know you two as well as everyone else are*

23

no doubt wondering why I would have Talinda hand deliver a letter to you that I could have easily sent by courier or certified mail.

Well the truth of the matter is this. Talinda, sweetheart, I figured that you would be very stressed by all the events that have taken place in your life up to this point and would be in much need of a break from it all. So, I planned a three week vacation for you to relax and start out on a new adventure of your life.

Bernard, I trust you will show her as wonderful a time as I had when I visited you several years ago. Enclosed you will find a letter addressed to each of you. I must forewarn you both that the contents of the letters could quite possibly and drastically change both of your lives. I pray that you will follow your hearts and let the Holy Spirit be your guide.

Love,

Brandon

Talinda's initial smile at the thought of a much needed vacation turned to uneasiness as she was handed the letter addressed to her from Brandon. She could feel her body start to shake inside from the anticipation. Her heart raced and she momentarily stared at the envelope half afraid to open it after Bernard handed it to her.

Her mind ran rampant, and she fought to keep her focus as she watched Bernard's reaction to his letter from Brandon. He was in tears as he read. This alarmed Talinda, and she realized that she was totally unprepared for what she may find.

Bernard,

I know by now your feelings and emotions are all over the place. As well as the guilt you feel about being in love with my wife.

Those words struck Bernard like a ton of bricks, and he gasped as he looked up into Talinda eyes. He had to stand and turn his back away from her to hide the tears that formed and began to roll down his face. His reaction sent her into alarm, and her hands trembled as she opened and began to read the contents of her letter. Bernard continued reading:

But rest assure twin, that it was all a part of the plan. I shared our love with you with the hopes and desire that you would take care of my wife in the event of my death.

He paused to catch his breath, and he whispered, "Brandon." He turned back toward Talinda, who now read her letter and tears had already started to roll down her cheeks. He continued:

"I know this is going to sound really out there considering your knowledge of my character. But I would rest easy knowing that my twin is taking care of my twins and my wife in every way. It's okay...smile Bernard.

He closed his eyes and breathed a heavy half smile half sigh. He shook his head at his cousin's divine foreknowledge that he would be struggling at this moment and would indeed need to smile. His cousin knew him well, perhaps better than he would ever know himself. He whispered to himself, "Twins...she's having twins." He looked at her and smiled before he continued to read:

I am asking you to marry Talinda, and I'm praying that your relationship with her indeed heads in that direction. The reason I know that you love her is because I initiated the love. I intentionally shared our most intimate moments with you and talked about our love and the genuineness of it constantly around you. I wanted you to desire her, not just physically, but spiritually. I knew you would respect us as long as I was alive. I had confidence in that because I know you. And I trust what God told me.

In the book of Ruth, Boaz, the next of kin male relative, fulfilled the tradition of God in caring for and marrying the widow of a deceased male family member. So, twin, don't think it strange that I would ask you to do this. And don't feel guilty, Bernard. This plan has been in the making for a while now. I set you up to love my wife. Bernard, I need to know that she is going to be taken care of, that she is going to be loved. God indeed blessed me to be able to leave behind enough money to take care of Talinda for the rest of her life. I love you twin, and I trust you. I will, however, make this one request, or I should say demand, of you.

Bernard continued with a bewildered look on his face, almost afraid to see what the next line of the letter would say:

Should you and Talinda decide that you will indeed marry, I must insist on you exiting from the military. Talinda is very delicate right now, and I do not want to put her right back in the same situation she just came out of –losing a husband to violence. I know you have deployed to war already on several occasions and I do not feel that Talinda can handle the stress of being married to a military man, especially in her condition. I know I am asking a lot of you because you have advanced considerably and are well on your way to retirement from the military. That is the reason that I insured that money would not be an issue for either of you. The inheritance that you received has nothing to do with Talinda. I simply wanted to bless my big brother.

This is a decision that you two will have to make together. I wanted you separate from both our parents and hers so you could come to a decision without outside interference. They, just as you, are receiving letters right about now. Their letters also explain my desires and wishes for the two of you. They are also being instructed not to bombard you with phone calls and to wait for you two to make first contact with them. That is the reason I had her to come to you instead of your being required to be present at the reading of my will. I knew you would both need privacy when reading these letters.

I have planned a very romantic three week vacation for you two. So for the next two days I gather you will probably spend time talking and sharing information about my request. Spend some time shopping, and on the night of day three open letter number three...alone.

Bernard, I love you and I know you love me. I have released her to love you, and I pray that she will, in the very near future, become Mrs. Bernard Alexander Travis.

Love,

Twin

Bernard let the letter fall to the ground as he walked away from it. He went to the balcony to gather himself. He stood and looked out into the city. He leaned slightly on the rail and shook his head back and forth and again whispered, "Brandon." He sat down in a patio chair, put his head in his hands and shed uncontrollable tears.

Talinda had been just as affected by Brandon's letter to her as Bernard had been with his:

Sweetheart,

I knew months before my death that it was coming. And I knew a few years into our marriage that we would not grow old together. So a short time ago, at the prompting of the Holy Spirit, I sat down with our lawyer and changed the will. That is when I wrote these letters and spent countless hours with our lawyer making arrangements for events to happen at specific times. Your visit to Germany has been well thought out and planned ahead of time. Upon my death, the lawyer knew what plans to put into action and when. So, Talinda baby, promise me you'll give it a chance. Promise me you'll experience the next three weeks with an open mind and an open heart. Knowing that I wouldn't spend the rest of my life with you prompted me to provide for your future. God prepared me for it.

"Oh Brandon," she thought as tears fell from her eyes. "What are you trying to say? Please don't...I don't know...Oh God. Brandon, please."

I know by now you have met Bernard and you are a little unsure about your feelings. He is so much like me that you probably think you may be falling for him and you are very confused, and maybe even a little guilty about feeling this way. After all, your husband has only been dead for a few months. And you don't want to hurt Bernard by just using him as a Brandon substitute.

"Leave it to Brandon to read me from the grave," she thought. She was afraid to look up at Bernard because she had begun to understand as she continued to read:

Sweetheart, I know you may think this is odd, but not every man gets the opportunity from the grave to choose who he would prefer to be his successor and take care of his wife.

27

She almost screamed out loud but somehow managed to hold her thoughts to herself. She screamed silently inside her head instead. 'BRANDON, NO! DON'T DO THIS TO ME! I'M NOT READY FOR THIS! I CAN'T TAKE THIS! I'M NOT EMOTIONALLY READY! OH, GOD, BRANDON! PLEASE! I DON'T WANT TO LET YOU GO! I DON'T WANT TO! If I ACCEPT HIM THEN I HAVE TO LET YOU GO! I WANT TO HOLD ON TO YOU! BRANDON, PLEASE DON'T MAKE ME! PLEASE DON'T MAKE ME!"

> Sweetheart, just as Boaz took Ruth because he was the next of kin living male relative, I am charging my cousin Bernard to take my wife and love her. It is no mistake that I shared our most intimate moments with him. I wanted him to desire you and the love that you have to share. Although I know that love is not mandated by man I would like for you both to know that my blessings are on any relationship that you two should decide to pursue. And my blessings are there as well should you both decide not to pursue.
>
> I know, baby. Your loyalty to me may have you feeling that you just couldn't do this to me. But I need to know that my wife is going to be taken care of. I prayed to God about you when he told me that He would grant our petition for another baby. But I also knew that I wouldn't be here to care for you or the babies. I did not want to leave you here alone to raise our children. I knew my parents, as well as yours, would be there to help you with them.

She paused, "Them? Brandon what do you mean "them"?" She placed her hand on her stomach and continued:

> But I wanted you to have someone to hold you in the middle of the night, and love you with a pure heart. You love too hard to be left alone. And as I shared with Bernard about our love I watched his reaction. I wanted to see that he was falling in love with you.

She stopped reading for a moment, and finally found the nerve to look up at Bernard. He had either finished or stopped reading his letter. She noticed that it was on the floor in the living room area and he was on the balcony. He was looking down and held his head in his hands. She continued reading:

I started to share with Bernard some very intimate things about our love; things the average man wouldn't share with another man about his wife. But I needed him to love you before he met you sweetheart, just in case. Tell Bernard I knew that was why he never came to visit us. He wasn't sure about his feelings for you. To keep him separated from you until now was all in Gods' and my plan.

By now you have probably already found out that you are carrying twins. If not, then congratulations sweetheart.

After she read that statement Talinda gasped and held her stomach. She smiled as she looked out on the deck at Bernard, who still had his head in his hands. She now understood what "help you with them" meant. She continued to read:

Just as God promised me, you have a baby boy and a baby girl growing inside of you, a manifestation of our love and precious gifts from God to you. Know that I love you sweetheart, and please, please consider my request. I am resting easy knowing that my twin is taking care of my twins and my loving wife. Not to mention the other blessings that I'm sure will come from the union that you will share with him. But sweetheart, don't feel pressured to do anything.

"Sure, Brandon...no pressure," she sarcastically thought.

I solely leave it up to you baby. If it is your desire to remain a widow then I trust that God will comfort you in that as well. Either way I am comforted by the Holy Spirit that you will be well taken care of. I love you, Talinda. I'm so sorry that I had to leave you so soon and leave you expecting.

Baby, it's okay to let go. I know that you love me. You made me extremely happy the last seven years of my life, and my life was so fulfilled in you. You are a wife, sweetheart. That's all you know how to be. That's what you were designed to be. You have mastered it, baby. And my death does not relieve you from that mandate from God. It does, however, relieve you of your commitment to me and opens it up for another to receive. It is my prayer that in the near future you will indeed become Mrs. Bernard Alexander Travis.

Wipe the tears from your eyes and rest easy sweetheart...rest easy.

Love,

Brandon

She again looked up at Bernard, who starred off into the distance. She gathered herself and walked out on the balcony. As she reached out to touch his shoulder, she was overwhelmed with emotion. She withdrew her hand before she made contact with him. He sensed her presence behind him but continued to sit in silence. He was afraid to face her.

They sat in silence for the span of half an hour. She read her letter over and over until she could no longer stand the silence. It was deafening to her. By this time Bernard had stood and was at the railing of the balcony. He still looked off into the distance.

She approached him. She touched his shoulder and whispered his name softly, "Bernard..."

He didn't respond to her voice or her touch. He just kept looking forward. She continued, not jarred in the least by his lack of a response. "Bernard, we can't just sit in silence for the next three weeks. We are going to have to talk about this eventually. Right now I know there are no words to describe what we both are feeling, but I..."

He cut her off, "Oh, Talinda. I wouldn't say that. There are a lot of words in my head right now. The one I can't shake is...," he paused and ran his hand from the front to the back of his head in frustration. "...You don't understand, Talinda. You are the kind of wife I prayed about. I used to pray to God that if he gave me half the woman that he blessed Brandon with I would be happy. And now Brandon has practically laid you at my feet and I feel...ugh...I feel so guilty. Why do I feel so guilty? Oh, God. I'm so ashamed about my feelings for you!"

"Bernard...you...," she started but was interrupted by him again.

"You don't get it Talinda" He exclaimed in desperation as he turned toward her to look her square in the eyes. "I'm in love with you! I have been since the first day Brandon started to talk about you. Don't you think it's strange that I never came to visit you and Brandon before? We were practically brothers and not one time in the last seven years have you ever met me or even barely spoken with me on the phone. I was in love with my cousin's wife! Oh, God! Please help me! This was so easy before when you were off limits...and now I am so ashamed about my feelings for you..."

"Shhhh," she said as she cupped the side of his face in her hand. "Oh, Bernard. Never be ashamed of love. It's God's most precious gift. I don't think its so much shame you feel as it is being exposed. Brandon has exposed both of our feelings today. I've struggled with

30

you since that day in the airport. When you sent the letter, I didn't respond because I was afraid...afraid that I would have to lie about my feelings to save face and protect my perfect little image as a youth pastor who had it altogether. Brandon has exposed our feelings, Bernard. As long as we could keep them secret, we were both okay. But now that they are out there we have to decide what to do about them."

"Brandon was so right about you," he said as he placed his hand over hers that was still cupped his face. "Your touch is magical, and you say all the right words to soothe a man's soul."

"Talinda, what are you doing?" she thought. She knew that he hadn't understood her touch. Or was it she that hadn't understood it? She silently chastised herself, "I have to learn to turn it off. I have to learn how not to be a wife." She had feelings for Bernard; however, she still wasn't ready to let go of Brandon, even though she had been released by him. "Oh, God," she thought, "Please help me. I can't do this. I'm not ready...I'm not ready."

She knew she had to choose her words very carefully because the one thing she was sure of was she knew her feelings did not match Bernard's. She took a deep breath and removed her hand from beneath his and replied, "Bernard I don't know how I feel. I mean my hormones are so unbalanced right now, and I just buried the man I waited for all my life two and half months ago. Not to mention I'm three and a half months pregnant with his babies. Babies we waited five years for after we lost the first one. Although I have feelings for you, I'm not sure that it's love. I'm not sure of the origin of these feelings. I don't want to be with you just because you look like Brandon. I don't want to hurt or use you."

Now in tears, she paused for a moment to gather herself enough to speak. "Bernard I don't know how to stop being a wife. I don't want to stop being a wife. I miss having a husband to take care of. But I don't want to use you as a default Brandon."

She felt herself starting to really lose it. Bernard pulled her into his arms and said, "Oh, God, Talinda. I am so sorry. Now on top of everything else...I feel selfish. This has got to be ten times harder for you than it could ever be for me."

Talinda was unable to respond. All she could do was weep. But even through her tears she realized she felt a strange comfort in his arms. She felt peace and she felt secure. As with Brandon, she felt Bernard's heartbeat and she could feel that her heart moved in unison with his. His voice both soothed and tantalized her at the same time. His manly smell mixed with cologne was a sweet aroma to her. She remembered thinking the first day that Brandon held her she felt like she belonged in his arms, like she belonged to him. But with Bernard it was a different comfort. It confusingly seemed more powerful. She felt like she was made to fit perfectly in his arms. She felt like...like she was made just for him. But how could that be? Brandon was the man of her dreams. He was the man of prophecy.

"But what if," she thought, "What if his job was to prepare her and introduce her to the man of her dreams? She thought back to the day at church when the Prophetess ministered to her about her husband. She desperately searched her memory for the exact words the prophetess had used. She was convinced that Brandon was indeed the man of the prophecy. Then it hit her...what if the man of the prophecy and the man of her dreams were not the same person? Although he fulfilled the prophecy, there were things that she shared with her Savior about the man of her dreams that Brandon did not fulfill. But what if she was not ready for the man of her dreams at that time, and the man of her dreams was still being prepared for her?

Maybe...just maybe she wasn't mature enough to handle the man of her dreams. She had secretly prayed to God for a man who would know how to completely satisfy her every need- spiritual, emotional and physical. Bernard's experience and aggressiveness would have terrified her seven years ago in her virgin state. Truly she had learned how to be a wife through Brandon. She had learned how to be the wife God designed. Through Brandon she had been molded and shaped into a true helpmeet. "Oh, God, what am I missing? Help me to understand." She confused herself with the many thoughts and ideas that ran through her mind. Startled by her thoughts and feelings, she gently broke the embrace and pulled away from him. She held her head down. She did not want to make eye contact.

As she wiped her tears, Bernard lifted her chin with his hand. He forced her to look him in the eyes as he said softly to her, "Talinda, you're going to be okay. We're going to be okay. We have three weeks to spend time thoroughly discussing this, and I trust God that He will be with us."

She smiled slightly, which warmed his heart all the more. "Yeah, He will," she replied.

He stared into her eyes and wanted so desperately to kiss her, but to her relief he just kissed her on the forehead instead.

"Okay," he said as he somewhat regained his composure. "I probably need to feed you."

"I'm not really hungry. Besides they served dinner on the plane," she replied.

He looked at her with that dazzling school boy smile that always said to her 'I'm going to rock your world' and said, "Yeah, and exactly how long ago was that, Mrs. Travis?"

She looked at her watch as she was about to answer. Then she realized that it had been much longer than she thought, she replied, "Oh wow, I didn't realize how long we've been here in the hotel suite. I guess it has been about eight hours from the time dinner was served over the Atlantic to now. But honestly Bernard, I am really more tired than I am hungry."

"I know baby, and believe me jet lag will set in on you very shortly here. So I need to get some food in you before you pass out from exhaustion," he replied on instinct, he had not realized what he had said until it was out there. It just seemed so natural to address her with a term of endearment. He quickly continued in conversation, and hoped she had not picked up on the fact that he addressed her as "baby." "I know you probably don't want to go anywhere for lunch so let's just look at the hotel menu."

Of course, she had heard him. But not being quite sure it was what she thought she heard, she decided to act as though she hadn't and replied, "That sounds fine to me. Since I have no idea what to order, I will leave that up to you. I am not very picky, but I would like to keep it light. I don't want to lie down on a lot of heavy or oily food because it's only going to come right back up."

He smiled and said, "Okay, I'll keep that in mind.

"Oh, God, please make him stop smiling at me," she thought but managed to just say thanks as she left the balcony. She sat down on the couch to wait on him to order room service.

He picked up the letter he had dropped as he reentered the room. He remembered it contained the knowledge of the third letter that Talinda was not to know about. He wouldn't have minded her reading it other than that fact. He folded it and put it away then proceeded to order room service.

Talinda was so tired she literally fell asleep while as she ate. Bernard took her plate out of her lap and placed it on the coffee table.

"Talinda...Talinda," he said softly to wake her so he wouldn't startle her. "Why don't you go lie down for a while and get some sleep?"

"Oh, wow," she said as she slightly stretched. "I guess I am pretty tired."

"Yeah," he replied. "Like I said, jet lag catches up with you pretty quick. Go ahead and lie down. I'll make sure you don't sleep too long so you can start to get calibrated with the time here and be able get some sleep tonight."

She responded sleepily as she rose from the couch and yawned. "I think I better, as long as you're going to be okay," she said as she headed toward the master suite.

He smiled at her response and said, "I'm fine. I'm in the right time zone, remember? It's just after lunchtime for me, but almost bedtime for you. Go ahead. I'll wake you in a few hours to go have dinner because you barely touched lunch."

After she disappeared into the master suite he retrieved the third letter from the envelope and placed it in his jacket pocket. He didn't want to take any chances that Talinda might view it by accident. He wondered if he indeed would have enough patience to wait until the third night to read it.

He checked in on her about an hour later and she was sound asleep. He stood and just watched her sleep for a few minutes. He silently had a conversation with God:

God,

She is so beautiful. As I stand here watching her sleep, I feel so fulfilled just being in the room with her. The anointing on her life just fills this place and I'm overwhelmed. Please grant my petition for her. I so desire to be her husband. God, help me to be her head, to nourish and protect her, to lead and guide her and to love her to satisfaction and fulfillment.

Amen

As he turned to leave the room he thought it quite curious that she had not locked the bedroom door. Relieved that she indeed trusted him he returned to the living room area and sat once again to read his letter from Brandon. He examined every word and took time to ponder every request. He then prayed to God that he would be with them in every decision that they made and that he would guide their steps. He so desired to be her husband and prayed that God would give her a genuine love for him.

~Chapter Five~

They spent the next two days talking as little about Brandon's letters as possible in spite of the intensity of Brandon's request. They found themselves quite comfortable with each and had very few awkward moments.

They shopped and dined regularly. They decided that it would be best if Bernard did not stay at the hotel with her because they wanted to make sure that everything was done in decency and in order. But secretly neither one of them trusted themselves to be alone together for so long a time unsupervised.

On the third day as they sat in the hotel room getting ready to go to lunch, the babies moved for the first time. Talinda cried out, "Oh my God!" and grabbed her stomach.

Bernard rushed to her side and asked if she is okay.

"The babies are moving!" she exclaimed with excitement. "I just felt them move for the first time. I'm only three and a half months...oh God!" Without thinking she grabbed his hands and placed them on her stomach. "If you press in right here Bernard you can feel them move. I can't believe I can feel them move so early in the pregnancy."

Bernard knelt in front of her in awe as tears filled in his eyes and rolled down his face. Talinda looked at him but before she could say anything he whispered, "What an awesome honor it must be to be a father. To know that the manifestation of love is growing inside the woman you shared that love with. Conception of life is truly amazing and mandated of God..."

This was a bittersweet moment for him. He grieved that Brandon would not be here to be a part of it. He was also honored that Brandon had entrusted him, should Talinda choose him, to be the father of the manifested love growing inside of her. He was amazed that he so quickly and easily had a fatherly love for those babies and silently prayed that Talinda would indeed accept Brandon's request concerning them. Oh how he loved her so and could feel himself taking on a husbandly protective nature toward her.

As he pondered his thoughts with his hands still on Talinda's stomach he got more excited with every movement the babies were making. He began to praise and magnify God, "God you are so awesome. You are truly the giver of life. The pure manifestation of love is life. Thank you, Jesus, for your love!"

Talinda was speechless. She didn't know what to do so she just sat there. She wanted to caress his face with her hand. She wanted to rub the top of his back at his shoulders as he kneeled down in front of her. She was a wife and a nurturer and at the moment realized that's all she would ever know how to be. Brandon was right she would never be relieved from that vocation. It just came natural for her. She forced herself not to touch him for two reasons: she didn't want to send him the wrong message, and she had seriously started to struggle with her feelings for him.

All she could do was watch and say, "To God be all the glory." Then she remembered the night that Brandon died. For the first time she connected all the dots. How could she have missed it and why had it taken her reading Brandon's letter to figure it out? Brandon had said to her, "*No, baby, Bernard is going to be a father.*" Tears rolled down her face as she realized Brandon had indeed planned this union for a long time. Just like his letter said he knew he wouldn't grow old with her himself but wanted a part of him to always be with her. He also wanted her to be loved and had made his request known to God of his choice.

As she looked down at him, she saw something in Bernard she hadn't seen earlier. She saw the genuine and earnest relationship he had with God. It was as though she wasn't even there, and he was alone with God. She also saw something else she had not seen because she had not been looking for it...she saw...a husband. He was going to be a husband. She knew he would be a loving and caring husband...but was he going to be hers would remain to be seen.

And for the first time she had to honestly admit to herself that Brandon was not in her thoughts although he should be. She was feeling their babies move for the first time and Brandon was far from her mind. She was in awe of Bernard and felt the warm fuzzy feeling she felt the first night she met Brandon.

She was suddenly very nervous and wanted his hands off of her because they brought emotions out of her she hadn't felt in a while. But she was captivated and just sat there stared at him as tears continued to roll down his cheeks and he praised his God for the gift of love and life. She also felt guilty that someone other than Brandon could make her feel this way. As she looked at him she didn't see a Brandon look alike, she saw a man of God full of love and in awe of his Lord's blessings.

She didn't want to stare at him because she knew that eventually he would look up into her eyes. And at that moment he would see what she desperately tried to hide from him. She was falling in love and felt very guilty about it. She forced herself to close her eyes and placed one hand on his shoulder and lifted the other to give God praise. She may have been better off to just stare at him because she sensed that her touch sent him just as strong a message. He looked up at her and caressed the side of her face in his hands as he now watched her closed eyes shed sweet tears as she thanked God for the lives that were growing inside of her.

She leaned her head into his hand and received his touch and said something that caught him totally by surprise. She whispered through her tears of joy, "God I thank you for the life inside of me and for the love to share it with."

Bernard had not expected that and wasn't sure if she meant the gift of love to love her babies or the physical and spiritual love of a man...more specifically...him...to share it with.

His heart raced at the thought that she could love him and accept him to take Brandon's place in her heart. He could feel his hand that cupped her face start to tremble and broke the touch. He stood and went to the restroom to get them both a cool wash cloth. She sat there and looked down afraid to make eye contact with him...her emotions were some place that she couldn't control nor understand. He was too afraid to ask her what she meant by "the love" because he would have been heartbroken if it wasn't directed at him.

He finally broke the silence. He sensed that she struggled with the moment and lighten the atmosphere as he said, "Life is an awesome gift from God. Women are truly blessed to be chosen to be carriers of life. I can't wait for these little ones to get here so big cousin Bernard can spoil them rotten."

He didn't understand why he had directed the path away from intimacy other than the fact that he did not want her to feel pressured by the high emotions of the moment or act on them. He would exercise patience and wait on the Lord.

She laughed slightly, thankful that he had broken the thickness of the atmosphere and she could now muster the courage to look up at him. "Yes, I guess we better be getting to lunch so I can feed them and keep them healthy."

"Yep" he replied. So they left for lunch and an afternoon of touring and souvenir shopping for everyone.

"Well are we driving today or taking the train like yesterday?" Talinda inquired at the conclusion of lunch.

"Today we are actually driving. I figured riding the bus wouldn't be as intriguing or comfortable for you. We're going to the maternity store on the other side of town my co-worker and good friend told me about. So finally you'll be able to shop for something for yourself," he said. He opened the door for her as they headed out of the dining area of the restaurant. He retrieved the jacket he left at the table in the Hotel restaurant just in case the weather turned rainy or cool. The forecast had called for rain that day. Late spring to early summer often brought cool showers in Germany.

They were going in and out of stores and enjoyed themselves when suddenly the heavens opened and there was a downpour. They had just enough time to duck into the entry way of a store before they got completely soaked. To their dismay the store was closed and they were stuck in the small entry way and had to huddle close together to stay out of the path of the rain.

She was suddenly very grateful that Brandon had her pack the old grey sweat suit. She remembered thinking its late spring I'm not going to need a sweat suit. She chuckled to herself as she shivered slightly. Bernard took off his jacket to wrap it around her. He said, "There are you warm enough?" She shook her head in affirmation but still shivered.

He smiled and said, "Come here, come closer to me so my body heat will warm you." He pulled her into his arms to warm her. She nestled into his chest and half moaned and half sighed which caught her and Bernard completely off guard. She was instinctively comfortable in his arms and longed to be there since they had read the letters the first night.

Bernard smiled and declared, "Girl, you drive me crazy when you do that."

"Do what?" She inquired in a soft daddy's little girl voice.

Bernard replied somewhat hesitant, "You know...when you snuggle into my chest and do that little half moan half sigh thing. You did it the night on Aunt Helens deck, at the barbeque and again at the airport. I remember the first time it almost sent me over the edge."

"Oh, I'm so sorry," Talinda replied. She attempted to release the embrace.

"No," he said in a low toned smooth sexy voice as he slightly tightened the grip. "I love it. It makes me feel strong. It makes me feel like a protector. It also makes me feel like you are completely satisfied with where you are. Girl you make a man feel like a million dollars. How do you do that?"

"I...I don't know," she answered as she snuggled back into his chest. This made him smile. "It just...happens. But obviously is doesn't happen with every man that hugs me because you and Brandon are the only two to ever say that to me. I mean I had boyfriends growing up. One in particular I was pretty serious about and none of them ever said that to me."

"Maybe because...," he stopped short of finishing his sentence.

She waited for him to complete his sentence. After they stood in silence for about a minute she inquired of him, "Because what..."

She could feel his heartbeat speed up slightly and he took a deep breath to regulate it. She prepared herself for what he would say and was excitedly and frightened at what his response would be.

He rubbed her back slightly and then with his right hand reached under her chin and lifted her face toward his. "You are so beautiful, Talinda. Maybe because," he paused again then continued, "Maybe because...none of them were destined to be your husband."

Those words penetrated past her soul into her spirit. They were captured in time and everything completely stood still. She could no longer hear the rain or feel the effects of it. She wanted to break contact and just run out into the rain to force herself back into reality. She wanted to get away so she could hide the feelings that manifested inside of her. She realized she had the warm peach fuzz feeling on the inside like she did when she first encountered Brandon. Just when she thought the moment would pass...it happened.

Nine months to the day after her wedding night as Nevette lay in her private room in labor and delivery in the early stages of labor, she thought back about how wonderful Justice had been to her throughout her pregnancy. She had enjoyed countless foot massages and back rubs. He had catered to her every whim and supplied her every need.

"You're going to be a good daddy," she said as she looked into his eyes between contractions.

Tears filled his eyes and he was unable to reply. He just kissed the back of her hand.

"Oh baby," she said as she stroked his head and fully understanding his tears. Justice was such a sensitive yet strong man's man.

They had elected not to know the sex of the baby beforehand. Justice was somewhat old fashioned in some areas and wanted to be surprised at the time of birth. His mother, Shaundra, had been a prominent part of Nevette's care the last nine months. She, wanting to know the sex of the baby, had elected not to be present when Nevette had undergone an ultrasound so she wouldn't spill the beans by accident.

They had gone with a pastel Noah's Ark theme which could go either feminine or masculine for the nursery.

"Now, Mrs. Goodfellow, are you sure you don't want an epidural?" the nurse asked.

She looked up into Justices' eyes. She smiled and said, "Yes, I'm sure. We want to go natural all the way."

Although Derrick's mom would be delivering the baby, Nevette had also regularly seen an obstetrician throughout her pregnancy to ensure everything was properly taken care of. He would also be in the room during the time of delivery to assist Shaundra should any problems arise.

Nevette's father and brothers, as well as Derrick's dad and sister, were all on their way to the hospital. They tried to discourage them from coming so soon being that she was only in the early stages of labor. Everyone was so excited. There was no keeping any of them away.

Lindsay called and said that she would be there after work hoping that by then Nevette would be close to delivery.

"You better get here before I deliver, godmother," Nevette teased in a serious tone. "I'm going to need my best friend to make me laugh at about seven centimeters dilated I'm sure," she said being cut short of all out laughter by a contraction.

"Don't worry," Lindsay replied. "I'm only about an hour from being done. You're just now getting to three centimeters so I have time. How is Justice doing?"

"He's awesome," she said as she looked into his eyes and smiled as she stroked his face with her free hand. Tears welled up in her eyes as she told Lindsay she had to go and she would see her when she got there.

"I love you so much, baby...thank you," Justice said as he leaned over to kiss Nevette as she hung up the phone with Lindsay.

She responded with a smile and said, "For what, Justice?"

"For loving me so much you would willing to endure the pain of childbirth to make me a daddy," he whispered almost in tears again.

Shaundra looked on and smiled as she enjoyed the love they share. "Truly they are God ordained," she thought.

After everyone arrived at the hospital they received permission for everyone to be present in the room for just a minute with the expectant parents. Nevette and Justice wanted her father to pray for the delivery.

They all joined in and laid hands on the young parents to be, as Theodore Sr. anointed and laid his hands on the belly of his daughter. He found himself struggling with the task. He was missing his lovely wife he had lost to cancer almost six years before. Instinctively Teddy moved over behind him and placed his hand on his father's shoulder for support.

Nevette said through teary eyes to her father, "I know daddy...I know."

He cleared his throat and began to pray:

Father,

We come before You in the mighty name of Jesus. God, we thank you for this union and the life You have produced through them. Father, as she enters into the final stages of labor we pray that You will be with Derrick and Nevette. We pray for an uneventful delivery God and for a healthy and normal infant. Father, we pray that her labor pains will be tolerable. Father, we thank You for the many blessings You have bestowed upon our family thus far. We thank You for Derrick's mother, Shaundra, who has the awesome privilege of delivering and caring for our grandchild. We pray that You will be with her as she assists in bringing the life You created into this world.

God, we promise that we will bring this child up in the admonition of the Lord and we dedicate him or her to You in advance. Father, we ask You to be with the parents as they leave the hospital with their first born child. While it is joyous and exciting, parenting can be a trying and somewhat scary task. So lead and guide them, Lord. Father we thank You for your presence in our lives. Lord, we thank You for a quick and complete recovery for Nevette. Childbirth is very stressful on the woman's body so God, we pray that You will keep Nevette and regulate her systems during the stress of the delivery. Father, we thank You for Derrick, and we pray that as he coaches his wife in labor, his touch will be soothing to her and his words will bring comfort in the midst of contractions. Father, as we return to the waiting room, help us to exercise patience in waiting for this miracle of life to come forth to greet us. We are so very excited, Lord...so very excited and we thank You and give You praise.

In Jesus' Name,

Amen

A few hours later as the contractions were stronger and came closer together, Nevette was way past uncomfortable. Lindsay and Derrick helped her to continue to breathe through the contractions.

"Okay," she said as she breathed shallow painful breathes. "This is way harder than I imagined it would be." She cried out, "OH GOD, JUSTICE! PLEASE HELP ME! AHHHHHH! MMMMMM!"

"Come on, baby. Try to take deeper, slower breaths," he replied. He grabbed her hand and stroked her face with the other. His touch soothed her and she smiled at him as the contraction subsided.

Shaundra came up to the bedside after she had checked to see how far she had dilated. "Okay, Nevette. You are about seven centimeters, sweetheart. Are you sure you don't want an epidural? Your contractions are about to pick up in intensity, and the time in between them is about to shorten significantly."

"No, mom," she replied. She breathed slowly during the break of the contraction. "I'm going to try to make it."

"Baby, are you sure?" Justice replied as he continued to stroke her face. "The last one was really hard for you, and we're not at the end yet."

"Let me go just a little while longer okay, Justice," she mustered a smile as she looked up at him and reassured him she was okay.

He listened, but didn't look at her because the monitor had his attention. He could see that another contraction was on the way so he grabbed her hand and braced himself for the squeeze.

"Okay baby. Start taking deep breathes," he coached as she entered into a contraction.

"OOOOH GOD! THIS HURTS...JUSTICE!" she yelled as the contraction hit a peak.

"I know baby...I know. I'm so sorry sweetheart," Justice whispered in her ear as he kissed her on the cheek.

Lindsay laid her hands on Nevette's stomach and started to pray and sing. Nevette loved to hear her sing. She smiled at her as the contraction subsided once again. She looked up at Justice, who has a worried look on his face. She reached up to touch him and said, "Oh, sweetheart. It's okay. It's going to be o...," she is cut off as another contraction started to build. "MMMMM.... WHOOO.... G...GOD... UHNNNN." She attempted to take deep slow breaths as the contractions indeed came stronger and closer together.

"Mom...," Derrick said in a whisper as he looked at his mother for reassurance that his wife is okay.

"She's fine DJ," Shaundra replied. "Childbirth is not an easy task. She is doing just fine, son. She's doing just fine."

He didn't reply. He just looked back down at his wife and began to kiss her. "I love you so much Naythia," he said as he kissed her.

She was about to respond but was hit with a contraction that almost lifted her off the bed. He held one hand and she reached into the air in an attempt to grab anything in the near vicinity with the other as she screamed out, "JESUS! GOD! OHHHH GOD! HOLY SPIRIT!!! JUSSTIIICE! OH, GOD! THIS HURTS!"

Derrick was beside himself as he held his wife's hand. He had absolutely no idea what to do and could feel he was about to lose control of his composure. The contractions were stronger and

42

coming quicker. The last few hours began to be unbearable for Nevette, and he felt absolutely helpless in her pain.

Lindsay saw his distress. She leaned down and whispered in Nevette's ear. "Now before you lose control and start to torment this poor man for putting you in this situation, remember he is the same man you were "gaga" over that day in the therapy pool three years ago."

Despite the pain of the contraction Nevette couldn't help but to laugh at Lindsay's remark. "Oh Lindsay! Whooo...don't make me laugh. OH GOD! Okay...okay," she said as she began to breathe easy as she neared the end of the contraction.

She smiled at Lindsay and then looked at Derrick. His eyes were filled with tears. She said in a reassuring tone, "I love you, baby. It's okay. I'm okay, sweetheart."

Justice was unable to speak. He was overwhelmed and in awe of the act of childbirth and the unimaginable pain his wife was suffering to bless him by bringing life into this world. A life he desired from the moment he laid eyes on her.

"LINDSAY! OH, GOD! PLEASE MAKE IT STOP! MOM...I CAN'T DO THIS! JUSTICE...I CAN'T DO THIS! PLEASE MAKE IT STOP GOD," Nevette screamed as she once again neared the peak of a very hard contraction.

"Sweetheart, do you want to take the epidural," Shaundra asked.

"NOOO...NOOOO!" Nevette screamed and attempted to control her breathing at the same time.

Justice, seemingly regained his composure and leaned in to her. He said in a calm and mild tone, "Okay, come on baby, and breathe deeply. You can do this...come on baby. I'm here, sweetheart. Listen to the sound of my voice. Concentrate on me baby...concentrate on me. Look at me Naythia. Focus baby...focus."

She mustered a smile and breathed in through her nostrils. She pushed the air out through her mouth as she relaxed back on the pillow. "I'm so tired Justice...I'm so tired."

"I know baby. I am so proud of you. You are so awesome. You're doing great, sweetheart...just great," he replied. He kissed and stroked her face.

The obstetrician reentered the room. He had been monitoring her contractions from the nurses' station. Upon checking her he beckons Shaundra to sit on the stool. He pats Nevette on the hand and said, "Okay little momma, we are ready to push. I need you to sit up just slightly and scoot all the way to the end of the bed. Okay, you two coaches. I need one of you on both sides to support her. Now, when the next contraction hits, Mrs. Goodfellow, bear down and push with everything you have."

"Okay...okay," Nevette responded, preparing to push because she could feel the contraction mounting up.

All of Justice's fears and anxieties instantaneously turned to excitement as he realized they would soon be holding their child.

"Okay baby, here we go," Derrick said supporting her back as she leans forward to get ready to push.

Alright little momma, push," Shaundra said with excitement.

Nevette let out a yell as she pushed through the contraction with all her might.

"Okay," the doctor said. "That was a good push mom. Take a few deep breaths and get ready to go again."

"Come on, Naythia. Push baby, push," Justice coached as he held her up with Lindsay on the other side coaching as well.

"OOOH, GOD! I CAN'T DO THIS JUSTICE! IT'S TOO HARD," Nevette screamed as she attempted to push through the next contraction. "I'm so tired Justice! I'M TOO TIRED!"

"Come on baby, you can do it. You have to. Now come on sweetheart, push. You're a strong woman of God. Come on, baby. With this next contraction push with all you might baby. Come on Nevette, push," Derrick said as he kissed her on the forehead.

She pushed and yelled out to God as she gave a strong effort.

"OH, GOD! I SEE THE HEAD! COME ON, NEVETTE! PUSH!" Shaundra yelled with excitement.

The declaration that her baby's head had crowned seemed to give Nevette new found strength and energy as she braced herself for another push. With the next push the head emerged.

"Okay," the doctor said to Nevette, "Stop pushing, little momma."

Through her tears, Shaundra suctioned the baby's nostrils and throat and prepared for the final push.

"Okay, Mrs. Goodfellow, one more push and we got ourselves a baby," the doctor declared.

Justice and Lindsay both supported her under her back and legs. They simultaneously said, "Okay Nevette, give it all you got."

"THANK YOU JESUS!" Nevette yelled as she gave it all she had.

Shaundra maneuvered little baby Goodfellows shoulders as Nevette's pushed and out he came. "IT'S A BOY!" she yelled with excitement.

Baby Goodfellow let out a healthy cry as he took his first breath outside his mother's womb.

"You hear him, baby? It's a boy sweetheart," Justice said to Nevette as he kissed her. "Oh baby, I love you. I'm so proud of you. You did it, sweetheart...you did it!"

"We did it Justice...we did it," she whispered through her tears of joy.

44

Lindsay and Shaundra were over at the table with the baby as the nurses went through the initial check. Lindsay took the first snapshot of baby Goodfellow. Justice stayed with Nevette, crying tears of joy. He showered her with kisses and expressed his love and happiness to her as the doctor delivered the afterbirth and began to stitch her up. He had decided beforehand that they would see the baby for the first time together.

"Okay," Shaundra said through tears as she took little Goodfellow over to meet his parents, "Derrick Justice Goodfellow III, meet your mom and dad. He is 8lbs, 6oz and 22 inches long."

"Oh, Justice, look at him. He's beautiful. Hey sweetheart. Mommy and daddy have been waiting to meet you for a while now," Nevette said through tears as she held her baby in her arms for the first time. Justice looked on in awe of God's power and love.

"He's perfect," Justice finally managed to say barely above a whisper.

Lindsay went out into the waiting room to let everyone know Nevette had delivered and was doing fine. "IT'S A BOY! 8LBS, 6OZ AND 22 INCHES LONG!" she exclaimed.

"Wow!" Derrick, Sr. said in excitement. "He is almost the exact same size that DJ was."

They were all overjoyed and couldn't wait until they would be able to see Nevette and the baby.

"I'm going to go back in. I have more pictures to take," Lindsay said as she headed back into the delivery room. "I'll also go find out when everyone can come in."

As she reentered Nevette's room, Derrick was holding his son with an absolute look of amazement on his face. Little Derrick was gripping his finger as he and his dad held their first glance of each other. She snapped the picture and said, "Priceless."

Nevette looked on with tears in her eyes. Lindsay snapped pictures like she worked for a professional photography studio. The doctor said that he would send the rest of the family in on his way out after Lindsay had inquired about visitation. The room was soon full of Goodfellows and Grahams as they each met and enjoyed the new arrival to the family.

The moment Talinda had secretly been waiting for with as much anticipation as Bernard had been was finally about to happen. As he held her in his arms, he looked deep into her soul and whispered to her, "I love you so much baby that it hurts." He moved his hand from under her chin to the side of her face and kissed her with a fiery passion. It was beyond the kiss of consummation she had received from Brandon on their first encounter. It was a kiss of ownership...of complete ownership. She melted in his arms and felt if he would have even slightly let up on his grip of her she would hit the ground. She was utterly consumed and wanted it to last forever.

Her eyes were still closed as he released her. The complete look of satisfaction on her face made him smile and he kissed her again as he placed both his hands on either side of her waist. He pulled her as close to him as her stomach would allow. She placed both of her hands on the sides of his head and gently caressed his neck as he continued to kiss her.

"Oh, God, I'm falling," she thought as her reaction told him that she never wanted him to stop. She had that inside the rainbow feeling again. They had come to a point that they could not turn back from. They both knew as they continued it was no longer a matter of "if" marriage would happen, but "when".

As they broke contact she looked out to the street and realized the rain had stopped. He just stared at her both amazed and relieved that she had received and responded to his kiss. Afraid of what would come out of his mouth next, she decided to cut the passion of the moment to let in fresh air.

"Wow...huh...way to steal a girl's attention," she chuckled. "I didn't even realize the rain had stopped."

"I guess it has," Bernard replied. He did not take his eyes off of her as he noted, "Considering that you have stopped shivering, I guess I kept you warm enough."

She placed her hand on the side of his face and softly caressed it as she smiled and said, "Yes...nice and toasty..." She paused and closed her eyes for just an instant as she lightly moaned and then continued, "...mmmm...inside and out."

He smiled as he replied, "Girl, you are something else." He turned his head and slightly kissed the inside of her hand that that she had on his face. "As much as I would love to stay right here, we better get going. I'm not sure when the store closes and we don't want to end up eating dinner too late."

"Okay," she replied barely above a whisper. But her eyes were telling a different story. They were saying kiss me again and hold me in your arms. She thought to herself that if he indeed was becoming one with her he would begin to be able to read her.

Before she could ponder any other thoughts in her head he pulled her back into his arms and kissed her again. He moaned lightly and said to her, "I love you. Your eyes are talking to my heart baby, and I love what they are saying to me."

All she could do was place her hands at the top of his chest near his chin and lean up to kiss him again. She screamed inside, "Oh, God! We're becoming one...we're becoming one!"

He looked her in the eyes and said, "Talk to me baby...what's happening here?"

46

She smiled and let out a light sigh. She replied, "I think we both already know the answer to that question. A connection has been made that we cannot ignore or can't turn back from. I guess what we have to ask ourselves is where do we go from here."

"Wow," Bernard said as he gave her a light peck on the forehead. "Everything Brandon said about you is...wow...you are amazing."

"No," Talinda replied as she ran her fingers across his lips and caressed the side of his face, "God is amazing."

He smiled as he placed his hand over hers and said, "Yes, He is. He is full of blessings and He has truly blessed me today." He moaned and looked up to the sky. "God, I want to stay here forever. But we better get going before another rain shower rolls in."

They found the maternity store fairly easily. They spent the afternoon in laughter, shopping, enjoying each other and sharing an occasional intimate moment.

Bernard decided to plan a more romantic evening for dinner. While on the phone making dinner reservations at one of the finer restaurants in town, he watched her pick out an evening gown at the maternity store. She held a gown up in front of her as she stood in front of a mirror. He rubbed her stomach and continued to marvel at life. *"I will praise thee for I am fearfully and wonderfully made,"* he said, quoting a portion of Psalm 139:14 as he stood behind her. He lightly kissed her neck while still rubbing her stomach. She smiled and was completely lost in the moment.

"Oh, God...wow. He is so loving...just like Brandon," she thought. She reached up with her right hand placed it almost on top of his head as he continued to parade her with soft kisses on the side of her face and neck. Her eyes were closed and she took in every element of the moment.

After she chose a gown for the evening, they checked out and headed back to the hotel. Bernard was loaded down with Talinda's bags. He felt very husbandly as he accompanied her back to the hotel room. After he placed the bags on the table, he turned toward her to let her know that he would be back to pick her up around six-thirty.

She smiled as he gave her a light kiss and replied, "Okay, I'll be ready." She closed the door behind him and breathed a sigh of relief. She went into the bedroom, held the dress up to herself as she looked in the mirror and sighed again. She was in such a state of satisfaction and was perfectly content with everything that was happening.

She sat down on the bed and read Brandon's letter once again. But this time she paid attention to every word, every suggestion from Brandon. She wanted to feel what he was feeling at the time he wrote the letter. She didn't want to miss anything. Her future depended on her having complete resolution from Brandon.

Random words began to jump off the page at her. "*Baby, its okay to let go... prefer to be his successor... my blessings are there...mandate...immediate future...become Mrs. Bernard Alexander Travis...wipe the tears from your eyes...rest easy, sweetheart."*

She felt the overwhelming power of the Holy Spirit enter the room. She felt comforted and sure...sure that she would indeed become Mrs. Bernard Alexander Travis very soon. She smiled at the thought of being a wife again. The last two and a half months she had felt so lost. She had felt so empty. Losing Brandon was part of it but the worst part of it was that fact she was no longer a wife. She was no longer fulfilling her destiny.

She then took some time to pray and thank God for his comforting spirit and for blessing her with Bernard. "Twice in one lifetime," she said aloud to God. "Twice in one life time, you have blessed me with the man of my dreams." She realized that making that statement to God was a declaration of her choice of Bernard. That she had indeed resolved to be his wife.

She shuddered suddenly at the weight that fell on her shoulder because she understood fully what had happened today. His kiss had taken her to a place that she could not return from. She smiled as she knew full well that not only could she not return she did not desire to return from there. Because it was there that she was once again made whole.

As she began to prepare for her night on the town she realized that she had not contacted her family since they read Brandon's letters. Knowing they had also received letters and were probably anxiously awaited any contact from her, she decided to wait a little while longer. She wasn't sure what they would think and so took Brandon's advice not to allow their opinions to enter into her and Bernard's decision about their future. She felt an excitement that she could not contain come over her. She felt like a school girl that waited to go out of her first real date.

Meanwhile Bernard sat down at his kitchen counter of his town house and proceeded to open letter number three. Twenty thousand dollars in traveler's checks were inside the envelope with the letter. He placed them on the table with no regard to their value. He knew the real value of the envelope was in the words contained within the letter itself. His hands trembled as he unfolded the third letter and began to read:

Dear Twin,

> *It is my prayer that you and Talinda have had some time to discuss your future together. I would hope that there has also been some sort of spark of romance between the two of you. Talinda loves hard, Bernard, and she is a very decisive woman. She said exactly what she means no matter how*

uncomfortable or uneasy a feeling her emotions may bring. Rest easy that if she has responded to your love it is indeed genuine. She is incapable of toying with your heart, and when you have hers you will know it.

Tomorrow you are to rise early because for the next five days you will be in Paris, France. I pray that your drive there will be full of flavorful conversation. The last page of the letter states all the reservations and arrangements for the day. Check in time at your hotel will be at noon and lunch has already been prepared for the two of you in the hotel suite.

After lunch you will separate for the afternoon. A limousine will pick the two of you up around 3 pm. She will be dropped off at a boutique to be prepared for your romantic evening. They will fit her with a ball gown designed especially for expecting mothers. She will have her hair and makeup done, not that she needs any mind you, and be ready for you upon your return.

You will be fitted for a tuxedo or high fashion suit which ever suites your taste. But I will give you a hint, Talinda loves black tie affairs. You will then be driven to the jewelry store where a necklace, earrings and bracelet have already been chosen for her and charged to my estate. Since you are probably not sure of her taste as of yet I took the liberty to help you out a bit...smile.

Bernard paused and smiled as he thought out loud, "Brandon, you have thought of everything. Wow. I'm so in awe of your love for us both." He continued to read:

The traveler's checks inside this envelope are part of your inheritance. They are also for your visit to the jeweler. Upon receiving the aforementioned jewelry pieces, you will then pick out an engagement ring and wedding band set. This, I cannot help you with. This choice must come from inside of your heart, not mine.

Bernard stopped at that statement as an anxious feeling came over him. Had Brandon expected him to propose to her tomorrow night? She had only been in country for three days. They had shared an intimate afternoon but...was he crazy...were they ready...more so was she ready? He continued to read:

Bernard, don't wonder if she is ready. Just follow your heart. Trust God that her heart, if she is indeed meant to be your wife, will match yours at the appointed time. I have reserved the Eiffel Tower for you. It will be closed to the public for three hours and the two of you will enjoy dinner with soft music accompaniment of a string and brass quartet at the base of the tower.

You will know if you are to propose to her that night. I cannot help you with that decision either. But as I stated earlier, follow your heart and trust God.

The limousine will be available to you for the five days that you are there. There are several dinner theatres to enjoy, not to mention all the sites for you two to explore together. I will leave the design of the rest of the remaining four days to the two of you. They will solely depend upon if she leaves the Eiffel Tower with your ring on her finger.

The remainder of the eleven days she is in country are on you twin. Talinda will be happy when she makes you happy so you don't have to think outside the box with her. However she does love to be surprised and on several occasions will surprise you as well. She can be very spontaneous at times...pleasantly spontaneous.

As Elijah cast his mantle upon Elisha to walk in his anointing, I place upon you authority to walk in my place. Know that I love you both and have been praying for the last several months for a successful marriage for the two of you. Just walk the path that has been laid out for you and watch God work...They two shall become one. Take care of my babies, all three of them. Well actually all four when you include Raymond. So catch your breath twin, and don't stay out too late tonight. You both have a very big day ahead of you tomorrow...and a wonderful full life in the making! I'm at rest, twin. Take care.
Love,

Brandon

He indeed needed to catch his breath. Brandon had thought of everything and he was overwhelmed at the power of the God he served. He prayed to God to please guide him and give him strength and courage to venture forward in this journey. He slid down out of the chair and knelt to pray. He prayed for Talinda that God would indeed prepare her heart. He prayed for her health and for the lives she carried. He prayed for Raymond that he would be receptive of him. He knew Brandon was a tough act to follow and prayed that God would lead him concerning Raymond. He had met Raymond as a close friend and relative to the family but to come back as his father figure was another thing.

He got dressed for dinner and proceeded over to retrieve his bride to be. He was so full of God and love that he could have just floated over on thin air. He decided he would not share the plans for the next day until they were on their way to Paris the following morning.

The knock on the door all but startled her because she was deep in thought pondering the events that would unfold that evening. She opened the door to a strikingly handsome Bernard.

"Well, hello there handsome," she said as she stepped aside so he could enter.

"Wow you look very beautiful," he replied as he entered into the room.

She closed the door behind him and as he turned to face her she walked into his arms and kissed him. As they released from the kiss he smiled and said to her, "Mmmmm...spontaneous tonight."

She only smiled and toyed with his shirt collar as she took a few steps away from him to gather up her purse and shoulder wrap off the table. As he watched her walk over to the table, the love in his heart for her radiated in the room. It was a love he knew she felt because as she turned to walk back into his direction her eyes were soft and inviting.

He wanted to get down on one knee ring or not and propose to her right then and there. But he knew the time was not yet and so held to the perfect plan that had been laid out for him. He placed his hand on her waist to guide her out of the room and they closed the door behind them.

They enjoyed a romantic candle lit dinner and beautiful conversation as soft jazz played in the background. On several occasions they held each other's gaze and he had her undivided attention. He would touch her face and she would momentarily close her eyes leaning into his touch. Many times he felt as though he could have told her the exact words she was thinking. "It's happening," he thought, "we're becoming one."

"Dance with me," he said. He rose from the table and held her hand to assist her to the middle of the restaurant where several couples were already engaged in the amour.

She placed her head in his chest and through the rhythm of the music their hearts began to beat in unison to each other. She enjoyed the sweet smell of his body mixed with the fragrance of his cologne and closed her eyes. As his strong arms secured her she realized that there was nothing left to be revealed. Bernard had stepped into the prophecy of everything she was told that her husband would be just as Brandon had walked into it. Like Brandon...he was fulfilling prophecy. The passion of his kiss earlier confirmed to her that he indeed was the man of her dreams.

She was complete, and she now knew that she was Mrs. Bernard Alexander Travis. She looked up into his eyes and stopped just short of telling him that she loved him. But she didn't have to say a word to him because her eyes told him everything he needed to hear. He rubbed his hands through her hair and paraded her with light sweet kisses.

"I'm done," she thought, "It's all over. I love this man!"

It was as if he could read her thoughts. He responded with a low, "Wow...hmmm."

"What," she shyly asked him.

"I think you already know baby," he replied as he again looked deep into her eyes, "You already know." He pulled her back in close to him and whispered through tears that had now formed in his eyes, "Thank you, God."

She just nestled into his arms and enjoyed his love. Her heart raced and she knew he could feel it. "How sweet it is to be inside love. It's such a powerful place," she thought.

He had not realized how much time had gone by because he was so caught up in the romance. He noticed the clock on the wall and remembered Brandon's warning not to stay out too late.

He escorted her back to the table and said, "I had better get you home so you can rest. We have had a very full day and much is planned for us on tomorrow."

"Okay," was all she could manage to reply. She was completely engulfed by the power of the love that grew within her for him.

After they arrived at the hotel he walked her up to her room and accompanied her inside to say goodnight to her.

"Thanks Bernard I had such a wonderful time tonight," she exclaimed with a sigh of satisfaction. She waited for him to kiss her.

"So did I baby. Everything was just perfect and you were gorgeous," he replied. He pulled her into his arms and they shared a very passionate kiss goodbye which reminded him why he chose not to remain at the hotel with her upon Brandon's request first day of her arrival. He knew that wisdom was speaking when it said aloud to him ringing in his spirit...No!

"Get rest baby, we have a full day tomorrow," he stated as he turned to leave the room.

"Okay," she replied. "Can I just get a little hint of what we are doing tomorrow?"

"Well, Mrs. Travis," he said. He toyed with a play on words. "You're just going to have to wait and see."

52

She smiled and kissed him again before he left. She closed the door behind him. She stood there momentarily and said aloud, "Uhmm...Mrs. Travis...Mrs. Bernard Alexander Travis." She chuckled and sighed as she walked to the bedroom to retire with her thoughts full of Bernard and anticipation of what the next day would bring.

He had stood outside the door and was about to leave when he heard her voice. An incontrollable smile came across his face as he heard her announce herself as Mrs. Bernard Alexander Travis. He walked away realizing he was about to receive a precious gift from God...love and matrimony.

~Chapter Six~

"Okay, Bernard, why again are we are leaving so early in the morning to go shopping?" she asked as she yawned for the fifteenth time ten minutes into their journey,

"Because we have to be checked into the hotel by noon and it takes about 4 hours to get there," he replied and shook his head in amusement. He felt so light to be so full of God's power, presence and love at that precise moment. He knew he was her husband and he was momentarily overwhelmed at what God was doing in his life.

"Where?" she asked sleepily.

"Paris," he said with a smile.

"Paris...as in France!" she squealed in delight and was instantly fully awake now. "Wow...Paris really! I've always wanted to go to Paris!"

He smiled and continued driving. He said that he wasn't sure about the room but he thought Brandon had, once again, reserved a single room for them which is, "Not going to work!" he exclaimed.

They playfully argue back and forth about being in the same room. "Bernard, you know Brandon probably reserved a suite with two bedrooms, so what are you worried about. We'll probably be in separate rooms...AND...separate beds," she said with a sarcastic chuckle.

"Well, I'll find out in a minute," he said. He pushed the button for the OnStar service to check the room reservation. A familiar voice to Bernard came over the speaker and confirmed Brandon had ordered a suite with a living and dining area. She did not, however, mention a second bedroom.

The OnStar operator knew Bernard because she received his calls most of the time. She suggested that he allowed her to download the route, even though he said he is sure of the way. While monitoring the controls of his car she said, "I notice you're driving slower than usual today Mr. Travis. That insures you'll arrive at your destination safely."

He looked over at Talinda and smiled at her as he replied to the voice coming out of the car speaker, "Well, I'm carrying very special and precious cargo with me today." His smile always penetrated past her soul and into her spirit.

The OnStar operator said something to him in Spanish and he responded. She heard the name Travis and something that sounded like babies. "Well, okay Mr. Travis. The directions should be downloading to your vehicle now. Mr. and Mrs. Travis enjoy your trip to Paris. Congratulations on the twins, Mrs. Travis."

Talinda thanked her and looked at Bernard, who shoots her an "I didn't do anything" smile. She whispered as she pointed to the rear view mirror. "Is this thing off?" she asked, referring to the OnStar.

He chuckled as he replied, "Yes."

She asked him with a suspicious look on her face, "What did you say to her?"

"She asked me what was so special and precious about my cargo," he replied. He paused to reach down and grab her hand, crossing his fingers in between hers and lifted her hand to kiss the back of it while still paying close attention to the road and cars driving around them. "I told her that the ladies name was Mrs. Travis and she was carrying twins...soooo....I guess she just assumed..." he said as he again hunched his shoulders up with a school boy smile on his face that just absolutely melted Talinda. She knew that her reaction had to show.

She smiled and shook her head. She didn't respond but thought, "Oh God I fell so fast...I've fallen in love with him. He is just adorable." She was guilty again about the feelings she had for Bernard so soon after just recently physically meeting him and her husband's death. She had thought she would mourn for years. But as she looked at Bernard she was beginning to see that that is exactly what Brandon thought she would do, mourn for years and he made sure that wouldn't happen by sending Bernard.

"Why do I get the feeling that there is something going on with you and Ms. Spanish OnStar?" Talinda said in a rather sarcastic tone.

"Why Mrs. Travis, I do believe you're jealous," he said as he toyed with her once again and flashed that million dollar smile of his.

"Stop it, Bernard," she said as she pulled her hand from his and playfully punched him in the arm. "I am NOT...jealous."

"Oh, I think you are," Bernard threw back at her again in a joking manner. Then he quickly glanced at her and said, "And you're blushing too."

"Stop...I am not jealous, and I am most certainly not blushing," she replied. She tried to hide the fact that while she wasn't jealous her face was indeed flushed.

"Sure," he replied.

"Okay...maybe I am blushing just a bit. But I am definitely NOT jealous, Mr. Travis," she responded in an okay you caught me tone.

He smiled, shook his head and grabbed her hand. He kissed it again as he continued to drive.

"Now back to this room..." he started to say but was interrupted by Talinda.

She placed her hand on his shoulder to get him to stop talking and listen to her, "Bernard, why don't we just wait and see there is probably a pull out couch or something. Maybe this was the only room Brandon could get. Let's not jump to conclusions and just see what happens when we get there, okay baby." Talinda surprised herself and Bernard when she referred to him as baby.

"Okay...okay, alright you're right. I'm probably anxious for nothing," he responded in a somewhat joyous tone. He secretly smiled inside at the security he felt that she had addressed him as baby. That was her first term of endearment toward him and his heart raced at the thought that they might actually leave Paris engaged.

They continued to drive along consumed in conversation and very much enjoyed each other. They took the time they were in the car to begin to fill each other in on their likes and dislikes, fetishes and pet peeves. All in all they shared a very pleasant drive to Paris.

They arrived in Paris and checked into the hotel. They found out that the room Brandon actually had reserved did indeed have two separate bedrooms but that wing of the hotel was currently under construction due to weather damage. Reservations had been changed for the entire guest lists that were preregistered in those rooms. They were also given a rather large discount and dinner of their choice on the house for their inconvenience. Talinda assured them that it was no inconvenience whatsoever for them. She was sure all their rooms were nice and adequate and they were perfectly okay with the arrangements.

With much persuasion from Talinda, Bernard finally agreed to stay in the same room with her. If it got to be too much, he would get a separate room.

Talinda desired for him stay in the room and said as she flashed a daddy's little girl smile, "I promise I'll be good sweetheart."

He shook his head and took a deep breath before he responded. "I'm not worried about you. I'm worried about me," he said with a smile that just took her temperature right off the chart.

"Don't be so sure about that, Mr. Travis. I am so struggling right now," she said with a serious look that let him know this was going to be a very tempting and interesting five days.

The bellman gave them a tour of the room. The bed in the suite was king-sized, and there is no sofa bed in the living room area. Bernard asked if one would be available. Talinda shook her head in amusement. The bellman was somewhat perplexed by the question but said that he would look into it for them.

Bernard filled her in on some details of the day as they settled into the room and ate the lunch that had been reserved for them. He told her they have special dinner plans later, but didn't disclose location. That of course drove her crazy with excitement and anticipation.

After they both showered and changed, the limousine arrived. The front desk associate called to inform them that their driver was downstairs whenever they were ready to leave.

They arrived at the boutique, and he escorted her in to get her settled. "I'm sure there is not a gown in this store that is as beautiful as this lovely lady," he said to the fashion consultant. "But, if you find one that is half as gorgeous as she is I'm sure she'll be stunning in it."

"I'm sure she will, sir. Don't worry we'll take very good care of her," the clerk said.

"I know you will," he replied as he turned back toward Talinda.

"Oh Bernard," Talinda replied with an embarrassed smile as she kissed him.

He cupped her face, looked into her eyes and said, "Okay, I love you baby." He didn't wait for a response, he just kissed her again. "I'll see you soon. I have to go take care of everything else."

As he turned to walk away he heard the sales clerk say, "Wow, your husband seems so romantic and he certainly takes good care of you."

Talinda responded, "Yes he is and yes he does. He's the man of my dreams and the love of my life. I got it so bad for him."

The clerk responded, "Oooo. I am so jealous."

"I am so blessed," Talinda added.

Tears filled Bernard's eyes and he smiled. He was glad that his back was to them so his reaction wouldn't show. As he reentered the limousine he is confident of one thing...he indeed had her heart. He looked up toward heaven and whispered, "Thank you, Brandon."

He headed to the jewelry store while his tuxedo was being hemmed. True to his word, Brandon had Talinda's ensemble waiting for him. "I need to see the top five most beautiful and elegant wedding sets you have available." The salesman asked if there was a certain price range that he desired to stay in the boundaries of. He replied not to worry about price to just show him his top five sets that he had available. He laid the sets out in front of him. Bernard was floored at the beauty of the diamonds. He gasps, "Wow these are beautiful."

He tried desperately to remember the set Talinda's wore the very first time he met her at Brandon memorial service. But just couldn't recall. He was about to say, "Alright Brandon which one?" when Brandon's words rang in his spirit, "It *must come from inside of your heart.*" So he changed his thoughts and said, "Okay, Holy Spirit help me. Show me the love I have for my wife. Which one?" As he began to look at them, the one in the middle of the five caught his attention.

So he made a decision. "I think I like this combination right here. What does the men's band look like that goes with this set?" he asked the sales clerk.

He was shown the wedding band that matched. "Perfect. I'll take it," he said.

"Okay, sir, this particular set is fifteen thousand dollars for the three," the salesman responded hesitantly.

"That's fine, where does that put me with tax and insurance," Bernard replied. He not so much as flinched at the price that was told to him.

"I will calculate that for you, sir. I'll be right back with your total," the salesman replied as he hurried off. He returned and told Bernard that the final cost would be nineteen thousand dollars.

Bernard, again did not flinch at the price, said to him, "Okay, what size is the set? She wears a size 6 ¾."

"This just happens to be 6 ¾," he responded.

Bernard replied, "Great, and I need an 8."

"Wow," the salesman replied. "This men's ring is an 8. We usually have to send out rings to be sized. Someone really wanted you to have this set today."

"Yes, someone did," Bernard replied. He couldn't control the smile that came across his face. "I'll take it. I plan on proposing to her tonight at dinner."

"Say no more sir," the salesman interjected. "We have a beautiful presentation box for the engagement ring and we will place the bands in the boxes the rings come in which is just as nice."

"Thank you," Bernard replied. I have twenty thousand in traveler's checks, and since you have been so helpful please keep the other thousand for yourself."

"Wow! Thank you, sir. That is very generous of you. I will get these polished and packaged if you will give me a moment," the salesman replied with excitement.

He offered Bernard coffee and croissants while he waited. Bernard declined, not wanting to spoil his dinner with Talinda. The salesman informed him that everything is ready. The jewelry had all been polished, and as he escorted Bernard to the door he thanked him again for his generosity and wished him well on his evening. He told Bernard that he hoped she would say "yes".

Bernard smiled and replied, "Thanks...but she's already said yes."

After he purchased the rings he had time to go back to the hotel to place the bands in the hotel safe and head out with her necklace ensemble and engagement ring in the inside pocket of his jacket to pick up his bride to be. Bernard was in awe of God as the limousine headed over to the boutique where Talinda was.

As he stood at the base of the stairs and awaited Talinda's descent, one of the fashion consultants of the boutique welcomed him back and told to him that they were advised not to accessorize her gown.

"Yes," he said. "I have those items with me. If you would assist me, I would appreciate it."

"Of course," she said as he showed her the jewelry. "Oh, my, how beautiful."

"Yeah...not as beautiful as she is but thank you," he replied.

"Oh," the consultant sighed, "Do you have a brother?"

He smiled with and chuckled as he responded, "Well, yeah, my twin. Unfortunately, he passed away a few months ago."

"Sorry to hear that," she replied. "Wow, there were two of you...whew," she said. She paused as she took a deep breath and fanned herself in an amusing gesture. She then laughed as she comically inquired and slightly bit her pointer finger on her left hand, "Ahhh...Any cousins?"

Bernard was almost in total laughter he answered, "Yeah, but trust me they are nothing like my brother and me."

They are engaged in conversation as Talinda rounded the corner. He had tears in his eyes as she descended down the stairs.

"Wow, baby, you look stunning," Bernard said to Talinda.

"Really?" She replied through a loving smile, "You like it?"

"I love it," he answered with a loving sigh. "Here, baby. I have your jewelry for the evening," he said as he opened the box.

She gasped, "Oh, Bernard its lovely. I was wondering why they didn't accessorize and then the consultant said that my husband was bringing it." She couldn't help but smile at her statement.

"Yeah, I wanted to present this part to you. I had a little help with picking it out. But sweetheart...it's not nearly as lovely as you," he replied.

She turned and he placed the necklace on her and put the bracelet on as the clerk put on her earrings. The consultant never even noticed that Talinda didn't have on a wedding ring. It never even occurred to her to pay attention to it. The love Talinda and Bernard shared filled the room and there was spiritually a sweet aroma of love in the air.

Bernard placed his hand on the side of her face as he declared, "You are so beautiful, and I love you so much."

She looked him in the eye and said, "I love you too sweetheart."

Both the fashion consultants stood there almost in tears and one of them said, "Wow, genuine love."

"Come on baby, dinner is waiting on us," Bernard said as he thanked the ladies and started to escort Talinda out.

Talinda replied, "Okay." She then turned to the two consultants and thanked them for making her so beautiful.

"You're welcome ma'am," they replied. Then the one who escorted her down the stairs said, "We will send your other gowns and items you selected to your hotel suite."

"Okay, thanks again," Talinda said as she gave them a wink and she turned back toward Bernard and said, "Ready honey."

After they left the two clerks let out a sigh and the one asked the other, "Where are all the men in the world like that? I want one like that."

"Oooo and he is nice to look at too," the other chimed in. "Did you see how he was filling out that tuxedo? I would love to be in that hotel suite tonight in her place."

"Tell me about it...whew...I'll have your baby too sweet thing," the one that helped her with the jewelry said as she was fanning herself.

They shared a silly school girl laugh as they head back upstairs still engaged in conversation about Talinda and her husband to prepare Talinda's gowns for transport to her hotel suite.

Once they were inside the limousine Talinda turned to Bernard and said, "Okay, am I going to find out where dinner is now?"

He smiled as he said, "You sure will...when we get there."

Talinda sighed, "Bernard...."

"You'll find out when we get there, Mrs. Travis," he said in a teasing tone. "I love you."

"I love you," Talinda said and finally concedes on getting the dinner plans out of him as she looked up and sees the Eiffel Tower. "Oh, the Eiffel Tower...oh Bernard can we stop here for a minute. I have always wanted to see the Eiffel Tower up close.

"Oh, I think that can be arranged," Bernard said. "Do you have your wrap? You'll need it."

"Yeah, it's right here," she replied.

Without Bernard even having the opportunity to ask the driver to stop he pulled into the Eiffel Tower entrance. Talinda finally realized that dinner was here. She said, "Ohhh Bernard."

"Welcome to dinner under the Eiffel Tower baby," he said as the driver opened the door.

"Oh my gosh," she gasped.

"It's closed off for three hours just for us. Come on," Bernard said through a smile.

"Oh my gosh Bernard...how did you do..." she said in total surprise.

"Don't thank me Talinda...this was all Brandon's idea. He set all of this up for us," Bernard replied.

"Brandon..." Talinda said almost in tears.

"Come on let's go have dinner. Wrap up, it will be cool until we get underneath. I was told they would have heaters blowing so we wouldn't get too chilly under there," he said as they walked toward the base of the tower where their table is set. The musicians had already started to play soft melodies.

"Oh Bernard this is amazing," Talinda said in total awe of the moment.

So they sat down to a seven course dinner. They conversed and just relaxed and enjoyed every minute. The music was playing and Bernard gently grabbed her hand and said, "Dance with me."

She rose from the table all smiles and totally enraptured in the ambiance of the love that engulfed them both under the Eiffel Tower. Then they sat for desert and continued in conversation. She looked into his eyes and tears filled hers.

She placed her hand on the side of his face and declared, "I love you. I love you so much. I didn't think that I could fall so fast and so hard but I did...I did and I love you Bernard. Not because you look like Brandon. Not because I want to replace him. But because you are the second man in my life that has fulfilled prophecy. I'm starting to see that you are probably the man of my dreams. I always called Brandon the man of my dreams. But in actuality he was the man of prophecy and so I placed him in my dream man category as well. But there are some things that I told God I wanted in a dream man that Brandon never fulfilled. He was the man of a dream. But I see now that I have met you, not the man of my dreams. He fulfilled everything the prophetess said my husband would be but he was not all that I told God I desired. Brandon was...well let's just say very reserved and conservative and what I described to God as the man of my dreams was anything but that. I told God I wanted a man who was spontaneous...who knew how to walk on the wild side erotically and keep it Godly. A man who would be domineering and take complete ownership of me without being too controlling. I am beginning to realize that God sent Brandon to prepare me for you. To teach me the God side of the spontaneously erotic man I desired. And has left in me a part of him so I don't ever forget the balance of the love a man should have for his wife. Don't get me wrong...my love for and with Brandon was strong and powerful and I wouldn't trade it for anything in the world. It was agape love all the way and I grew and blossomed in it. I was so ready to spend the rest of my life with him. I never thought that I would ever be able to love another man after Brandon. I thank God for you. I..."

"Shhhh," he replied. He took the ring out of his pocket and got down on one knee and he opened it.

"Oh, Bernard," she gasped.

"Will you marry me?" he asked.

"Oh my God, Bernard...oh my God," she responded.

"Oh my God Bernard is nice. But, 'yes Bernard' is what I need to hear right now, sweetheart," he declared.

"Oh my God...yes Bernard...yes...yes...yes!" She cried out.

He smiled and chuckled, "That's even better." He stood and pulled her up into his arms and kissed her. "I love you, Mrs. Travis." He declared in between kisses.

"Mrs. Bernard Alexander Travis," she said.

He smiled with a sexy manly chuckle and said, "Yeah, that, too."

They danced and enjoyed each other in their awesome evening filled with love. They sat back down and talked about everything imaginable and all that they have to plan over the next few months. While they are talked she looked at him and noticed that tears fell from his eyes. She wiped them and said, "Oh baby what is this?"

He replied, almost completely choked up through his tears, "I'm just overwhelmed at how much God loves me. That he would give me the woman of my dreams. That he would give me everything that I have asked for in life. That he would bless me. And for Brandon...that he would trust me with his wife and with his children...I'm just humbled by his trust in me and God's love for me."

"Oh, baby," she said as she wiped his tears. She got up from the table and stood beside him and pulled his head into her bosom. She said, "Ohhh...I love you so much."

"Oh, my God. Even in my tears you make me feel strong. Oh, God. How do you do that? How do you do that? Even when I'm weak you make me feel like I'm everything. You magnify my strengths. You don't exploit my weaknesses and you build me up with a simple touch. A man can be a man and the same time be himself around you," he said as he enjoys the touch of her hand.

"I love you, baby...I love you. Mmmmm...It's okay to be yourself around me. In my arms is one place you don't ever have to be afraid to be Bernard. I guess I learned it from my mom. I watched her with my dad. I watched how she made him the center and the head in the home. I watched how she nurtured him, how she loved him. Even in his mistakes, she comforted him. I watched her. She and I weren't very close growing up because she had a lot of things going on. But I still watched her...how she was with daddy. I watched how he was when he was around her. I asked God show me how to make my husband feel that way; show me how to touch him and soothe him and bring him peace at the end of a stressful day. I asked God to show me how to make him feel like he is the best man in the world when he has just made the biggest mistake in the world. I prayed and it just happened. I mean...I don't know...it just happened," she said as she stroked his head.

He sighed as he declared, "I am so blessed. I miss Brandon. But I have to admit I'm selfish because if he were here then I wouldn't be. But you would be complete. You would be here with the man whose babies you're carrying."

"Bernard," she said in no uncertain terms, "I am complete...I am. Brandon made sure of that. I miss him too and you're right, if he was here then you wouldn't be...but he's not here...you are. And I am complete. As far as the babies go...like Brandon said the night he lay dying in my arms, Bernard is going to be a father. You are their father...these are your babies, okay. These are YOUR babies."

"There you go doing it again, making me feel so secure," he replied. "I want our little girl to be the same way...just like her mother."

She smiled and said, "I'm sure she will be. And she'll have a little bit of her dad too."

Yeah," he replied, "Brandon..."

"Bernard, I'm not talking about Brandon's baby. I'm talking about the ones that we're going to have together," she replied.

"I love you so much," he said as he rose from the table to embrace her. "Come share a last dance with me. Our time is almost up. Come on..."

"Alright sweetheart," she replied. She accompanied him to the center of the base of the Eiffel Tower and they danced to the last song. But for them time seemed to stand still as they moved together as one with their heartbeats in perfect unison.

As he placed her wrap around her shoulders, that was the limousine driver's cue to opened the car door. They exit the base of the Eiffel Tower. It was very chilly coming from under the tower where the heaters were blowing. Once they were inside the limousine, Bernard thanked the driver for having a temperature warm for his wife on the inside.

They rode back to the hotel with Talinda tucked securely in Bernard's arms. She was in total awe of the majesty of God in her life and all the lengths that he and Brandon had gone through to bless her and heal her soul and spirit. The babies moved and she placed Bernard's hands on her stomach and he smiled and kissed the side of her face. There was no need for words. The love they shared spoke volumes.

Once they got back into the hotel room Talinda was ready for a hot shower and a relaxed evening with her husband to be. They climbed on the couch in their pajamas enjoying hot cocoa with marshmallows and sat talking and just enjoying everything about what had transpired that day.

She started to yawn and Bernard kissed her forehead. "You're tired," he said.

She replied with a daddy's little girl smile, "Yeah, but I don't want to be without you. Come lie down with me."

"Talinda..." he responded in a 'that's NOT a good idea' tone.

"Oh baby I just want you to hold me in your arms until I fall asleep. We have on pajamas and we can lie on top of the covers. We're fully covered Bernard," she replied softly as she yawned.

"Why do I get the feeling that you are going to get your way a lot? That it's going to be hard for me to say no to you...you're spoiled," he said to her.

"Uh huh, I sure am," she said as she yawned again. "Besides its too late now...I've got the ring on my finger and I'm not taking it off...ever. Please sweetheart, just hold me until I fall asleep. I just want to be in my husband's arms," she said with a smile as she yawns again leading him into the bedroom.

"Alright...I can do that," he responded as he allowed her to lead him to the bedroom.

They lay down and he held her in his arms. She shivered slightly so he pulled the blanket up to cover them with. She talked to him until she fell asleep. But when he tried to move she sighed and held on to him as she snuggled into his chest. He realized, "She is not going to let me go. I'm not going anywhere tonight." So he decided since he couldn't we would pray over her. As prayed she stirred but showed no sign that she was indeed awake.

Father,

> *As I lay here holding her in my arms all I can say is thank You. There are simply no words to describe the love I feel in my heart for You and for her. I am overwhelmed at how consuming Your presence is. Part of me is afraid to fall asleep for fear that when I wake in the morning I would find that is has all been a dream and will wake to find myself back in my townhouse in my own bed clutching a pillow. Lord, I thank You for Your blessing and I promise that I will not only cherish her but I will always love her and keep her. I will protect her and lead her as I continue to follow you. I have to admit that I am a little intimidated of my predecessor. He was such an awesome and loving husband and his unconditional love was and is so agape. I pray that I will be able to satisfy her every need as I am sure he did. He is my brother, Lord, and I miss him. Although I am in total bliss at this very moment my hearts aches at the loss of my twin. I know there will be times of sorrow and remembrance in her life. I pray that You will use me to minister and comfort her in those times. She is so very special, Lord, and is the epitome of what a wife is and should be.*

> *God, as I place my hand on her stomach I pray now for the lives that she carries; the seed of your servant, Lord. I pray that You will lead and guide me concerning their care. I feel so much love for them and I thank You for allowing me to be their father, a responsibility that I do not take lightly Lord. I solicit your guidance concerning them. I already have a love for them and Raymond. He is such a special young man, Lord, and I feel I will learn as much from him as You place in me to teach him. We seem to have a special bond already and I look forward to the life we*

will all have together. I am in awe that You would bless me and deem me worthy to care for and love them as well as being loved by them. Lord, my heart races with anticipation of holding little Brandon in my arms. I know it will be a bitter sweet moment for us all Lord and I pray that You will be with us.

I thank you for all things, God, and pray in your son Jesus' name,

Amen

She lay there in his arms and fought off the tears that welled up in her eyes because she didn't want to alert him that she was awake. "Truly," she thought to herself. "This man is ordained of God to be in my life to care for me for such a time as this." He continued to stroke her temple and pray for her until he drifted off to sleep. He held her secured in his arms.

~Chapter Seven~

"Baby I can't sleep in the bed like this with you," he said when they rose the next morning.

She completely ignored his declaration. Still nestled in his arms she looked up into his eyes and said, "Make love to me."

He gathered himself before he responded to her. "Talinda...,"

"Shhhh, make love to me Bernard," she said again. She cut him off and climbed almost on top of while him as she kissed him.

"Talinda, baby...please....this cannot happen," he said as he tried to move from underneath her.

She knew he would not be rough with her because of the babies. So she took full advantage of the situation. She fully straddled him and said to him again, "Make love to me baby."

He grabbed her slightly pulled her up so she could look into his eyes. "Talinda...what are you doing...you are NOT Mrs. Travis yet."

"Oh, but I am Mrs. Travis," she declared as she kissed him again.

"Sweetheart you know that just a play on words. You are not "my" Mrs. Travis yet, Talinda..."

"Oh, I became Mrs. Bernard Travis that night on the deck in Athens. I just didn't know it then," she replied.

Before he could say another word she kissed him again. He broke the kiss and said, "Talinda, please don't do this."

She started to kiss him in a seductive way. She gently caressed him and kissed him all over his face and neck. He started to lose control of the situation. He said, "Oh God, please help me...God please. Talinda, I want to make love to you so bad. Please don't do this. Oh, God. Girl, please stop! I don't want to push you off me baby...I don't want to hurt you. You gotta stop, Talinda. God, please help me!"

She looked him square in the eye and said, "Oh no baby. God is NOT coming into our bedroom. You are on your own in here, sweetheart. Make love to me, Bernard."

≈

Lindsay and Nevette sat at a corner table in the hospital cafeteria at Northside Hospital and enjoyed lunch. She was on temporary assignment from the Falcon's for specialty training and she and her best friend Nevette were back in college mode again. Nevette and Lindsay were still extremely close although they didn't attend the same church. They met for lunch regularly. Also, Lindsay was Tre's godmother so she was a frequent visitor at the Goodfellow residence. Lindsay lived just outside Atlanta in Forest Park and worked on the therapy team for the Atlanta Falcons. She attended Grace Tabernacle Christian Center in Decatur, Georgia, which happened to be the same church Nevette's brother Teddy and Talinda Travis attended.

Nevette, however, still somewhat uncomfortable with male patients, elected to work at Northside Hospital on the physical therapy ward. She had no desire to work with an all-male professional athlete team to Justices' relief. He hadn't wanted her in close proximity for the opportunity for all those male athletes to come on to his wife on a daily basis. Nor did he want his wife's hands on them. He knew all too well that her touch can be somewhat arousing even when she hadn't intended for it to be. She is an anointed woman and the anointing can be very attractive to believers and non-believers alike.

As they sat and conversed, Dr. Trevor Johnson from OB/GYN walked into the cafeteria to grab a quick bite between his rounds. When Nevette saw him she kicked Lindsay under the table and said, "There he is, girl. He is the one I told you about...Dr. Trevor Johnson."

"Well I have to admit he is cute," Lindsay said with a sly smile. "But girl you know I'm not the settle down type. I'm here for training not to find a man. Besides girl I have a whole team full of men to flirt with if I need the entertainment."

"Girl, you need to settle down. You are not getting any younger and your clock is ticking," Nevette said with a matter of fact look on her face and her head slightly tilted.

"My clock is not ticking because I unplugged it years ago. Girl, I am not trying to be anybody's momma. I am satisfied being Tre's godmother because I can send his little tail home when the momma game gets old," she said as she laughed out.

Nevette laughed, but sensed that something else was behind her friend's declaration. She decided not to push the issue. There always seemed to be something that was just not quite right with Lindsay. She always laughed and praised God but there was still so much pain in her eyes.

Just as they neared the end of their lunch break and prepared to leave, Dr. Johnson saw Nevette and came over to speak. As he approached Nevette and Lindsay smiled at each other and shared a private conversation with their eyes. Lindsay gave her a 'you better not' look and Nevette silently replied back with an, 'oh I most certainly will' look of her own.

"Well, hello there, Mrs. Goodfellow. How are you today?" Trevor said as he looked in Lindsay's direction. "And hello to you, too, Mrs..."

"Ahhh, that's Miss and its Lindsay," she replied as she kicked Nevette under the table.

"Oh, yes. I'm sorry. How rude of me," Nevette replied. "Trevor, this is my best friend Lindsay. We met in college and have been close ever since. And Trevor I've told you about this Mrs. Goodfellow stuff, we're co-workers so it's Nevette."

"Nice to meet you Dr. Johnson," Lindsay replied before Trevor could respond to Nevette.

"Just Trevor is fine and the pleasure is all mine," he replied as Lindsay playfully kicked Nevette under table again.

"Well, I certainly hope you're here to join the staff, Lindsay," Trevor asked.

"No, I'm just here for training," Lindsay stated. "I work on the therapy team for the Atlanta Falcons."

"Oh, well I'm sure I'll see you from time to time while you are here then. It was very nice to meet you but I had better get back upstairs. Mrs. Storm is at seven centimeters and one of my high risk patients. Her first child was almost three months early. Besides, with twins you never know when things are going to take a quick turn," he said. He looked at his watch and said goodbye as he smiled as walked away.

"Well?" Nevette asked.

"Well what, Nevette?" Lindsay replied. She knew full well what "well" meant.

"You know well what," Nevette said with a sly smile. "What do you think about Trevor Johnson?"

"Okay, I have to admit he is 'sexy fine' girl, but I'm not trying to get tied down in a serious relationship. That's just not me," Lindsay responded and hoped the subject will change but Nevette hammered down on her instead.

"Girl, you are twenty seven years old and I think you have sowed enough oats," Nevette said teasingly. "Come on Trevor is a sexy, fine and cute doctor. Besides he can give you all your yearly exams and deliver all y'all babies' free girl."

At that comment they both crack up laughing as Lindsay said, "At the rate you and Derrick are going, I won't need to have any of my own."

"What do you mean girl?" Nevette chuckled. "You act like we're throwing them out like rabbits or something. Tre is four and we are two months pregnant with our second."

"But seriously, Lindsay," Nevette said in a more serious tone now. "What are you so afraid of? I mean I'm not saying you have to marry the guy tomorrow. I'm just saying you seem to go through guys like a snowball rolling down the hill. You gain momentum and pick up

68

everything in your path and leave snow dust flying everywhere girl. Just maybe it's time to settle down...I mean, I'm just saying."

"Okay...okay I swear between you and Talinda I've been lectured to death this week," Lindsay said as she rolled her eyes with a sly smile on her face. She tried desperately to hide the fact that Nevette's words had struck a deep wound.

"Talinda? Who's that?" Nevette asked.

"Oh, she is the youth pastor at my church. You know you two really ought to meet y'all are just alike. I don't know why you and Derrick are over at Shiloh Tabernacle anyway girl. It's drama central over there."

"Girl, you know I don't want to be there but I'm 'letting Justice lead'," Nevette said with a sigh and made the quotation mark gesture with her hands. "He didn't like where we were going and Teddy said I need to let him make the decision on where we are going to fellowship. Teddy said that he has been struggling being in my shadow spiritually all these years. Lindsay we both know I let him lead the household but sometimes spiritually he doesn't see the whole picture. He has only chosen this church because the pastor has him in position training him to be his assistant. I don't really think Justice is ready for that big a responsibility but I'm backing off girl and being submissive and supportive. Girl, if I go visit your church he will probably feel betrayed."

"And you want me to settle down...why again?" Lindsay asked sarcastically. They exit the cafeteria still engaged in conversation and laughter as they headed back to the physical therapy ward.

As the weeks and months went by, Dr. Trevor Johnson was finally successful to get Lindsay to go to lunch and dinner with him from time to time. Training had long been over and she had returned to her job at the Falcons' training camp. She had to admit that she did enjoy his company. There was something different about him compared to all the other guys she had run through in her lifetime. He seemed to ignore her many sexual advances toward him.

She assumed underneath all his gentlemanly manners he was indeed just like everybody else. She decided it was time for his true colors to manifest and so she accepted his invitation to cook dinner for her at his house. She had only been in his house once before and marveled that he hadn't come on to her and really was just interested in her opinion on a recent decorating overhaul he had done on his great room.

She noted that he looked strikingly handsome and was his usual well groomed self as he opened the door to invite her in. "Mmmmm he always smelled so nice," she thought as she passed by him. As she entered the kitchen she commented on the aroma of dinner he was still had in preparation.

"Thank you," he replied as he followed her into the kitchen. "My mother was determined that I would be a domestic man. She ensured that I knew how to cook and clean and do laundry..."

"You're hired," Lindsay interrupted and they share a laugh.

He smiled as he continued with his previous comment, "Nah, seriously. She always said that I should desire a wife, but not need one because anything a man desired he would take special care of once he acquired it. He wouldn't abuse it but would understand its proper use and love and protect it."

Lindsay's laughter was completely stunted by his comment and she was left without a response. She was suddenly very uneasy with him. Not because she feared what he would do to her, but what he would bring out of her...her past. Something she had been very successful thus far at hiding from the world outside of Faith Temple located in small town Mississippi. She kept it tucked away in recesses of her mind.

He felt that she was very much uneasy with the current conversation so he decided to let her off the hook. He walked over to the refrigerator and asked, "Can I get you anything to drink while we're waiting for the dinner rolls to finish in the oven?"

"No I'm fine," Lindsay said in a somewhat shaky tone.

He totally changed the subject to a work related conversation which seemed to relax Lindsay. They went through dinner with fun conversation and laughter and she found herself enjoying his company. She felt so different with him and out of sheer fear decided that she would sabotage the potential relationship herself. She realized at that moment that she had absolutely no idea what real love was. She neither knew how to give nor receive it. She needed to gain the control of the atmosphere and so shifted the situation in a different direction.

She stood up from the dinner table and walked over to his side of the table. She grabbed him by the hand, pulled him up from the table and led him into the living room. He followed her with a look of bewilderment on his face and eyed her with much curiosity. She led him to the couch and started to unbutton his shirt. She kissed him lightly on the cheek and was about to plant one on his lips when he grabbed her hands and leaned back out of her reach.

"What are you doing, Lindsay?" he said as he looked her square in the eyes.

"Showing my appreciation for dinner and giving you what you have been building up to these last six months," she replied. "But I have to admit you're good, you're probably one of the few who have actually earned this."

"Earned what, Lindsay?" he replied. He knew full well what she had referred too.

"Come on, Trevor, we both know why I am here tonight," she replied. She started to feel more confident because she felt the situation was about to go the way she expected from every other man she has ever dated. "I mean you have wined and dined me for months. Why else would you invite me to your house tonight and cook me such a nice dinner? I have to admit, you have smooth game brother. You even seem genuine in church."

She smiled and started to try to unbutton his shirt again. He stopped her and grabbed her hands as he again took a step back and away from her. He had a look of total disappointment on his face.

"Wait a minute," he replied with a hint of frustration in his voice. "Is that what you think this is? You think I have pursued you all these months and cooked dinner for you tonight to get you into bed? Lindsay I didn't have to cook dinner for you to do that. You have been throwing yourself at me since the first day I took you to lunch six months ago. If sex is all I wanted I could have had that on the first date or whatever the heck it was you called it. I spent half that evening and countless others ignoring your seductive advances and excusing myself when the temptation escalated to a level beyond my control. I resent you referring to my unfeigned love and respect to worship God and my relationship with him as an avenue to get you into bed. What happened so bad to you that you don't understand when a real Christian man is trying to love you? I have been abstinent since I gave my life to Christ five years ago. The next woman that I give myself to in physical love will be my wife on our wedding night."

She realized that she had insulted him and out of sheer fear, she decided to finalize the possibility of having any type of relationship with him after tonight. She could feel herself began to unravel on the inside. She walked back up in front of him and tried to kiss him. "Come on Trevor let's just get this over with so I can go on about my way and you can too."

He grabbed her and looked her square in the yes and spoke barely above a whisper, "I am not trying to have sex with you Lindsay. My God what did he do to you? Don't make me pay for his mistakes. But you're right about one thing...this is over." He released his hold on her and walked over to the front door. He opened it and gestured for her to leave as he said, "I'm sorry that things didn't work out between us. I guess you're not who I thought you were."

These were the last words she heard from Trevor as she walked out the door. For the first time she felt shame in her actions. Tears streamed down her face as she drove toward Nevette's house. It was Sunday evening and Justice and Tre were away at the father-son overnight retreat with the church. Nevette was now eight months pregnant with her daughter. She had on pajama bottoms and one of Justices big t-shirts relaxing on the couch with a good book when the doorbell rang.

She got up off the couch and put her feet into the slippers. "Just when I thought I would have some time to myself...who can this be," she thought out loud sighing as she opened the door. "Lindsay..."

"Oh, Nevette I messed it up...I didn't think...I don't know...I didn't realize!" Lindsay yelled as she walked past Nevette into the living room apparently talking to herself.

She remained calm tried to assess the situation. Nevette replied, "Lindsay you're not making any sense. What are you talking about?"

Lindsay replied in total despair and confusion, "I thought he wanted...I mean...Trevor...he....Pastor Miller...I...he's not like the others...but he did it...it wasn't me Nevette...it wasn't my fault!"

She started to feel panicked but was still unable to put the pieces together. Nevette closed the door and followed Lindsay into the living room. "Lindsay you're not making any sense at all. Dr. Johnson has always showed you respect even though you constantly throw yourself at him. Lindsay what has happened?"

She fell to her knees and started to scream as she began to unravel her past. "I HATE THEM BECAUSE THEY EXPOSED ME! THEY SAID I WAS THE ONE THAT WAS WRONG. HE CAME ON TO ME...I WAS JUST A BABY!"

Nevette slumped slightly and she knelt beside Lindsay as she touched her friends shoulder for support. She realized what Lindsay's dark secret was.

Lindsay continued, "NOBODY PROTECTED ME! THEY MADE ME GET AN ABORTION TO PROTECT HIS IMAGE SO NOBODY WOULD KNOW THAT THE PASTOR FATHERED AN ILLEGITMATE CHILD WITH A MINOR!" She sobbed as she began to speak in a lower tone but with just as much anger. "I was labeled a Jezebel because I liked to look nice. They blamed me and they protected him! And I hated them, Nevette. I hated my mom. Mother Carver blamed me and my mom did nothing. She agreed with them. How could she, Nevette? How could she? I was her baby. I was only fifteen!

Nevette fought back tears as she responded, "Oh God, Lindsay. So, that's been it all these years. Please tell me this isn't true."

Still down on her knees, Lindsay rocked back and forth and cried as she continued as though Nevette hadn't said a word. "They said it was my fault because I came to church with clothes that fit! They weren't even tight. I never exposed my chest and my mom always made sure my bottom was covered. He had a lustful spirit. Pastor Miller was having sex with almost every young girl in the church and nobody would stop him and they knew what he was doing. And they made me give up my baby to protect him. Why is everybody so caught up in ministry that they can't see what real ministry is? It wasn't...my...fault!

She collapsed in Nevette's arms. She held her and began to pray for God to give her the words to say. "Oh God it wasn't your fault Lindsay. You've been pretending all these years that you were okay and carrying such a heavy load. Oh God...Lindsay I am so sorry this happened to you. Oh God help me know what to say to her...God give me the words...please God."

She just sat there and held her and waited on God. God did indeed give Nevette the words to say. He gave her words of comfort and words of deliverance. Scriptures fell into her spirit and out of her mouth and hope and love filled the room as Nevette laid her hands on Lindsay and began to pray for her mind her womb and her wounded spirit. She began to bind the enemy and take authority over promiscuity that had taken over Lindsay's life as a result of her molestation at the hands of Pastor Miller.

She prayed a prayer of deliverance and healing:

Father,

Oh God I come before You asking for the comfort of the Holy Spirit to rain down upon us Lord. God I don't understand why such ugly things happen to innocent children but God I pray now that You would begin to restore her Lord. Begin to put the pieces of her shattered childhood back together. Just as You said in the book of Joel that You would restore what the palmerworm the cankerworm and the caterpillar hath eaten up. Restore her God...cleanse like only You can. God the blood of Jesus covers a multitude of sin. Father You said in Isaiah that You would give them that mourn beauty for ashes, the oil of joy for mourning, the garment of praise for the spirit of heaviness; that they might be called trees of righteousness, the planting of the LORD, that he might be glorified.

Father You said You would wipe every tear from our eye. Jesus You are a Savior that is acquainted with grief. And You are our high priest. But You are not a high priest which cannot be touched with the feeling of our infirmities; but was in all points tempted as we are, yet without sin. And Father since we know that You are our high priest and care for us. We realize that we can come boldly unto the throne of grace, that we may obtain mercy, and find grace to help in time of need. Lord when we suffer and know not how we shall escape from the pain and the torment of our mind You hath said that your grace is sufficient for us Lord and your strength is made perfect in weakness. For when we are indeed weak Lord You are strong.

Father I pray for her innocence Lord that even though she feels that it has been stolen. Father I pray that You will restore purity in her body Lord. I pray that You will heal and open her womb God. That as she repents and cries out to You Lord, we pray that You will wash away all residue of her past. That You gird up the loins of her mind Lord by sanctifying her emotions God so that they will not work against her in the coming months of her complete healing and transformation Lord. Father I pray for her wounded spirit that You will comfort like only You can. I ask that You would fill her with the power of the Holy Ghost baptizing her with fire.

Father I also pray for Trevor that You would give him an understanding heart. Obviously Lord you have sent him into her life. So I pray that You minister unto him as well God. Satan I bind you with the authority that has been given unto me by the shed blood of Jesus Christ. Your assignment concerning this vessel has been canceled. You are exposed and found out now you must repay seven fold. God I thank You that You will indeed insure that she is blessed beyond measure that she will not have room enough to receive.

Spirit of depression you are relieved from your assignment on this vessel. Spirit of promiscuity you are now relieved from your assignment on this vessel. Spirit of despair, deception and delusion you have all been relieved of your assignments on the mind of this vessel. Low self-esteem you will vacate the premises now because your tenure here is up and you must go. Oh God my soul cries out Hallelujah and I thank you for your healing power.

As Nevette prayed Lindsay could feel the Lord's presence overshadow her begin to cleanse her. Nevette remembered what the mothers of the church would say about deliverance services and she rose, opened the door and commanded the spirits that had oppressed Lindsay to vacate not only Lindsay but leave her home as well.

~Chapter Eight~

Bernard looked at Talinda. He appeared to give in and kissed her. He then got a good hold on her and sat up with her. "Go take a cold shower Talinda Travis. You need to cool off! Look, obviously neither of us is a virgin here. You are a pregnant widow and I haven't been saved all my life. But, I have taken a vow before God baby, and when I stand before God at the altar, I want to stand there with clean hands. I want to be able to say that I did not fornicate with you...that I did not defile you. I want to be able to enjoy you on my wedding night without any guilt what so ever. So baby I can't do this. Oh and God did come in this bedroom because we are not married yet. He rescued me from myself."

She replied nonchalantly in a school girl tone as she hunched her shoulders and hopped off of him, "Okay."

She headed to the bathroom to brush her teeth and get ready for breakfast. After she left he continued to sit there on the bed completely confused. He desperately attempted to figure out what the heck just happened. He sat there and analyzed the conversation. "God, what was that?" Then it came to him, "It was a test!" He laughed to himself, "God it was a test." He got up and went into the bathroom.

"Talinda...were you testing me?" he asked her.

She smiled and kept looking in the mirror as she brushed her hair. So he turned her around toward him, looked her in the eyes and said to her, "You were testing me."

She looked at him a put her hand on the side of his face lightly caressed him. She said, "You passed." Then she walked back into the bedroom.

He walked into the bedroom after her. He grabbed her softly by the arm and said, "Talinda..."

She shushed him before he could say another word and said to him, "I wanted to know that you were a real man of God. I wanted to know that you weren't going to let me push you to a place of temptation. I needed to know that you weren't going to put me before

God. That you were going to have enough man of God in you to say no to me when I'm trying to take us into a direction that we should not go in. I needed to know that you would love me enough to say no to me. That you weren't going to let me tempt you pass where you were supposed to go. I needed to know if you were going to listen to the Holy Spirit and let Him lead your life and not your manhood or your thoughts. I needed to know that the man of God that is going to be my husband is not going to let me take him there to the point of no return. That he is going to be a real man of God that can tell me no when he really wants to say yes because he hears God say don't go in that direction. I needed to know that Bernard." She kissed him on the cheek and said, "Come on baby, let's get ready to call room service for breakfast. Afterwards we can get dressed and enjoy this wonderful day that the Lord has made." Without giving him a chance to respond she walked into the living room area leaving him standing there to gather his thoughts.

He stood there stunned, and thanked God that he hadn't given in because he knew that in his heart of hearts he wanted to. Once again at a crucial point in his life he had listened to the Holy Spirit. This time the command was, "Don't." He thanked God and he realized, "Today...I just became her husband."

He smiled within himself because of the victory God had blessed him with through the power of restraint. All through breakfast he could hardly contain the love that flooded his heart for her. They continuously looked in each other's eyes and had numerous conversations without saying a single word.

Talinda broke the silence. "Bernard now that you got your thoughts back together, here is another mind blower for you. If you would have given in to me, I would have made love to you. The truth is Bernard..." She reached up and gently glided her fingers across his lips and said, "...You are so sexy." She paused and dropped her head and sighed with a teasing smile. "I know it was really hard for you to say no and believe me when I say, I am so struggling right now. Everything in me strongly desires to make love to you." She paused and again closed her eyes. She shook her head, "Oh...God..." She looked up at him and continued, "...I want to be one with you. Completely one and completely yours...But I know that we can't."

"Sweetheart, we are going to have to trust God that he will keep us," Bernard replied. He attempted to sound completely in control.

She cupped his face and declared, "Baby that only works if we want to be kept. And right now Bernard...I don't want to be kept."

He broke contact and took a few steps away from her at the table. He declared as he looked up, "Oh God...Brandon what are you doing to me...why are you tempting me?" He turned back toward Talinda and said, "Baby I have to step out of the room for a minute...if I don't...Oh God...I'll be back sweetheart."

He turned to walk away and Talinda grabbed him by the arm and said, "I'm sorry Bernard, it's me that is not going to be able to deal with it...baby I am..."

"Shhhh," he placed a finger over her mouth. "Talinda it was only a matter of time before we were going to end up here. We were going to have to deal with our physical emotions sooner or later. The last twenty four hours have been pretty intense. We have shared some very intimate moments. But we cannot cross that line. Baby do you want me to get another room?"

"No, Bernard, please...don't," she replied in tears and placed her hand on the side of his face.

"Baby...wisdom is screaming at me right now," he replied as he wiped the tears from her eyes.

"Then marry me," she said. She looked deep into his eyes.

He smiled and chuckled, "I asked first...I beat you to it." He attempted to lighten the mood. Her statement threw him and he was unsure how to react to it. He wanted so desperately to be her husband. He knew he wouldn't have been able to handle it if she were merely teasing him and not sincere in her declaration.

"No, Bernard," she replied. "I mean marry me today."

"Talinda," he softly exclaimed. "You've been in this country for only five days. The first three we spent in Germany trying to figure out how we felt about one another. I proposed last night and now on the fifth day you want to get married? Talinda I have been preparing for this for quite a while. The emotions of the last few months for you may prove to be..."

She cut him off, "Bernard, time doesn't measure love. It is a gift from God. Paul said that it is better to marry than to burn. He is not talking about burning in hell. He is talking about burning with unquenchable passion for your espoused mate. Besides this is the fifth day. Five is the number of grace. God's grace will be with us and we know that we have His and Brandon's blessings already. What sense does it make to have a long drawn out courtship? What reason could we possible have to justify for putting it off? Everything we need to know about our life and courtship is written in Brandon's letters and in our hearts. Ask yourself this, why would Brandon have me to bring my birth certificate with me? There is no need for it. I have both my passport and social security card. Obviously he was hoping that I would leave this country as Mrs. Bernard Alexander Travis. He said it in his letter to me that it was his prayer that in the immediate and near future that I become your wife. So marry me Bernard Travis...marry me today."

Bernard sighed and said, "Oh, sweetheart, I don't want this to be a response based purely on emotion and passion."

"How can you say that Bernard when love is an emotion that leads to passion? Are you saying that I don't know whether or not if I'm in love with you?" She asked him quite frankly.

"No, baby that's not what I mean," he replied. "Sweetheart, you just buried Brandon a few months ago. I'm prepared to wait to give you time to get over him. I don't want you confused about who you are with or have any regrets about this because you feel rushed. Baby I will refrain from you, so don't feel like you have to do this for me..."

"Newsflash," she cut him off. "If you want to wait for me to get over Brandon we should just call this off right now because sweetheart I am never going to get over Brandon. I just have to continue on with my life. That's why he had me bring the birth certificate. He wants me to marry you quickly so I won't talk myself out of it and end up in mourning for years. I mean...what other logical reason is there for me to have it. And baby," she said as she cupped his face. "I am not confused about anything. I know exactly what I am doing and who I'm doing it with. Love is mandated by God not man. I've been your wife since the day you walked into that funeral home in Athens...I know that now. So I guess the real question is...are you ready Bernard Alexander Travis?"

"Of course I am. I've waited for this for over a year. I mean not you exactly, but a woman like you. But I was never able to shake the love I had for you. That's the reason no other woman has been in my life the last year and a half. I kept comparing them to you and baby they just couldn't measure up. Oh Talinda...girl you have just turned my world upside down this morning. Besides I don't even know if it's possible. We are in Paris and I have no idea what to..."

"Then let's leave and go back to Kaiserslautern to the airbase and get married there. We can come back here for our honeymoon. The room is reserved for the next three days anyway. I still have the room at the Lieberitz as well," she replied before he could protest any further.

Bernard shook his head and smiled, "You're serious about this aren't you? You have it all planned out. Sweetheart I would have to call to find out if we could even get married today at the base."

She picked up his cell phone and handed it to him. He smiled as he took it out of her hand and called the office to speak with CPT Thomas. She is one of his closest friends and works in the squadron administrative office. She was out to lunch and he got the number to the legal office from the airman on duty.

He smiled and shook his head at Talinda as he dialed the number. "Yes, this is Major Travis and I have a quick question for you. My fiancé is here visiting from the United States and I was wondering how difficult it would be for us to get married while she is over here...really...are you serious...well we are in Paris right now...okay I can do that, she has hers but mine is back in Kaiserslautern...really...okay we should be able to do that with no problem...okay...attention Staff Sergeant Williams...okay got it...thanks. We're on our way."

He hung up the phone and said to Talinda, "You are not going to believe this but all I need to do is fax our passports social security cards and your birth certificate in to them and they will start the paperwork. We need to get there by fifteen hundred...I mean three pm today with all the originals and we can get our license notarized today. I will call Chaplain McGhee on the way back. I would at least like for my pastor to marry us rather than a judge at legal.

She jumped into his arms and said, "Oh, Bernard."

He laughed and said, "Let's go get married baby!"

She kissed him and as they release their embrace he teased, "You'll be Mrs. Bernard Travis by four o'clock today, and you know that means, turnabout is fair play with all this teasing and testing this morning."

She put her arms back around his neck and kissed him again and said, "Mmmmm...promise?"

He smiled and laughed at the same time, "Ooh, boy do I promise...I do solemnly swear...."

Lindsay began to cry out to God for his forgiveness and thank him for loving her enough to expose her painful past. She prayed for Trevor that the Lord would indeed give him an understanding heart. She called on the name of the Lord and poured her heart out to him. She confessed the many sexual sins she had committed with countless men over the years of her pain and revenge. Nevette continued to pray over Lindsay, herself and her house as well anointing all the windows and doors as she prayed a prayer of protection over her home. She also prayed for the protection of her unborn child as she laid her hands on her stomach.

Then suddenly, Lindsay began to sing under the anointing and inspiration of God and peace filled the house. Nevette knew that there would be nothing to worry about and she indeed would have peaceful sleep that night. She went and made her and Lindsay a cup of hot herbal tea and they sat down to talk.

Lindsay looked up from blowing her tea to cool it and said, "When my mom passed away I remembered being emotionless and relieved. I felt that was one person from my past that God had dealt with and I secretly prayed that he would kill all of them."

Nevette replied with a sigh, "Now, Lindsay, you know that is not..."

"I know, Nevette, and I have since repented for those thoughts. It feels so good to have that weight off my shoulder," Lindsay said interrupting her and started to cry again. "Thank you for being who you are in God...a woman of authority and compassion. You know Nevette I thank God that he kept me all those times. I started giving men what I thought they wanted...what they all were expecting. To me there was no such thing as real love. You give a man what he wants, you satisfy him and then you move on. If I was going to have to give it up then it would be on my terms and under my own authority to whomever I wanted. That just kind of just became my motto. Thank God I didn't get anything all those years. So many times I probably could have been HIV positive or acquired some other disease. God...thank you so much for keeping me. I did some ungodly things with some ungodly people. I did it because somehow I thought that showing them what they created in me would hurt them. But I wasn't hurting them I was only hurting myself."

Nevette shook her head in a disbelief but compassionate manner as she replied, "Now it makes sense why you never went home, even on school breaks you always stayed in Athens. You even went home with me to Columbus several times. Wow, now it all makes sense. You know you have to forgive them Lindsay. Not for them but for your peace of mind."

Lindsay breathed in heavy and nodded her head in agreement, "I know Nevette, and I also know that I have to go back."

Nevette said as she grabbed her by the hand and looked her in the eyes, "Lindsay are you sure that's a good idea I mean it was over ten years ago. Just let God..."

Lindsay interrupted her, "No, Nevette, I have to. Pastor Miller is probably still there doing the same thing to other young girls that he did to me. We don't need any more Lindsay's out here. I have to go back. Who knows how many more Lindsay's there have been there since I left.

Nevette understood, agreed and said, "Okay Lindsay do you want me to go with you?"

Lindsay fought back tears as she replied, "Please...I don't think I can do it without your support and your strength."

Nevette smiled and hugged Lindsay. "Alright we'll go this weekend. I'll tell Justice we're going out of town, and we'll go this weekend, okay?"

Lindsay lost the battle to her emotions and started to weep again. "Thank you, Nevette. You have always been there for me."

"Hey girl, I love you. You're the godmother of my children. You know I got your back and you have mine," Nevette replied.

"Oh, Nevette, I am so ashamed of how I acted with Trevor tonight," Lindsay exclaimed. "He is so perfect. I just didn't know what to do when confronted with real love."

"Well, you just said the magic word Lindsay," Nevette replied. "If he indeed has real love for you then it will also consist of an understanding heart. Just go talk to him tomorrow. He, just like us has probably spent the night in prayer."

"Yeah...you're probably right," Lindsay said in relief. I think I'll stop by his office tomorrow to formally apologize to him."

The next day she called in to take the day off and said a silent prayer before she entered the hospital to talk to Trevor. Nevette escorted her up to Trevor's office and then had him paged to come to his office on the pretense that he had a patient waiting to see him.

"Okay, girl he should be here is a few minutes are you ready?" Nevette asked as she gave Lindsay a reassuring smile.

"Guess I don't have much choice but to be ready. Oh Nevette what if he orders me out of his office. I don't blame him for never wanting to see me again," Lindsay replied feeling the tears build up.

"Well at least you would have apologized to him. You do owe him that at any rate," Nevette replied.

"Yeah I guess you're right," Lindsay said.

Nevette hugged her as she said, "Ok, I'm going to leave now. Don't worry. I got a hunch about this one girl." Lindsay managed to muster up a smile as Nevette turned to leave the office. She sits and silently prays to God for strength. But no sooner than Nevette left Lindsay could hear him enter the outer office and greet Nevette.

"Okay, Nevette I didn't expect to see you here. I mean I know you're expecting but you're not a patient of mine," Trevor said jokingly.

"No, I'm not the patient Dr. Johnson. She is waiting in your office." She gave him a knowing look that let him know the patient who waited for him in his office was Lindsay.

"Oh...okay," he replied as he took deep breath and smiled at her as she exited his office. He entered and of course found Lindsay sitting in the chair facing his desk with her back to him.

"Well, I must say that I am really surprised to see you here today Lindsay. Let me first apologize to you. I allowed my emotions get somewhat out of control last night," he said as he approached the chair where she sat.

Lindsay stood and shook her head in protest to his apology. "No Trevor please don't apologize to me. You have shown me nothing but love from the beginning. I am the only one who should be apologizing here," she said. She paused and put her head down. She felt so much shame in his presence.

He walked over to her and lifted her head and smiled at her and said, "Hey, are you okay?"

"I'm fine Trevor. I was hiding some big demons. You kind of struck a nerve yesterday and they started surfacing. I had really been subduing them. I thought I was over it but in the presence of real love everything just fell apart," she said as she lowered her head again.

He smiled and lifted her head back up so he could look into her eyes. He softly and gingerly said, "What is it, baby? What has consumed you with so much hurt and pain all these years?"

"Oh God," she said as she took a few steps away from him. With her back to him she began to talk. "When I was fifteen I was molested and impregnated by the pastor at my church."

"Oh God baby," he replied. He did not make any advancement toward her. But his tone was loving and reassuring.

She continued to talk as though she were the only one in the room. "All the women there they...they blamed me...they said it was my fault. Because I wore clothes that fit instead of clothes that were two sizes too big like all of them. But it wasn't my fault...it wasn't I know that now. I just liked to look nice...I mean I couldn't control the shape of my body it was just there you know. But my mom and all the other deaconesses in the church they made me get an abortion. They didn't want it to get out that the pastor had fathered my baby. They were so busy protecting the pastor and his image and nobody, not even my mother, ministered too or even seemed to care about the damage to me or any of his victims. We were casualties of war so to speak. They told her that I was lying to protect some little boy that I was seeing and she believed them. So when I left home I decided I would control my body. I would give it the way I wanted to give it, and who I wanted to give it to. There was no such thing as real love to me and it was like I became a sex magnet. All men want is sex anyway so just give them want they want and get them out of my face...you know. I never wanted to go to another church where there is a deacon or a deaconess ever again. Real full fledge ministers...they keep the pastor in line...they make him accountable. I think that deacons and deaconesses is such a bogus office where any and everything is allowed."

"You don't mean that and you know it. A deacon is an office appointed by God with strict guidelines that some men and women elect not to follow. You're just hurt sweetheart," he said as he walked right up behind her and put his hands on her shoulders but doesn't turn her around to face him. He didn't want to make her feel pressured in any way.

She sighed and dropped her shoulders. She said in a solemn voice, "I know and now Nevette said that I have to forgive them...ugh...I have to forgive them. But there is only one thing wrong with that...they never asked for my forgiveness. They act as though I should be asking for theirs. But I know she's right...if I don't forgive, they keep the power and my relationship with God will forever be strained."

"Not just your relationship with God, but with everybody else as well," he said as he now gently turned her to face him. "The first day I saw you sitting in the cafeteria with Nevette God told me you were special. He told me to nurture and protect you because you had many wounds. He told me that you needed to know how special you were to him. I didn't realize that in the process of protecting and nurturing you I would fall in love." He pulled her into his arms because she had

82

started to weep. He just held her and prayed over her wounded heart and echoed many of the declarations that Nevette had prayed the night before.

As he continued to hold her and pray for her he could hear the Lord say that it was time. He held her tighter as he said, "You know baby Nevette is right, you're going to have to forgive them...all of them. Because you and I can't be whole...and we can't be one...and we can't be happy in our marriage if you don't forgive."

"I know I just...what...wh...what did you say?" It took a moment for what he had said to register and caught her quite by surprise to say the least.

He lifted her head so he could look her in the eyes as he repeated, "I said...we can't be happy in our marriage if you don't forgive." He reached into his desk and got the ring out that he had purchased for her just weeks prior and got down on one knee. "I was going to take you to dinner and be all romantic but I hear God say that now is the time to ask you...Will you marry me Lindsay?"

She just cried and said, "I don't deserve a man like you."

He smiled, "Oh baby you deserve me and then some. Don't ever say what you don't deserve. You deserve to be happy and loved. You deserve to be pampered and taken care of and I plan on doing all of that and then some baby. Please say yes."

Through her tears she was able to muster up enough voice to say, "Ye...yes."

He put the ring on her finger and they shared their first kiss. He held her in his arms and said, "Its okay, baby. Go ahead and cry. I got you and you don't ever have to be afraid anymore. You don't ever have to wonder about a man's true feelings and intentions toward you anymore. You're special and you deserve to be loved the right way by a real man...one that has been groomed just for you. I'm going to show you love...I'm going to show you real love. I love you baby and I am going to be so good to you. I'm going to treat you like a queen because you are a queen. You are my queen."

She was beyond words and try as she might she could not utter a word. She simply rested in his arms being consumed by his love and felt secure for the first time in her life.

"Wow...okay, God you're really going to do this to me? You're going to make me wait?" he said as he had a conversation with God with Lindsay still tucked securely in his arms.

"What?" Lindsay asked. "What do you mean God is going to make you wait? Wait for what?"

"You sweetheart, he is going to make me wait for you. He just dropped into my spirit that we cannot set a date to be married until exactly one year is fulfilled," he answered. He looked up and shook his head in amusement.

"Fulfilled...what do you mean fulfilled Trevor," she asked. She did not make any notion to move from his arms because it just felt too good being there.

He smiled and said, "Until your one year of preparation is complete." He chuckled and looked up as he said, "Oh God...you really are going to make me wait for her. Sweetheart just like Esther was prepared for her night with the king God is about to minister to you this year. I am to set up for you and pay for a weekly massage with a masseuse to anoint and massage you with frankincense and myrrh. He said we are to spend this year studying the book of Esther and scriptures of marriage together. We are to study no less than weekly. We are to totally dissect and understand the power and security in the love God has given to a man and his wife. God wants you to know how special you are. There are things that God said he must bring to the surface still and heal you from. If we are going to be happy and healthy we must follow God's instructions baby."

"Wow, God really does love me," she said still nestled in his arms. "You know, I think I get it Trevor. I mean God knows I can pay for the massages myself but I think he wants me to learn to yield to you. I need to allow you to minister to me. I need to give you control over my body and trust you with what happens to it. I get it Trevor...I get it."

"When God gets through with us this year," Trevor replied. "All I can say is...wow...we will be so ready for matrimony...we will be one. Whew...this is almost too much God." He kissed her again as his pager is going off.

She felt the vibration of his beeper attached to his waist and she sighed, "Oh, I could just stay right here in your arms forever but you are at work so I guess I'll see you later."

He kissed her again and said, "Mmmmm you'll definitely see me later but unfortunately it will be much later. I just came on shift about two hours ago."

"Don't worry, I'll wait up for you to call me," she said. She had a silly school smile plastered on her face as they finally release their embrace.

"Call? Baby, I'm stopping by to see you on the way home. If only just for a few minutes," he smiled as he kissed her again.

"Okay," she said. She was in total awe at the intensity of his words and the love he had for her.

They left his office and said their goodbyes. He headed down the hallway to check in on patients. Lindsay headed down to physical therapy to see Nevette.

When she walked into the physical therapy ward Nevette was coming to the desk with a patient to get him set for his next appointment. She saw Lindsay and said goodbye to him as the office attendant sat up the appointment.

"Judging by the smile on your face I assume it went okay with Trevor," Nevette said as she approached her.

"Oh, it went more than okay," she said. She held out her hand to show Nevette the engagement ring.

Nevette gasped and grabbed her by the hand. She pulled her into her office hardly able to contain herself until they are inside.

"Oh my gosh, Lindsay that's an engagement ring on your finger!" Nevette exclaimed in sheer delight. "Okay girl tell me everything and don't you leave out one jot or tittle!"

Lindsay proceeded to tell Nevette about the conversation and events between her and Trevor. Nevette cried tears of excitement and joy for her friend.

"Wow, Lindsay, this is going to be a magnificent year for you. I am so happy about what God is getting ready to do in your life...and Trevor's," Nevette said through tears that are now forming in her eyes. "You deserve it...you have been so hurt for so long."

Lindsay, now crying again herself, said, "Yeah I know. God loves me...he really does Nevette."

"Of course he does," Nevette said as they embrace and shed tears of joy together.

Lindsay did indeed go back to her home town in Mississippi to confront and forgive the members of Faith Temple. To her dismay there had been other Lindsay's...other young ladies whose purity had been robbed of them at the hand of a pastor who preached a turn or burn message from a soiled pulpit every Sunday. Lindsay stood in church almost unrecognized by the church mother and the other deaconesses as a visitor when she introduced Nevette and proceeded to peel back the covers of her distorted past.

There were many in an uproar and some tried to no avail to silence her but she would have her say. She stood strong and firm and exposed the horrible truth of her past that unfolded at their hands. There were sobs all over the building as Lindsay spoke. She realized that there were so many Lindsay's still sitting there among them and she fought back the tears as she continued to peel away at the onion skin of her distorted past. Anger rose up against the pastor and deaconess board and some had to be restrained now realizing that they had been masterly manipulated and lied to. In the end however God would use Lindsay and Nevette to minister to the young ladies.

Lindsay stood face to face as she rubbed her fingers across the ring on her finger for comfort and forgave them with sincerity and no anger in her heart toward them. She realized that too much was at stake to harbor any anger or resentment toward them. She didn't want anything to stand in the way of her present and future happiness with Trevor. As she walked out of the doors of the church she knew that day would be the beginning of the end of Faith Temple.

85

Not long after Lindsay's expository debut they closed their doors forever. After much investigation it was discovered that several of the small children in the congregation were indeed fathered by the pastor. He and the mother of the church and several others were eventually arrested for child endangerment and sexual abuse. The pastor was charged with several accounts of rape and sex with a minor. Lindsay could finally put the past behind her knowing now that her year long journey with Trevor would be an experience she would never forget.

~Chapter Nine~

"So this is the lovely Talinda Travis I've heard so much about," Chaplain McGhee said as he shook Talinda's hand.

"Yes sir, it is," Bernard replied.

"Well considering she is a youth pastor and has been married before and knowing your character as well son I see no need to prolong this marriage with counseling. I can't come against a match divinely put together in heaven. So let's get you two married. Do you have your witnesses?" Chaplain McGhee inquired.

"Sir, we'll just use the people here in legal. I kind of want to surprise all my friends. We will be going back to Paris for our honeymoon and won't be in church on Sunday so I would appreciate it sir if you would keep it a secret for now," Bernard requested.

"No problem, son. Okay Pastor Travis are you ready?" he asked Talinda.

She smiled and replied, "I most definitely am sir."

As they reach the part of the ceremony where the vows are repeated Chaplin McGhee said, "I understand that you two would like to speak from your heart your own personal vow to each other."

"Yes sir we would," Bernard replied. He looked into Talinda's eyes and declared:

Talinda,

> *I take you now to be my wife. I have dreamed of this moment all of my life and I have prayed about a wife like you for the last two years. I thank God that He loves me and He has blessed me with the woman of my dreams. Outside of God, Jesus and the Holy Spirit, you are everything to me. Baby, I promise I'll love you...I'll cherish you...I'll honor you...I'll always satisfy you...I'll take care of you no matter what. As I shared with you under the Eiffel Tower you are a*

nurturer and a wife and I love you so very much. I take
you now to be my wife and I say...I do...I will...I must.

She smiled as she began to declare to him:

Bernard,

> *I didn't think that it would be possible for another*
> *man to come into my heart and even remotely come*
> *close to Brandon. But not only have you come into my*
> *heart...you have taken over. You've taken ownership*
> *and you've loved me. I promise I will cherish you...I*
> *will nurture you...I will take care of you...I will satisfy*
> *you...I will be your wife. There is nothing...nothing on*
> *this earth that will ever separate me from you. I am so*
> *blessed to have a man of God full of wisdom...full of*
> *honor...full of integrity and full of authority. I love you*
> *baby and I do...I will...and I must.*

Chaplin McGhee continued on with the ceremony. "We will now exchange the rings and the couple has also elected to share their own personal ring vows as well."

Talinda said through her tears, "You did remember to bring the rings didn't you?"

"Baby, you know I did," Bernard replied. He took the ring and placed it on her finger as he said:

Talinda,

> *With this ring, I thee wed. As I place it on your*
> *finger, it is a symbol of my undying love to you. It is a*
> *vow that I will always be true to you. It is a promise*
> *that our love with never end and I will love you as*
> *Christ loved the church. I promise that I will give*
> *myself for you. It is a symbol of a love that will never*
> *fail...that will not degrade or disrespect you...but will*
> *cherish, honor and defend. It is a promise that I will*
> *be a father to Raymond and our two unborn children.*
> *It is a constant reminder of God's presence in our life.*
> *Two become one. I love you baby."*

Bernard,

> *With this ring, I thee wed. And as I place it on your*
> *finger I do declare my love for you. A love that will*
> *not fail...a love that will submit to your authority and*

rule...a love that will always support...that will always lift up and not tear down...a love that will encourage...and when you look at it, it will remind you that I am forever lifting you up before God. I will follow you as you follow Christ.

Chaplin McGhee stood in awe of the vow they made to each other and could feel the power of the presence of God in the room as he declared, "By the power invested in me according the United States of America...citizens married abroad. I now pronounce you husband and wife. Minister Travis you may kiss your bride."

As they released from the kiss Chaplin McGhee said, "Congratulations Major Travis & Mrs. Travis. Well when shall we expect you back?"

"Well, we'll miss this Sunday, sir, but we'll be back next Sunday. We're headed back to Paris for our honeymoon," he said with a smile and quick wink to Talinda.

"Sounds good, and you enjoy the rest of your time in this country Mrs. Travis," Chaplin McGhee said as he shook both their hands.

"I'm sure I will," she said as she looked into Bernard's eyes and smiled in response to his wink.

"Remember sir, I would like to surprise everybody," Bernard said.

"Oh, don't worry. I'll let you introduce your bride yourself next Sunday," Chaplin McGhee replied. "Well, get out of here and go enjoy your honeymoon you two."

"Yes sir. Thanks again for marrying us," Bernard replied.

He said a hearty you're welcome as he smiled and walked away.

Talinda through tears said to Bernard, "Bernard...I'm your wife."

"You're my wife baby, YOU'RE MY WIFE!" he declared as he picked her up being careful not to squeeze her too hard. He spent her around kissed her again.

"Yes...I am," she said through tears. "I guess we better call our family huh."

"Yeah I guess we better. We haven't talked to them since you landed on Friday. I know they are just on pins and needles in an attempt to figure out what we decided to do. It's probably taken all Aunt Helen has to not call us," Bernard said laughing. "But first I want to take my wife to a reception dinner. Where do you want to go baby?"

Talinda replied with excitement, "I don't' know and I don't care. We can go to a gas station and get potato chips and a coke. I'm Mrs. Bernard Alexander Travis...that's all that matters to me."

Bernard was speechless at her declaration and excitement. All he could do was pull her into his arms and kiss her. As they released he whispered in her ear, "I love you baby. What did I ever do to deserve you?"

Talinda moaned and said, "You are amazingly perfect for me Bernard and I am so...so happy. I am inside joy."

As he opened the car door for her he kissed her again. Once he got into the driver's seat he said, "Okay sweetheart, do you want to spend our wedding night in the Lieberitz hotel or at home?"

"Home?" she replied. She had not fully understood.

"Sweetheart, remember I live here? I'm a Major in the Air Force so I don't live in the barracks. I have a townhouse off base. Sooo...," he said as he kissed her hand. "...We can spend the night at the hotel or at home. It's up to you," he replied. He knew full well what her choice would be.

"Ahhh, Bernard, why haven't I seen your home before?" she said with a 'you're in trouble' smile.

He laughed and said, "We haven't had time baby and I just never really thought about it."

"Well, I think I would like to make love to my husband for the first time at home," Talinda said with a smile. "I mean that is unless you have to go clear all your ex-girlfriends pictures of the wall first." She said with a sarcastic smile.

He laughed as he said, "Okay, you got jokes." Then he looked into her eyes and declared, "The only pictures of any woman that has been in my house for the last year and a half are of you. I mean not printed pictures, but as a screen saver on my lap top. I told you Talinda. I was ashamed of the fact that I was in love with my cousin's wife. "

She smiled and replied, "Uhmm...wow, Bernard...really?" The pure presence of love overwhelmed them both and they fought hard to keep their composure.

"Yeah baby...really. I was so guilty about my feelings about you," he managed to say.

"Let's go home," she said as she stroked his face.

He smiled and they drove away. They went by the Lieberitz hotel to check out and retrieve all of Talinda's things. They also stopped at a local restaurant on the way home and picked up an entrée, salad and bread sticks for dinner.

As they pulled up in the driveway Talinda marveled at the architecture of the home Bernard lived in. It was exquisite and very ornate. He got out of the car and walked around to open her door for her.

He stopped short of going into the house after he unlocked the door.

"Okay, Mrs. Travis. Here we go," he said as he swept her up and carried her over the threshold. He went back to the car retrieved the food and joined her in the kitchen. "Go ahead Mrs. Travis you know you want to go look around. Be my guest as I prepare our plates for dinner."

Talinda was impressed with his decorating skills. Most bachelors you could tell were indeed bachelors by their choice of furnishings.

As she re-entered the kitchen area she complimented him on his decor.

"Thanks, but I can't take the full credit for it. My mom came for a visit plus one of my closest friends' wife Tasha, had a lot to do with it as well," he replied.

≈

"Oh, Justice I do believe it's time," Nevette said. She breathed heavy between contractions.

"Okay baby, I'll call mom and everybody to let them know we are on the way to the hospital," Justice replied beginning to run around like a chicken with its head cut off.

"Relax baby, we've done this before remember," Nevette said as she smiled through the contraction.

"I know, but the excitement of life entering the world never gets old baby," he exclaimed. He grabbed her overnight bag as he escorted her to the car.

Tre was with Teddy and would arrive at the hospital with him. The gang was soon all there and in much anticipation of the addition to the family. They could hear the sounds of labor from the waiting room across the hall and all gasped as they heard the faint cry of baby Goodfellow just after she entered this side of creation.

"Oh wow, baby, she is so beautiful. She is just like you," Justice said as he and Nevette hold their new baby daughter. Their son Tre has finally been let into the labor and delivery room and is eager to meet his new baby sister.

"Wow mommy, she's little! Her hands look just like mine except they're little," Tre said in amazement to his new baby sister. "She has pretty hair mommy it's so soft and curly."

"Be careful Tre when you touch her head okay," Nevette said. "She has some areas that are really soft and she can be hurt if you touch them to hard."

"Okay mommy," Tre replied still in total awe of his new baby sister. Justice was also beaming with pride.

Lindsay was on the job taking pictures of any and everything that moved in the room. Soon everyone started to enter the room to see the addition to the Goodfellow family.

Shaundra had the honor of delivering her as well as teased DJ and Nevette. She declared, "If you guys keep having babies I may have to change my profession from pediatrician to obstetrician." Everyone laughed as they took turns holding little baby Goodfellow.

"Okay, what name did you guys finally decide on?" Jason inquired.

"Callisha Renee Goodfellow," they both said in unison.

Shaundra looked up with tears in her eyes. Nevette said, "We decided to use my mom's and your middle name, mom."

Her dad smiled and reflected on all the events that had happened in his life over the last several years that his wife had missed.

≈

Back in Athens at the Travis', Raymond and Talinda's parents were enjoying an evening meal. Her dad had journeyed back down from Virginia to spend a few days with his wife who after returning had decided to stay with Raymond until Talinda returned.

"Okay," Roger said as they finished dinner and adjourned to the family room. "We all are thinking the same thing so we may as well just talk about it."

Victor nodded in agreement and said, "Yes, I would say that was a fair assessment of the situation."

Valetta stood as Helen entered with a tray with a coffee pot full of delicious smelling gourmet coffee. She helped her to fill the cups with coffee and serve everyone. As she sat down, she tapped her spoon on the side of her cup. She smiled and said, "Well I for one am not surprised by the letter from Brandon. I fully expect that they will get married soon if they haven't already. I think Talinda will return from Germany Bernard's wife. Marriage is the only job and ministry she has ever wanted to have. She is a wife and she's not happy unless she has someone to nurture. She loves to love and be loved. I think she actually grieves the loss of her marriage just as much as she grieves the loss of her husband."

"Well, I think it's a swell idea," Raymond said as he cracked the seal on a can of his favorite soft drink. "I like Bernard. He's a lot like dad. Dad and I talked about him a few months before he died right before he changed the will."

"Wait a minute...Raymond you knew?" Valetta asked.

"Yes ma'am," Raymond replied. "Dad told me that if anything ever happened to him that he would ask Bernard to marry mom and take care of us. He said that Bernard would love me the same way that he did. He made me promise not to say anything. So I already knew dad wanted him to marry mom and I hope they do. Mom is too young to be alone, she needs a husband. This way she won't have to change her name and when she finishes adopting me my last name will still be Travis." Raymond's comment brought laughter to the room.

Roger eyes his wife and attempted to read her take on it all. He decided to just ask. He cleared his throat he said, "Honey, you've been pretty quiet. How do you feel about all of this?"

Helen sipped coffee and said as she placed the cup back in the saucer, "I think I agree with Valetta. Talinda is a wife that's her gift. She misses being a wife. I watched Bernard when he was here for Brandon's service and the love he had for her just filled the room. He tried very hard to hide it but there were times when I would catch him staring at her. At first I was a little disappointed that he could be in love with his cousin's wife. But after getting Brandon's letter from the attorney it all makes sense. I am actually a little relieved to know who her next husband will be. I don't think I could have taken a total stranger coming in to raise Brandon's baby."

Victor stood to retrieve another lump of sugar for his coffee. As he stirred his coffee and returned to his seat he said, "I must join my wife in saying that I am not surprised. The day he left he shook my hand and when I looked in his eyes I saw a familiar look. The same look Brandon had in his eyes when he first stepped into our home a little over seven years ago. What I saw was love. More specifically the love of a husband for a wife and I wondered who was the special woman that was in his life back in Germany. But as he lowered his head from my gaze I realized that special woman was standing in the room. At the reading of the will when Brandon requested that Talinda hand deliver a letter to Bernard that sort of sealed my suspicion concerning the matter. One thing is for sure, they are being very careful to make the decision on their own. They have not called to allow our opinions to cloud their own. All the more reason I feel that they probably will, like Valetta said if they already haven't, marry soon."

Valetta added, "When it boils down to it, their ideas, feelings and concerns are the only ones that really matter in this. I mean what could we do about it if we didn't want them together anyway? Brandon has set this whole thing up and specifically asked Bernard to marry his wife to take care of her every need.

"You are so right, Valetta," Helen replied. "I guess we'll know soon enough. I don't think they will take a lot of time in their decision. For now I'm going to enjoy my coffee and plan my shopping day tomorrow for that grandbaby. Valetta I hope you will join me."

"Wouldn't miss it," Valetta declared in no uncertain terms.

They continued in conversation and enjoying family games as the evening roles on. Each of them harbored their own secret anticipation of that much awaited phone call from overseas.

"Okay, Bernard, we really need to call our families," Talinda said as she took a seat at the kitchen counter.

He took a deep breath and replied, "Yeah I guess we can't put it off any longer. I'm really nervous about how my mom and Aunt Helen will take this."

"Well I am certain my mother will be fine," Talinda said. "I'm not quite sure about my dad. I feel like Raymond would be okay with it too he really likes you."

"Okay so who do you want to call first," Bernard asked.

"I think I'll call Raymond," she said as she dialed the number.

Raymond felt his phone vibrate as he headed upstairs to get more chips and dip. Everyone else was still downstairs enjoying coffee and conversation. He saw the number and knew it was his mom and

Bernard. He tried to control his excitement as he answered the phone because everyone anxiously awaited to hear from them since they had all received the letters from Brandon's attorney.

"Hey, mom," Raymond said with excitement. "Grandma and grandpa all got the letters. How are you and Bernard doing?"

"Well son, as a matter of fact Bernard and I got married today," she said with a little hesitation.

"WHAT! NO WAY MOM! YOU GUYS GOT MARRIED TODAY? NO WAY, MOM!" Raymond yelled out in total exhilaration.

"Yes, son. We got married today. Are you alright with that?" she asked not sure to the origin of his reply.

"Sure mom, why wouldn't I be alright with it?!" Raymond responded with excitement still in his voice. "Grandma and Grandpa are here at Nanna and Papas' house. We are here for dinner. So, I'm gonna go back downstairs and put you on speaker phone okay."

"Alright Raymond," Talinda replied relieved at his excitement. She turned toward Bernard and took a deep breath, "Okay...here we go."

"Maybe I should go in the other room and use the house phone to call my mom before Aunt Helen beats me to it," Bernard inquired. He wanted to escape the task of facing his aunt and uncle.

"No you don't Mr. Travis, you are not leaving me to face Brandon's mom by myself. I want you to be here to hear their response. We'll just tell her to give us time to call your parents first," Talinda said as she grabbed his arm to hold him beside her.

"Hey, everybody! Mom just called me! She and Bernard are on the phone!" Raymond yelled with excitement as he descended down the stairs. He jumped down the last five steps in excitement to get to everyone so they could hear the news. "I'll put it on speaker. Okay mom, you can talk now."

Bernard and Talinda say hello to everyone at the same time. Then Talinda started to speak but was cut off by Helen who said, "We've been waiting to hear from you guys."

Talinda took a deep breath and replied, "Yeah, things have been pretty crazy over here. We know you guys all received letters from Brandon's attorney. Our letters took us quite by surprise and I'm sure yours did as well."

Valetta said, "Oh, dear, they didn't take your dad and me by surprise. We were kind of thinking all along that there was something there."

"Well..." Talinda started then she stopped and whispered to Bernard, "Do you want to tell them."

He nodded yes and cleared his throat, "Well Aunt Helen, Uncle Roger, Mr. and Mrs. Thomas we will now introduce ourselves as Mr. and Mrs. Bernard Alexander Travis."

"OH MY GOSH," Helen gasped. "You guys got married?"

94

"Yes...we got married today...just a few hours ago," Talinda said almost in tears. "We had an awesome time this weekend and we saw no reason to wait or have a long courtship. Brandon laid everything out for us. Bernard kept asking me are you sure, are you sure, are you sure? I don't want you to feel you have to because of Brandon's letter. Give yourself some time to get over him. I told him I am never going to get over Brandon. I just have to move on because Brandon wants me to. I know what you guys are thinking and I do love Bernard. There were some things that happened this weekend that were just amazing...truly amazing. His love for me over took me and I fell...very hard and fast. I can look into his eyes and tell him with all sincerity that I love him. Mom...dad you know me. I'm not going to play with his heart."

"We know dear," her dad said. "Rest assured, Bernard, if she tells you she loves you...she does."

Bernard replied almost in tears, "I know sir...thank you. I promise I'll take care of her."

"I know you will, son...I know you will," he replied. "You're a Travis."

Talinda jumped back in, "We didn't call earlier because we took Brandon's advice. We didn't want any outside influence because the decision had to be ours. I didn't want anyone telling me how I felt or didn't feel. Every day I fell further and further in love with him. The first day I saw him at Brandon's' service in Athens there was an attraction."

"Well, as long as you guys are happy," Valetta said. "That's all that matters."

Bernard asked hesitantly, "Aunt Helen...Uncle Roger...how are you guys feelings about this?"

"Oh, Bernard," Helen said almost in tears. "Honey, let me tell you something. Brandon has given you the highest honor that any man can give to another man. He has entrusted you to take care of his wife and his child. You are like my son Bernard and I love you. Honestly, I don't think I could have handled Talinda marrying anybody else but you, Bernard."

Those words took Bernard over the edge and he began to sob. Talinda caressed his back and she herself shed tears.

Helen continued on, "I would have struggled with the thought of a stranger coming in to take care of my grandbaby. Talinda is a wife...that's what she does. That's the air she breathes. She doesn't know anything else. Half of her struggle these last two and a half almost three months was that she wasn't a wife anymore. Like she said she is never going to get over Brandon...none of us are. She like us has to pick up the pieces and continue on. And with you she is going to be able to do that easier. Congratulations to you both...she is just not taking my grandbaby overseas. She is coming back here to have him," she said in a joking but serious manner.

Talinda laughed through her tears, "Speaking of that I called Dr. Harrell to get permission to extend my time over here for a few more weeks to spend some time with my husband. So I'll be back in about a month from now." Then she thought, "They don't know!" She said with excitement, "Hey by the way you guys Brandon informed me in my letter that I'm carrying twins a boy and a girl. And they are moving around like crazy already."

Valetta and Helen both screamed at the same time. And Helen exclaimed, "We were right Valetta we were right. Oh, two babies. God is so good!"

Talinda, somewhat surprised, said, "Wait...you guys knew already? How did you..."

Valetta replied, "Well that echo and heartbeat in a heartbeat you heard that day Veronica came over gave it away. We didn't want to say anything until we were sure."

Roger finally spoke up and addressed Bernard. "Bernard."

"Yes...sir?" Bernard answered.

"Listen, son," Roger continued. "We have always loved you like a son. You, indeed, are our son and Brandon's big brother. Do not take lightly what Brandon has done for you. Cherish and savor every moment of your life together. Love each other hard and strong and give it everything that you have. Brandon lived a life of no regrets. He personally designed this experience for you and Talinda. Brandon was a man of love and now he has entrusted you to carry that love...physically, emotionally and spiritually. Always keep communication open and listen to each other. Son she is going to have some good and bad days ahead so keep an understanding heart...okay son...keep an understanding heart." Talinda's father sat there and shook his head in affirmation. Roger had literally taken the words right out of his mouth.

"Yes sir," Bernard replied and began to sob once more.

"I couldn't have said that any better Roger," Talinda's father chimed in. "The only thing I'll add is this princess and I'm sure I speak for everyone here. How were we going to protest something that your husband blessed? So it doesn't matter what any of us thinks. This is what Brandon has laid out for you guys to do. Princess, you take good care of him. He's going to need you as well. You both are going to experience some powerful emotions so be there for each other. And don't worry. Your mom will be at the house with Raymond."

"Yes, daddy," Talinda replied and began to shed tears again. Everyone had been emotional basket cases the last few months.

Bernard said, "Aunt Helen...Uncle Roger, I will be getting out of the Air Force. That is the one thing that Brandon did ask of me. Because of my job and many deployments Brandon understandably requested that I did not place my wife back in the same situation that she just came out of. So I will be going to my commander next week when we return from Paris to both extend my leave and request a compassionate reassignment until my date of separation from service. There is really only one place in Georgia that I can be assigned to so please pray for favor." They all agreed that they would.

"I love you, mom," Raymond said. "Bernard I'm glad you're going to be my new dad. Dad said you would be loyal and take care of me...he said you would." Raymond began to cry and Victor pulled him into his arms for comfort.

"Oh, Raymond I love you," Talinda replied.

"I love you Raymond," Bernard finally managed to say. "Brandon was right son. I'm going to take good care of you. Hey I haven't forgotten my promise. School is out in a month or so and you guys can start planning to come for a visit. We'll call back later in the week to talk about it."

"Yes sir," Raymond replied still in tears.

"Okay," Talinda said as she gathered herself. "We need to call Bernard's parents as well so we better go. Please you guys give us about twenty minutes or so before you call them. Bernard said that his mom will kill him if she finds out from someone other than him."

They all laugh as Helen said, "Yeah she will. Don't worry we'll wait for her to call us. She will as soon as she gets off the phone with you guys."

Bernard added, "Once we get back there and Talinda has had the babies we will have a ceremony at church at the one year anniversary so my mom can see her baby boy get married."

"Oh, that will be great," Helen replied. "Alright you two you make your other call so you can get back to your honey moon."

"Okay, can you guys please inform pastor and first lady Tills so they can let everyone else at church know? That way we don't have to make so many phone calls today," Talinda asked.

"Sure princess," her dad said.

"Okay, goodbye everybody," Talinda and Bernard said as they hung up the phone.

"Okay...that went well," Talinda said as she breathed a sigh of relief.

"Yeah, but here comes the real challenge...my mom," Bernard said as he dialed his parent's number. He put the phone speaker mode and placed it on the counter.

"Hi mom," Bernard said when she picked up.

"Hey, baby," she said with excitement and relieved to finally hear from Bernard.

"Hey, mom, is dad around?" Bernard asked.

"Yeah, he's right here in the kitchen," she said.

"Okay, can you put the phone on speaker mom," Bernard asked her.

"Sure, sweetie," she said. "How is Talinda doing, is everything okay?" she asked as she switched the phone to speaker.

"She's fine mom she's right here beside me and everything is great," Bernard replied as he looked at Talinda.

Talinda then greeted her as well. "Hi Mrs. Travis I'm fine thanks for asking."

"You're welcome sweetheart. Well...how is everything going son?" His mom said. "We received the letter and we've been praying for you both. Are you okay?"

"Yeah, mom we're fine," Bernard said as he took a deep breath and continued, "Well mom...dad I wanted you both on the phone so Talinda and I could talk to you about our decision to Brandon's request."

"Alright son...although I think I know the answer to this already," his dad said.

"Mom...dad, Talinda and I got married today," Bernard said.

His mom gasped, "Ahhh...wow...okay...I thought you just that you were just discussing what you were going to do."

"We were mom, but we got married today," Bernard said again and waited for the fireworks to start. He had his hand on Talinda's shoulder for support and reassurance. There was silence on the other end of the phone, so he continued. "We decided that there was no good reason to wait. Believe me mom, we talked about it thoroughly. I even questioned her if she was ready, because I didn't want to rush her. I wanted to give her time to get over Brandon. I didn't want this to be a rebound decision because of her emotions. She said we can't wait for me to get over Brandon because that's not going to happen. I just have to move on with you. Mom...dad, our love has grown this weekend. God has put us in situations where we've had to love...and the passion was weighed everything else. I asked, she said yes and we got married today."

Teresa replied, "You know son, when we got the letter I told your dad. I said Reginald they are going to get married and if I know Bernard it's going to be soon. Remember the conversation you had with your dad a little while back, well he told me about it when the letter from Brandon came. He said he wasn't surprised because he knew that you loved her. That's why you never went to visit them because you struggled with your feelings for her. And her being your cousin's wife made you feel extremely guilty."

"Yeah mom," Bernard replied.

Teresa continued, "All we can say is congratulations. Make sure that this is what God called you to do and you're not doing it because Brandon asked you too. Love has to be real and pure between a man and a woman."

"It is Mrs. Travis," Talinda responded. "I love him. When I look into his eyes I don't see Brandon or a Brandon look alike. I see a man who is fulfilling prophecy in my life."

"I believe you Talinda," Teresa replied. "I hear the genuineness in your voice." She smiled and with a slight chuckle said, "You can call me mom by the way."

Talinda sighed in relief and replied, "Thanks mom."

Teresa said with a new found excitement, "Well I guess I'm going to be a grandma finally huh? Helen and Valetta are going to have to share that grandbaby with me."

"Yes they are," Talinda replied as she laughed out. "And you've already have one...Raymond."

"Yes I do, don't I!" Teresa exclaimed as she remembered Raymond. "Guess I better up my Christmas list this year."

"Yes," Talinda replied was a laugh of relief.

"So, his adoption is final?" she asked Talinda.

"Well no ma'am, not yet. But I'm hoping to hear something by the time I get back from Germany. I mean he's seventeen now so we really don't need anyone's permission. He is eager to be a Travis. I just wanted to respect his mom by including her in the process." Talinda replied.

"By the way, mom and dad," Bernard added. "They will have to share more than one baby with you. Talinda is carrying twins."

"OH MY! Reginald did you hear that, two babies," she exclaimed in pure delight.

"That's great news son," his dad said. Then he took a more serious tone and called his son's name, "Bernard."

"Yes, sir," Bernard answered. He knew by his father's tone he was about to receive words of wisdom and instruction.

Reginald took a breath as though he pondered his thoughts and continued, "Brandon has placed great trust in you son. You've gone from being a single care free man, to a married one with a teen aged son and two newborns on the way. That's a heavy responsibility son. It should not be taken lightly. If you have ever been a praying man you will become one now. You must pray for direction in leading your family. Everything in that household is your responsibility and your liability. Get into His word, son. Get to know God like never before because you will need him like never before."

"Yes sir," Bernard replied. "I understand completely dad. Mom, dad there is one more thing. Brandon also requested that I exit out of the military. I have decided to honor that request because of my job and the state of the nation at war. He and I both agree she needs stability and reassurance from the possibility of losing another husband to violence."

"Oh Bernard...thank you Jesus," his mom said unable to hold back tears. "I, for one, am glad you are exiting out of the military. Every time you deploy I age son. Thank you God." She declared again.

"Well, alright son...and Talinda, you guys get off this phone and enjoy your honeymoon. Congratulations baby girl, and welcome to the family."

"Thanks Mr. Travis," Talinda replied.

"Dad," he said.

"Okay...dad," Talinda replied barely above a whisper because she had was once again lost her composure.

"Congratulations son. I know she was a beautiful bride," Reginald said to Bernard.

Bernard looked at Talinda and replied, "More than you'll ever know dad. More than you'll ever know."

"Okay son, by now you're looking deep into her eyes and we're about to hear something we don't want to hear. So get off this phone and go enjoy your honeymoon," Reginald said.

"Okay dad," Bernard said with a chuckle because his dad was so on point with his comment. "Mom, don't worry. We're going to have a ceremony on our one year anniversary. By then I'll be back in country and Talinda will have recovered from labor."

"That's all I ask," she said. "I'm only going to get to do this once."

"Okay, love you mom...dad. Goodbye," Bernard replied.

"Okay son," his mom replied. "Love you both. Goodbye. Bernard and Talinda both say goodbye and hang up the phone.

Talinda turned to Bernard, took a deep breath and let out a huge sigh of relief. "Well, that went okay. I was really nervous. I didn't know what to expect from your parents. I thought they would think I was playing with your heart."

"Yeah my mom took it way better than I thought she would," Bernard replied. "She has always been so protective of accomplishments in my life wanting to be present for all the first events. She would say I'm only going to get to do this once Bernard. She would fly in for every promotion or school graduation. I mean any big or small achievement. She would be there for every deployment departure and return that was allowed. I thought for sure when she found out that she wasn't here for the main event that she wouldn't handle it very well."

"Well, we had the clerk video it on your phone. Why don't we just email it to everybody," Talinda suggested.

"Yeah, great idea, baby," Bernard said.

Talinda got up from the chair, "I'll download it to your laptop and send it out now."

"Whoa, whoa, whoa Mrs. Bernard Travis, no you won't," Bernard said as he pulled her into his arms and kissed her. "You are about to eat dinner and make love to your husband. The video can and will...wait."

"Mmmmm," she moaned as he kissed her again. "That's fine with me Mr. Travis. I can't wait until we get back to Paris tomorrow. We're going to have an awesome honeymoon. There are so many sights to see and dinner theatres on the...."

"Hey," he said as he cut her off with a kiss. "Have I told you how much I love you?"

She smiled and said as she stroked his temple, "Awwwee...oh Bernard...I'm so blessed. I love you so much."

They sat down to eat and forced themselves to at least take in a little food. Neither one of them really had an appetite for food because their appetite for love had taken center stage.

"Bernard, we are wasting time with this meal. We'll eat later. Come on baby," she said as she rose from the table. She took him by the hand and led him toward the master bedroom.

Halfway to the bedroom she stopped and looked at him. "You can't run from me anymore Mr. Travis," she said as she kissed him.

"I wasn't running from you baby, I was running from temptation," Bernard said as he returned the kiss.

Once inside the bedroom he said, "Come on sweetheart let's take a shower and get the road off us so we can relax."

"Okay," Talinda said as she ran her fingers across his lips and down his chest. "Oh wait I need my bag," she declared. She turned to leave the bathroom to go get it.

Bernard stopped her as he said, "Oh, baby, trust me. You don't need clothes for the trip I'm about to take you on."

She chuckled and smiled as she said, "Oh trust me...you want this. I'll be right back." She left and retrieved her overnight bag. When she returned Bernard was already preparing the shower.

The shower was heavenly and they enjoyed the soothing caressing effects of the water as it paraded over them. He held her close and kissed her like she was going to disappear.

After they emerged from the shower he proceeded to dry her off. He was about to carry her into the bedroom when she protested. "No Bernard. You go ahead and I'll be there in a minute."

"Baby...," he started to say.

"Shhhh...no questions. Go. I'll be there in five minutes," she said as she kissed him again.

He let out a sexy chuckle eyed her with much curiosity, "What are you up to?" he replied.

"You'll find out," she said as she escorted him to the bathroom door and closed it behind him. She then took a purple maternity negligee she bought in Paris out of her bag. It was delivered to the room with the rest of the gowns she purchased that day. She oiled down, sprayed on a light mist of body cologne and was ready.

When she emerged from the bathroom, Bernard was in the center of the bed with a towel still wrapped around his waist. When he saw her he sighed. As he got up to meet her he said, "Wow....when did you have time to slip away to buy that?"

"I'm not telling," she responded with a sexy smile as she bit her bottom lip. She looked up at him as he approached her.

"Uhmm...who told you my favorite color was purple?" he said as he began to lightly kiss her on the neck.

"I am not revealing my source, Bernard Travis," she replied leaning her head back as he continued to kiss her on the neck.

He picked her up and carried her over to the bed and he said, "I have my ways...I'm going to love it out of you."

She moaned and replied, "I am going to enjoy you trying, but I'll never tell. My lips are sealed."

"Oh, they were sealed," he said with a seduction chuckle as he kissed her.

The sound and aroma of love engulfed the room as he fulfilled his bride and she enjoyed her groom.

~Chapter Ten~

They returned from Paris the following Monday morning. For the second time, Talinda's honey moon was everything she thought it would be. It was full of dinner theatres and tours and shopping. Although she was much too excited and happy to think much of food, Bernard consistently coached her to finish her meals. They toured the country side and enjoyed the history of the old world part of the country. Talinda declared that she would have been happy even if they never left the hotel room. She was amazed how many nostalgic moments she had about her and Brandon as she enjoyed her honeymoon with Bernard. They were alike in so many ways it was oftentimes very scary but never uneasy. She was completely comfortable and in love with Bernard.

"I'm so glad that I was able to get Dr. Harrell to let me stay an additional two weeks," Talinda said as they pulled into the driveway back in Kaiserslautern.

"Yeah, now I just have to check with my squadron commander to see if I'm up for any missions for those two weeks so I can extend my leave," Bernard said as he put the car into park.

"Oh baby, if you can't that's fine, too," Talinda said with a smile. "You know I'll be home waiting on you after work every day. I just want to be here in the same country with you a little while longer. We have so much we still need to learn about each other."

He walked around and opened the door for her. He handed her keys to the front door as he started to retrieve the bags out of the car. He turned around just in time to see Talinda attempting to lift one of the heavier suitcases.

"Talinda, what are you doing baby?" He said as he approached her and picked up the suitcase to carry it in.

"Bernard, I really could have gotten that," Talinda said in an 'am I in trouble' tone.

"Sweetheart this first trimester is a very fragile time for you and the babies. So please...don't take any chances okay," he said as he kissed her and then led her into the house so she wouldn't attempt to help him any further.

She smiled and was obedient to her husband. She walked into the kitchen and looked into the refrigerator. She asked Bernard what he would like for her to prepare him for lunch. He informed her most of the items in there should probably be thrown out but they could run by the commissary after leaving the commanders office.

"Okaaayy," she said as she closed the refrigerator. "Then we're going to have to stop to get something to eat on the way because my appetite has come back with a vengeance."

He smiled and said, "Sure baby. We'll stop by the food court and grab something before heading to my unit."

Talinda found the everyday life of a service man very fascinating and was full of questions for Bernard about the many activities that are going on around them. As they pull up into his unit he informs Talinda he will get her situated in the day room before he goes to meet with his squadron commander.

He introduced her to the commander and proceeded to escort her to the dayroom when the Colonel asked if she would like to accompany them into the office. She respectfully declines and elected to wait in the day room for Bernard. While she is there Captain Thomas walked by and stopped to ask her if there is anything she could help her with.

"Oh, thanks. I'm just waiting for...," Talinda paused. She tried to remember just what it was that Bernard addressed himself as when he was on the phone. "Ahhh...for Master...Travis," she said in an 'I have no idea what to officially call him' tone.

Tasha smiled. "You mean Major Travis. Oh, you must be Talinda Travis, his cousin's wife who is here to visit with him." She said as she extends her hand to Talinda.

"Yeah, I am really not familiar at all with military terms and prefixes for people. I just call him Bernard. You must be...Tasha he told me about you," Talinda said as she stood and shook her hand. She decided she would let Bernard inform her of their relationship status.

"Oh boy, just when I thought we were going to be friends. Travis has messed it up," she said laughing. "Hey would you like to join me in my office while you wait on Travis to come out?" Tasha asked her.

"Yes I feel somewhat awkward out here just sitting as people pass by staring at me," Talinda replied in relief.

Inside the commanders office Bernard informed his leader that he was recently married and would like to extend his leave to entertain his wife during her stay. He talked to him about the contents of the envelope from Brandon and discussed the circumstances of him exiting from the military. They also discussed the possibility of him obtaining a compassionate reassignment to Georgia. Bernard was surprised by his commander's knowledge of the bible because he had never really shown much of any sign of Christianity before.

"So he asked you to be her Boaz huh Travis?" The commander said as he as jotted down notes about their conversation.

"Ahhh...yes sir, and we were married last Monday here at the jag office sir. Chaplin McGhee preformed the ceremony for us," Bernard said. He felt the presence of God fall upon him.

They spend about fifteen minutes and discussed all Bernard's request and the commander informed him that although he really hated to see one of his top pilots end his career he certainly understood the special circumstances that surrounded his decision. He informed him that he would have Captain Thomas begin the paperwork and see what favors he could pull in for him. Bernard stood and shook his hand as they both exited the office.

In the meantime, Talinda talked to Captain Thomas and thanked her for telling Bernard where she could find maternity clothes there in Kaiserslautern. She also complimented her haircut.

"Oh, thanks girl, and no problem. Hopefully, we can get some more shopping in before you leave to go back to the states," Tasha said with a smile and a 'girl you're good' hand gesture.

The Colonel addressed Talinda and congratulated them. He gave Tasha the note pad and asked her to meet with him briefly after lunch to discuss some options for Major Travis. She agreed as the colonel walked away. She glanced at the paper to see what Bernard had requested of the commander as Bernard addressed her.

"Hey Captain Thomas. I see you met my wife," Bernard said with a sly smile and waited for Tasha's explosive response.

"Whoa...wife! When did you...I thought she was..." Tasha replied. She smiled and looked at Bernard like the cat who just stuffed the canary in his mouth.

"I know, I know. It's a long story," Bernard answered with a knowing smile.

"Yeah, I bet," she said very sarcastically as she gave him a 'you go boy' look. "I'm only your best friend and you run off and get married without telling me! Wait until I call Jaison and tell him about this." She turned to Talinda and said, "Girl we sat here talked for over ten minutes and you neglected to tell me you were married to Travis."

"I...ahhh...," Talinda said unsure how to respond. Bernard came to her rescue.

"It was one of those let's do this right now kind of things. Come on now Tasha you know you're my little sister girl. You and Jaison are family," he apologetically said.

"Well, anyway, congratulations to you both," she replied with a half chuckle and big smile as she shook her head in amusement. She rolled her eyes at Bernard and she threw Talinda a 'he's not even in the room smile' as she said, "Anyway Talinda, I hope to see you again before you leave the country."

"I'm sure you will, it was nice to meet you," Talinda said as she returned the smile.

They left the office. When they got back into the car Talinda turned to Bernard and said, "What would you say if I wanted to get my hair cut?"

Bernard paused and asked, "Sweetheart, is this a trick question?"

She said, "No I'm serious."

He said, "Baby, what am I supposed to say? I mean, I'm a little lost here."

"Would you mind?" she asked with a very inquisitive look on her face.

"Sweetheart, it's your hair why would I mind?" he replied.

"Well, I was thinking about getting it cut like the lady we were just talking to inside," Talinda said in an almost scared to ask tone.

"Captain Thomas?" Bernard asked. "Wow, you want it short. Ahhh...I think it will be sexy," Bernard responded still not exactly sure why she is so apprehensive about the situation.

"You mean you wouldn't mind?" Talinda asked again.

Bernard gave her a perplexed look, "Mind? Why would I mind? Talinda it's..."

She cut him off, "I won't if you don't want me too."

He looked at her with a 'are you serious' look as he responded, "Baby, you don't need my permission to cut your hair. Sweetheart listen, are you still going to be Mrs. Bernard Travis after you get your hair cut?"

"Well of course," she replied. She shook her head and smiled. His demeanor totally relaxed her. She marveled at his ability to disarm her and how completely comfortable she was with him after such a short time.

"Then what's the problem baby?" he said.

She looked at him in no uncertain terms and said, "Brandon would have nev...."

"Shhhh," he cut her off. "I'm not Brandon. Listen baby. Brandon and I are alike only in a couple of ways and totally different in everything else. I think it will be sassy...and sexy. I just want you to make sure you want it that short. I've never seen it short in any of the pictures I've seen of you. Because once you cut it off, you can't go back. Do you even know how to style short hair?"

Now totally relaxed she replied, "I guess I'll have to learn. I just want a change. You know I came over here as Brandon Travis' wife. But, I want to go home Mrs. Bernard Travis."

He shook his head in amusement and let out a sexy chuckle and stroked her cheek as he said, "Sweetheart you don't have to cut your hair to do that, you already are Mrs. Bernard Travis."

106

"I know," she replied. She smiled as she placed her hand over his and moved her head slightly in response to his touch. "I've always wanted to try it short and Brandon...even though he didn't have a problem with women cutting their hair...liked mine long."

"Well baby, cut it if you like. Come on," he said as he gets back out of the car.

"Where are we going?" she asked.

"To talk to Tasha and see when Stacy can get you in to cut your hair. I know that's who does hers and we are all friends," he answered.

"Really," she squealed in delight. "Oh Bernard, thank you so much." He smiled and shook his head in amusement again as they walked back toward the building.

Tasha was just about to leave for lunch when they caught her. He asked her to give Stacy a call to see when she would be available to cut Talinda's hair.

"Sure," Tasha replied, "How do you want it cut?"

"Like yours," Talinda responded.

"Are you sure...all that beautiful hair half way down your back...Talinda are you...?"

"Yes, I'm sure," Talinda cut her off.

"Okay," she replied. She agreed and called over to the post salon and asked for Stacy. She winked at Talinda because she couldn't help but toy with Bernard after Stacy answered the phone.

"Hey Stacy girl, can you do a haircut and style anytime soon? Oh, not for me. It's for Travis' wife," she said in a school girl sarcastic tone. She held the phone out from her ear so Bernard could hear because Stacy yelled out her response.

"Travis' what...who...girl, you better be kidding me! Travis did not get married without telling us. To who? It better not be who I think it is. Tasha talk to me, girl! Never mind. Is he there? Put him on the phone!"

"Yeah girl, he's right here," Tasha said sarcastically. "But he's scared to come to the phone. None of his so called friends were invited. It was a "private" ceremony."

Bernard continuously shook his head in amusement. Tasha proceeded to set up an appointment for Talinda. From time to time she would eye Bernard with a very sarcastic smile. Talinda was somewhat uncomfortable at first with the conversation that unfolded. But nevertheless, she marveled at how comfortable they were with each other and how genuine and pure their friendship was. She realized for the first time that she lacked something in personality compared to Tasha and Stacy and already looked forward to getting to know them better.

"Okay that'll work out great I'll let them know," Tasha said as she hung up the phone.

"Okay," Bernard said. He shook his head once more with a smile. "Now that you are done throwing me under the bus, when can she get my wife in?"

"You brought that on yourself Travis. You thought we were bad...just wait until Jaison and Terry find out about your "new wife." Anyway..." she said with a sista-girl roll of the neck. "She's off tomorrow but since we were going to the Heidelberg Fest she'll come in early in the morning and do her hair. Then we can all spend the day together. We were meeting up at our house about 1-ish tomorrow to head out to the fest. Since you had pulled a disappearing act on us the last week we were going to call you to see if you and your cousin's "wife"," she said with a smile and wink at Talinda. "Wanted to go to the fest with us. You know...I mean since we hadn't been "introduced" to her the whole time she had been here."

"Okay...okay enough Tasha," Bernard replied. He chuckled and shook his head. He turned to Talinda and said, "Is that alright with you baby?"

"Sure, but she doesn't have to come in on her day off I can wait until her next work day," Talinda replied.

"Oh girl, you gotta learn us. She is just fine with that. Hope you're an early riser, because I told her I would have you at the salon around zero eight in the morning. But considering your pregnant I can change that."

"Zero eight...?" Talinda replied in total bewilderment as Bernard explained.

"Oh, that's 8:00 am in the morning baby. Remember the military operates on a twenty-four hour clock. That also means we have to get up around 6:30 am. Tasha, Jaison, Terry and Stacy all just live down and across the street from us but it's about fifteen to twenty minutes from the base salon. So she'll have to get you early so you guys can all get there by 8 am," he interjected.

"Oh, okay," she laughed at herself that she had not figured out the whole zero eight time thing. "No that will be fine. We'll be there at 0800. Please thank her again for me," Talinda replied.

"That's going to be a long day baby. Are you sure?" Bernard asked her.

"Yes I'm sure sweetheart. I'll be fine," Talinda assured him.

"Okay," Bernard replied.

"Okay, 0800 it is, then. We can all ride together," Tasha answered. She turned toward Bernard and said very sarcastically, "Well Travis looks like you got one more night to play in that hair. Oh and don't keep her up all night either."

"See Tasha, you gonna stop it!" Bernard shot back at her just as sarcastically it had come at him. He couldn't help but smile because he was so incredibly happy with how God had blessed him.

Talinda just smiled and realized she was about to get acquainted with some really down to earth and aggressive sisters. Something she was obviously and desperately missing in her life.

"Bye, Major Travis," Tasha said with an eye roll as she passed by Bernard to address Talinda. "See you in the morning girl, and don't let him keep you up all night."

"I won't," Talinda replied teasingly. "I'm not missing this haircut in the morning. Thanks again."

"You're welcome. See you two in the morning," Tasha said as she exited the building.

Bernard and Talinda leave as well. They decide to go have lunch out in K-town in the Markplatz. Talinda was very fascinated with German cuisine and had enjoyed every meal up to this point. They spent the rest of the day in shop mode and enjoyed the love moments the shared with each other.

~Chapter Eleven~

At the salon the next morning after all the formal introductions are out of the way, Stacy pleaded a loss cause to Talinda not to cut her long beautiful hair. On top of that she chose a haircut that was much shorter that Tasha's. She realized she was bound and determined to cut it all off so she asked if Talinda would like to keep a lock or two for a keepsake. If so then she would know to be meticulous with the first cut. Talinda replied that she would indeed like to keep a lock for Bernard and one for a scrap book she would soon start about her and Bernard's life together.

As Stacy made the first cut, Talinda asked her to please turn her away from the mirror. She wanted to be totally surprised at the end result. Stacy neared the end of the hair cut when suddenly Tasha looked up and whispered, "Oh God, anybody but her."

That made Stacy and Talinda look up. Stacy sighed and looked up towards the ceiling. Talinda just sat quietly, not quite sure yet what it all meant.

Tasha greeted the woman who, has now walked into the salon, "Hey, what's up Hayes. What are you up too?"

She did not respond to Tasha because Captain Hayes looked at the hair on the floor and said, "Wow, tell me you did not just get all this beautiful hair I see on the floor cut off of your head. Girl, I would die for your hair."

Tasha mumbled under her breath and touched her temple and slightly looked away like she lost something on the ceiling as she said, "Yeah, she would die for your man too."

Hayes replied, "What was that, Thomas?"

Tasha responded with a slight hint of sarcasm as she is fanned herself, "Nothing, girl. I was just saying I would die for a fan...whooo it's hot in here." It is all Stacy can do to keep her composure. Talinda just sat in silence. Because she realized this girl either has or had an intimate connection with Bernard.

110

Hayes replied, "Speaking of to die for. Girl, where is that fine Travis at these days. I haven't seen him in a little minute?"

This comment, of course, got Talinda's full attention and she looked up and slightly pulled her hair out of Stacy's hand. Stacy gave her a gentle reassuring pat on the shoulder as she cleared her throat. That was Tasha's cue to handle the situation, which pleased her greatly.

"Oh," Tasha said in a high, soprano 'thought you knew' tone and attitude. "Girl, he's been on leave the last few weeks." She then paused for a millisecond and continued sarcastically. "Oh, and how rude of me. Allow me to introduce you to his wife...Talinda."

Talinda looked up and spoke. Hayes did not respond. She just stood there with her mouth open as she thought about what her response would be to Tasha's introduction to Bernard's wife.

Stacy turned her head she wouldn't out and out laugh in Hayes' face and escorted Talinda to the shampoo bowl leaving Tasha out on the cutting floor with her.

"What? Excuse me, when did Bernard get married? I mean I didn't even realize he was in a relationship with anybody?" She said to Tasha with a slight look of disgust on her face toward Talinda.

Talinda looked up again at that statement and Stacy put a hand on her shoulder to calm her. Tasha replied as they both walked over to join them at the shampoo bowl. "Oh girl. It was something of a long distance relationship for a little minute now. She just came to visit him from the states. Girl, they got married earlier this week. It was a private ceremony of just his "close friends" you know. Girl, not only is Travis married, but he is also about to be a father. His wife is what," she said and turned toward Talinda who tried very hard to keep her composure and her cool, "four months pregnant now...and if I remember correctly when Travis called about location of the maternity store, with twin's right?"

Stacy cleared her throat. She mentioned she needed more shampoo and dismissed herself to the supply room to fully enjoy the moment.

Hayes in total shock did not to reply to Tasha news and called out to Stacy instead. "Anyway...Stacy where are you? I came in to check on when my appointment is next week. I didn't even expect you to be here today. I thought you were off?"

Stacy replied as she walked back around the corner without any shampoo mind you, as she tried to regain her composure. "Girl, I am off. I came in early to do Travis a favor and cut his wife's hair before we all went to the Heidelberg Fest later today. Still can't believe she's cut off all that beautiful hair."

Talinda finally replied. She was surprised, to say the least, at her desire to be sarcastic and vengeful. "Stacy, like I said earlier, it's just hair. I was ready for a change and Bernard doesn't care. So I decided hey...new husband...new babies...new haircut...why not?"

Tasha replied in an 'I'm loving this just a little too much' tone, "I heard that girl," as she gave her the 'you go girl' gesture, with a flick of the hand.

In the meantime, Stacy went over to the counter to check her books. She still struggled to keep from laughing under her breath as she turned around and told Hayes her appointment day and time scheduled for the next week.

She thanked her and walked out without saying goodbye to anyone. As soon as she hit the door Stacy totally lost it.

"Y'all are bad," Talinda replied as smiled and threw her head back further in the shampoo bowl in amusement. "Who was that girl and do I need to be worried about her?"

Stacy replied, "A Travis wanna-be girl, and nobody you need to be worried about...trust me."

Tasha added as she chuckled aloud, "Girl, later on when she thinks about it, she's going to be trying to figure out how Travis could have fathered your children four months ago when he was still in Afghanistan."

At that comment they all burst into all out laughter.

"Oooo you guys are wrong for that." Talinda said in a more serious tone. "Tasha, why did you give that girl the impression that I got pregnant out of wedlock?"

Tasha replied, "Girl, if you going to hang with us you're going to have to let your hair down! Ooops...sorry. I guess you can't do that anymore because...ahh...you just cut it all off! Anyway you're going to have to lighten up."

They all shared in laughter at Tasha's comment.

"Don't worry," Stacy replied with a sarcastic chuckle. "She just married Travis...trust me, she'll lighten up."

Tasha replied to Stacy's comment with a slight chuckle and flip of the hand and tilt of the head, "Girl I know that's right." She looked down at Talinda who was still laid back in the shampoo bowl and said, "Don't worry she is too upset about Travis to worry about you. Your youth pastor image is safe...trust me."

They continued in laughter and conversation as Stacy set and dried Talinda's hair. Stacy gave her a quick curl and spike look and turned her around in the mirror.

"Oh my Gosh!" Talinda replied as tears welled up in her eyes.

"Are you okay?" They both ask in unison.

"Yes...I love it...I just love it! I hope Bernard likes it," Talinda responded.

"Oooh," Stacy breathed easy, "I thought you were about to say you hated it and burst into tears." They all laughed. To Stacy's protest, Talinda paid her quite generously.

As they walked out of the salon Tasha said, "Girl, why did Bernard let you wear this outfit and shoes to go to the fest. He knows better than this. You'll be dog tired and your feet swollen by the end of the day. You need something a lot more comfortable. Not to mention better shoes. Let's hit the maternity store again before we head back over to the guys."

They all agreed. On the way to the store Stacy couldn't help but ask Talinda the question that was in everybody's mind. "Talinda, you know I have to ask. Girl, how did you and Travis end up at the altar on Tuesday?"

Talinda gave them the short version of the story. They especially loved the dinner at the Eiffel Tower where Bernard proposed just last week. They thought the whole story was just as romantic as it was awesome.

Finally after they spent the whole morning doing hair, engaged in conversation and shopped they were on the way back to join the men at Tasha and Jaison's' house.

As they drove Tasha said to Talinda, "I wish you were staying here. I get the feeling we would all be very good friends."

"Yeah me too, but hey something tells me we'll end up together again somehow," Talinda replied. As they near Tasha and Jaison townhouse Talinda nervously asked, "Do you think Bernard will like it?"

Tasha said, "Like it...girl he's going to love it. He thinks short hair is sexy. Let me put it this way, if you weren't already pregnant then you probably would be by the time you left Germany."

They were engaged in laughter as they entered the house. Bernard took one look at her and said, "Wow, baby, that is sooo short!"

Talinda replied in alarm, "You don't like it!"

"No, baby, on the contrary I love it! You are more beautiful than ever. If you weren't already pregnant girl, you would be in trouble," Bernard replied.

The girls burst out laughing as Tasha said, "Do I know my big brother or what?"

"Wow Stacy, thanks it's beautiful," Bernard said as he gave her a hug.

"You're welcome Bernard," she replied.

"Hey guys where are the babies?" Tasha asked.

"They're asleep, sweetheart. Alicia's in her crib and TJ's in our bed," Jaison replied.

Talinda winked at Tasha and Stacy as she turned to Bernard before he could introduce her to Jaison and Terry and said, "Hey baby, exactly who is this Hayes girl that gave me such a hard time about you today?"

Bernard looked up in Stacy and Tasha's direction and yelled, "Tasha!"

She held her hands up and answered, "What...I didn't do anything...what...why do you have to think I had something to do wit...?"

He cut her off, "Because I know you Tasha. Why would my wife who has never been to Germany or known anyone I was associated with ask me about my ex-girlfriend?"

"Now hold on, wait a minute Bernard," Talinda interjected. "Tasha had nothing to do with it. She walked into the salon while Stacy was doing my hair and asked where that fine Travis was among a few other things. And as far as ex-girlfriend goes you have been the first person all day long to mention that fact sweetheart."

At that comment Jaison and Terry both gave Travis the "Oooo" sound with their hands over their mouths.

"Baby, wait a minute...listen," Bernard said, in an attempt to back paddle his way out of the conversation. He rubbed his temples slightly and looked down. He tried hard to think of the right words.

"I'm listening," Talinda replied. She tried to keep a straight face. She was glad Bernard had looked down. Jaison and Terry caught on because of Talinda's countenance and decided to turn up the heat on Bernard.

"Come on Travis answer the woman," Jaison replied.

"Oooo...this ain't the Travis I know," Terry added.

"Man would y'all stop it...please," Bernard said to Jaison and Terry.

He then turned back to Talinda who had regained her composure and is ready to play the joke out to the end.

"Baby listen...that girl is not going to be a problem," he said as he attempted to touch her face.

Talinda slightly turned her head away from Bernard which sent him into a bit of a panic. "Talinda...baby look at me...I swear she is a non-issue," Bernard replied with an 'I'm very sorry' tone.

Jaison jumped in and said, "Girl, you got to be the real deal because I have never seen Travis like this before." He then turned back to Bernard, "Brother you better get to explaining yourself."

Talinda just looked at Bernard with the straightest face she can muster up.

"Jaison...man please...you're not helping me. Could you guys just give it a rest for a minute and let me go talk to my wife," Bernard said in desperation.

Stacy who couldn't hold it in any longer burst out laughing and said, "Talinda girl please let him off the hook before he passes out!"

As soon as she said that Talinda and everybody in the room erupted in uncontrollable laughter.

Bernard, finally realized that he had been toyed with and said, "See all of y'all are wrong," Bernard said relieved. He attempted to play of the fact that he was alarmed at Talinda's response to him. "Baby I cannot believe you conspired against me with them."

Talinda laughed so hard that she could barely talk. "Oh sweetheart, I'm sorry, but you just walked right into it. Believe me you should be thanking Tasha because she put her in her place."

Tasha could hardly catch her breath to reply for laughing at Bernard's expense. "Travis, right now she probably trying to figure out how you fathered children four months ago when you guys were still in Afghanistan."

That statement brought more laughter in the room. Bernard had to even draw a smile on that one as he declared, "Okay...I admit you got me good...that was good. Baby I can't believe you did your loving husband like that."

He turned toward Tasha and Stacy and held up four fingers in their direction as he exclaimed, "Four hours...you two had my wife for four hours and look at the damage you've done. Already she's starting to act just like you two."

Talinda replied as she walked back over to stand between Tasha and Stacy, "I don't know sweetheart...I mean I take that as a compliment. I'm in very good company."

Tasha and Stacy both gave her a high five as they say in unison, "You know that's right, girl!"

"That's it, Talinda! You cannot be alone with these two ever again. They are NOT suitable playmates," Bernard responded.

Tasha replied, "Now that's the Travis I know!"

Bernard shook his head in amusement and beckoned for Talinda to come back by his side. As he touched Talinda on the shoulder he said, "Now that you all have had fun at my expense, sweetheart let me introduce you to the guys. This is Terry Stallworth, he's Stacy's husband."

"Nice to meet you," said Talinda as she shook his hand.

Tasha went over to Jaison's side and gave him a playful hug as Bernard said, "And this is Jaison, Tasha's husband."

Talinda greeted him and shook his hand. They continued in conversation as they gathered up the babies and get ready to head out to the car for a fun filled day at the festival in Heidelberg.

"Hey give me my god daughter," Bernard said as Tasha came out of the room with little Alicia.

"Be my guest," Tasha replied a she handed her over to Bernard.

"While you're at it, go ahead and change her diaper. You need the practice," Jaison said as he patted Bernard on the back.

"Man, you know I've changed her before so don't try to act brand new on me," Bernard replied as he proceeded to change Alicia.

"See girl, Travis is a professional...ahh so don't let him try to get over when the twins arrive," Stacy said with an 'uhn huh I told your girl' gesture.

"Wow I see," Talinda replied with a smile. Bernard just smiled and shook his head as he finished.

After they got the babies all packed up they all climbed in Jaison and Tasha's SUV. It was big enough that they could ride together in one vehicle. They had a car set in the middle of each row and the adults sat on either side of the car seats.

≈

Later after the festival Bernard decided to skip the late night cappuccino run the gang usually had after the festivals to wind down.

"Hey guys we're going to skip the cappuccino run. I am going to get my pregnant and tired wife to bed. See y'all at church tomorrow," Bernard's said as they all hug and said their goodbyes.

"Wow. It's good to see Travis really happy like this," Jaison said.

"Yeah," Stacy replied. "And so different. He was never this loving and considerate with Hayes."

Tasha let out a sarcastic chuckle and rolled her eyes. "Girl, please...look who you talking about...Hayes. Uhmm...she is nowhere near Talinda's league. Talinda is good for Travis. Besides, he's been in love with her for a long time. That was part of Hayes' and his problem. She just couldn't measure up to Talinda."

"Heck, even before Talinda came into the picture, the more Travis got into God the more he realized Hayes wasn't the one," Stacy replied.

"Yeah, you guys are certainly right about that," Terry interjected. "Hayes was just a good sleeping partner before Travis really got into God. He changed after his cousin came to visit him almost two years ago. He stopped drinking and everything. He was the main reason why we all straightened up. His cousin lit a fire under him and it just sprayed all over us."

"Yeah," Jaison recalled. "I'm really happy for him. He's wanted to settle down ever since we all started having kids. I think us settling in made him see he was missing the best part of life. What's success really worth without having someone special to share it with?"

~Chapter Twelve~

When they arrived home, Bernard made Talinda a hot cup of decaffeinated herbal tea to relax her for bed. As they lay in bed Bernard smiled as he played in Talinda's short, spiky hair. "I really like it, baby. It's very sexy."

"Mmmmm you really, do don't you?" Talinda replied. "Talk to me baby until I fall asleep."

He smiled and they began to talk about their life together and made plans for the future. They talked about Raymond and the babies. Then all of a sudden Bernard began to pray over her and praise God for her. This excited her and she looked at him and realized that he had not received the baptism of the Holy Spirit. As he praised God and prayed for her she asked him had he ever spoke in tongues. After he replied no she began to teach him what the scripture said about receiving the baptism and asked him if he was ready to receive it. He excitedly said yes and knew that was what he missed in his spiritual walk. He knew he could lead her emotionally but questioned his spiritual ability to be her head. He was saved but always felt like there was still something he missed in his life when it came to God.

She laid her hands on him and began to pray over him. He continued to praise God and the Spirit of God flooded the bedroom and filled him. Bernard started to speak in unknown tongues. Talinda praised God and sang the victory as her husband enjoyed the Holy Ghost ride that swept through the room and carried him away in the spirit. He just couldn't stop speaking in tongues. He went to sleep speaking in tongues. Spoke in tongues in his sleep and rose up the next morning still in the spirit.

When they arrived at church he was still in awe of God's presence. Everybody marveled at the glow that seemed to surround Bernard. They knew it was more than just the excitement of married. They were all lay ministers and had to be at church early because they had several duties to perform before church started at 12:30. Their service was the last one at the chapel every Sunday. Talinda told them about the events the night before and Tasha said, "I have always wondered about it and wanted it. Can we pray Talinda I want the fullness of God in my life."

Talinda, very much ready to oblige and be used by God, gathered them all in a circle and began to pray. Bernard had already begun to speak in tongues, which excited the rest of them. By the time Talinda was done, they are all laid out in the foyer and spoke with unknown tongues as the spirit gave them utterance. The chaplain appeared in the doorway to because he heard the commotion from his office and realized what had happened. He knew about the baptism of the Holy Spirit and privately envied it but never really had enough faith to believe God for it and so never taught on it to any great extent.

When he came out, his five lay minister's spoke in tongues as Talinda prayed over them. The minute Talinda laid eyes on him she knew he has never spoken in tongues. She started to pray over him and he was slain in the spirit and spoke in tongues. People begin to enter because it was close to the time service usually began. Everyone that crossed through the foyer began to speak in tongues. Almost the whole 12:30 service was slain in the spirit. Talinda spoke into people's lives and confirmed what they had heard from God as the spirit led her. They spoke in tongues and praising and worshipped God to the point they are still there two hours later before the chaplain could get enough control on his tongue to speak English to the congregation.

As they finally gathered some sort of order to the church Chaplain McGhee stepped up to the pulpit. "I know you are all just as in awe with God and what he has done here today as I am. As much as I would love to say that your chaplain was the origin of the outpouring for the spirit today I cannot take the credit. This is...well I think I will just let Minister Travis introduce this anointed woman of God to you."

"Gladly sir," Bernard said as he escorted Talinda to the pulpit. "This beautiful woman of God is my newlywed wife Youth Pastor Talinda Travis. Our story is very unique and comes straight out of the book or Ruth. She indeed was married to my cousin who passed away tragically a few months ago and he desired that I love, marry and take care of his expecting wife. She is visiting here from Decatur Georgia just outside Atlanta and Chaplain McGhee married us just a day short of two weeks ago."

Bernard smiled and handed Talinda the microphone. She smiled at him. "Truly God is the originator of his manifest power here today. I am just a willing vessel available for His use. He has visited us today and shown himself mighty in our lives."

Chaplain McGhee stepped back to the microphone as Talinda stepped away from it. "She is being very modest, ladies and gentlemen. There was a glow around her when I walked into the foyer that revealed to me that God had indeed exposed my shortcomings to her. I know she is only going to be here for a short while but I would like to extend the invitation to her to return to minister to our youth."

Bernard addressed Chaplain McGhee and the congregation, "Pastor it's a wonderful coincidence that you would request that because some of her youth indeed are planning a trip to come here within the next month or so. I am sure with a little coaxing we can persuade them to minister to both us and our youth while they are in country. Originally, I had invited several of the young men but I am sure the young ladies would be more than willing to accompany them. They are anointed young people full of the Holy Spirit and they are powerful when they minister."

"Well," Talinda replied, "I'm sure they will be excited about that. So, I guess all I can say is we look forward to seeing you again soon."

They all praised God as Chaplain McGhee stated that there was nothing he could possibly do to compete with what the Holy Spirit had done today so he dismissed the congregation and many stayed behind to talk to Talinda and Bernard. Chaplain McGhee invited Bernard and Talinda along with his other four lay minsters to have lunch and fellowship to discuss the details of the next visit. They enjoyed an afternoon of food, fun and fellowship.

≈

They cuddled up in the bed and talked the night before she was due to leave. "I can't believe my time is up," Talinda sighed. "These five weeks have gone by so fast. I miss you already baby."

He sighed as he said, "I am going to be so lost without you Talinda. I'm going to miss rubbing your stomach and talking to the babies and feeling them move. I'm going to miss holding you in my arms and feeling your love flood the room."

"Awe, baby," she sighed. "It's going to be so hard to leave you tomorrow Bernard. Are you sure I can't stay any longer?"

Bernard smiled as he said, "As much I would love that sweetheart you know you have to get back. You have responsibilities and you need to get in for your doctor's appointment. I need some pictures of my babies and Raymond's adoption and name change paperwork is probably waiting on you. Not to mention if I don't get you back soon Aunt Helen is going to have me court order summoned to get you home."

They laughed and continued to just enjoy their conversation with each other. She moved in closer to him as she moaned. She sighed and said, "Mmmmm, make love to me Bernard...I need you."

"Oh, I love you so much, Mrs. Travis," he said as he pulled her even closer to him. He kissed, comforted and consumed her with his love.

≈

She rose early the next morning so she could prepare breakfast in bed for her newlywed husband once more before she departed the country to return home to the United States. He awoke to find his wife absent from bed and smiled as the fragrance of breakfast filled the room. She entered the room and approached the bed with a tray full of all his breakfast favorites.

"You are just spoiling me too much Mrs. Travis," he declared and smiled as he kissed her good morning.

She returned the smile and welcomed the kiss but her eyes told a different story. She looked like she would almost cry.

"I know, sweetheart," Bernard said as he kissed her again. "I don't want you to go either."

They finished breakfast and she loaded the dish washer as Bernard loaded her luggage in the car. She took a deep breath as they backed out of the driveway and got on the autobahn headed toward Frankfurt.

He lightly squeezed her hand and pulled it up to his lips and kissed the back of it as they drove to the airport. She carried a much heavier load for her journey home than she had arrived with. She had four suitcases full of clothes and souvenirs for everyone. Two suitcases alone were packed full to the brim with all sorts of goodies for Raymond. She had also bought some newborn clothes for the twins which found a home in another suitcase. The fourth suitcase contained items for all the grandparents. On top of that, Bernard would still have to mail two huge boxes full of clothing items for twins as well. She decided to forego buying anything for the youth until they made the journey back with her in about a month.

She felt her emotions begin to rise to the surface as they pulled into the airport. Bernard had already begun to be able to read her and ministered to her through his love and touch. No words needed to be said his touch told it all. After he got her all checked in they went to grab a quick bite to eat together. They had arrived a few hours early so they wouldn't feel rushed and could cherish their last moments together.

The two hours flew by and it was almost time for her to proceed through the security check. She could feel herself begin to lose the battle to her tears as he pulled her into his arms.

"Oh, Bernard I am going to miss you so much baby," she said through her tears. "I feel like I am leaving you for a lifetime."

He squeezed her a little tighter, smiled and declaring yet again, his love for her. "Ohhh, I don't want to let you go. A month seems so far away. I pray my compassionate reassignment is approved because I am not going to be able to stay away from you for eight months until my release date from active duty.

Through her tears she looked out over his shoulder as four familiar faces came toward her. She exclaimed, "Ohhh, Tasha...Stacy!" She broke her hold with Bernard to greet them. "I can't believe you guys came down here."

"Hey girl, you're family now," Tasha said.

"We wouldn't miss your send off. Besides we thought we may have to drive Travis back in case he couldn't see straight through his tears."

"Funny, Tasha," Bernard said as they all laugh. But he silently thanked them for interrupted the solemn moment.

Tasha hugged Talinda as she said, "Well Stacy and I both got you a card. We started out looking for a goodbye gift but decided...what do you buy a millionaire?" They laugh and Tasha continued, "So we both got you cards expressing how we felt about these last few weeks here with you. I'm going to ask you not to open and read mine until you get on the plane because I told myself I was not going to cry."

"Okay," Talinda said as she fanned her eyes in an attempt to prevent the tears that had formed from falling. "That's a good idea."

Stacy said, "You taught us so much Talinda. We all received the baptism of the Holy Spirit."

Jaison said, "Yeah, our chapel will never be the same."

"Our chaplain either for that matter," Terry added and they all laughed again.

"You know he is waiting for you to get back over here to spark a revival in our youth. He is so looking forward to it. I have never seen him this excited about anything," Tasha declared.

"Well the Holy Spirit has that effect on you," Talinda replied. "I am looking forward to it. I am always excited about sharing the gospel and exercising the gift given to me by God."

Tasha grabbed her by the hand and said to her, "Truly it was a divine appointment for me to meet you. I have learned so much from you. I do see some things in my life I need to change..."

Talinda squeezed her hand as she interrupted her, "Well, don't change too much. I love your spontaneity and outgoingness. Your sense of humor is a gift and makes you very approachable especially with youth. So don't change too much."

They laughed and talked until her flight came up. Talinda realized it is now time to go through security. She started to give everyone their goodbye hugs. She turned back toward Bernard one last time to hug him. He pulled her into his arms and kissed her and declared his love for her.

"As soon as you touch down, you call me, baby okay?" Bernard said as he finally let go of her.

"I will, sweetheart," she replied. She had begun to feel the pressure of the moment again.

"Thank you guys again for coming to see me off," Talinda said as she got in the line to go through security.

"Hey, like we said. You're family now, girl," Stacy declared. "You're not going to get rid of us that easily. We're lifers!"

"Well, I say "I do" to all of you. Goodbye for now," Talinda said as she walked through security. Right before she rounded the corner out of sight she turned to throw Bernard a kiss and yelled that she loved him. He yelled back and she walked out of his sight.

He turned to his friends and expressed his thanks to them again for coming. Their arrival had made it much easier to say goodbye to her. He decided to call Raymond to let him know his mother was about to board the plane and he would need to be there to help her with her luggage on her end.

Bernard breathed heavily as he dialed the phone. "Hey Raymond I just wanted to call and let you know your mom was boarding the plane. You're going to have to meet her. I know she came over here with no luggage, but she is coming back loaded down. It's mostly for you, so make sure you're available for her, okay?"

"Sure dad, that's no problem. Just text me her flight information and I'll meet her there. I miss my mom and I can't wait to see her." Raymond replied.

"What did you say, Raymond?" Bernard asked, unsure if he had heard him correctly.

Raymond replied, "I said that's no problem."

Bernard replied, "No, Raymond, after that."

"I'll...meet her there?" Raymond replied with an unsure tone in his voice.

"No son. Between those two statements...what did you call me?" Bernard asked. He felt an overwhelming sense of pride.

"Oh," Raymond replied. He now understood what Bernard had referred too. "You don't want me to call you dad?"

"No Raymond," Bernard said. "I didn't know you felt that way. I'm honored son."

"Well, my father loved my mom. If he has given her to you it's a package deal. I mean...I come with it. If my dad loves and respects and trust you enough to give his wife to you then you have to take his son also," Raymond replied.

"I'm honored Raymond," Bernard replied. "I know your dad has some big shoes to fill. But I will love you and take care of you to the best of my ability son."

"Love is all I require dad. It's always been enough for me and it will continue to be enough," Raymond declared. "I love you dad."

"I love you too son," Bernard replied. "I'll text you the information as soon as we hang up okay...goodbye."

"Goodbye dad," Raymond said as he hung up the phone.

Jaison ask Bernard, "Are you going to be alright man?"

"Yeah," Bernard said in a low whisper still in awe of the moment.

Terry patted him on the back as he said, "I know how you feel man. Every day I look in my baby's face I'm in awe of the honor of fatherhood. I'm thankful to God for choosing me to be a father and I pray for guidance that I will lead in a Godly manner."

"Yeah," Bernard said. "Exactly."

≈

Talinda's plane touched down right on schedule and she disembarked with her backpack and a smile. She looked forward to seeing Raymond. As much as she didn't want to leave her new husband she seriously missed her son. She couldn't wait until they would all be together one big happy blended family. She marveled at how good and powerful God was. "You never know the direction the footsteps that God has ordered for you will take you in. All you have to do is place your foot in them and let them lead. Faith is such a powerful weapon," she thought.

She almost walked on top of Raymond before he recognized her.

"Wow mom! Look at your hair!" Raymond exclaimed. "It's so short."

"Do you like it," she asked him.

"I think it's great, mom. You needed a change. You look awesome!" Raymond replied with excitement.

"Thank you baby, I missed you so much," Talinda declared.

"I missed you too mom. Dad called me when you got on the flight and said I needed to meet you here because you had a lot of luggage. So Jonathan dropped me off so I could drive you back home. I know you're probably tired," Raymond replied as he gave his mom a big hug.

"Dad?" Talinda said in a surprised but joyful tone as she smiled at Raymond. "Raymond I'm glad you're alright with this. I was really worried you would be offended that someone would try to take your father's place so soon."

"Dad and I talked about Bernard months before he died mom. He told me all about him. He said that if anything ever happened to him I could depend on Bernard to step in and take care of me like a father," Raymond said with a smile and hugged his mom again.

"Oh Raymond...I missed you so much," she replied. "Come on let's get the luggage and go home."

"Tell me all about Germany mom," Raymond said as they walked toward the baggage claim. They retrieved her luggage and are soon on highway 20 east headed back toward Decatur, Georgia. They laughed and enjoyed each other as they get stuck in rush hour traffic and Talinda told him all about Germany.

They finally arrived home shortly after 7:00 pm. Raymond unloaded the car and reminded his mom several times that she was not allowed to pick up any suitcases. She finally gave and walked into the house and let him be the man. She noticed on the table in the foyer there was an official letter from her lawyer. She opened it carelessly with the thought that it was probably some final information about Brandon's and her estate. But to her surprise it was the information she had been waiting for. Raymond's adoption had been finalized and his name change would go into effect as soon as they went to the lawyers' office for him to sign the necessary paper work. There was also a letter enclosed addressed to Raymond as well. She marveled at how God worked. She assumed that it was because Raymond was seventeen that she would have no more legal battles with his mother because the decision was now his. But this was not the case at all. Just when she was about to rejoice she flipped to the final page and her heart stopped. She paused and looked up at Raymond who was still busy unloading suitcases. She fought back the tears as she once again looked down at the paper. She reread it. She could not believe the words that were on the page:

Dear Mr. Raymond Rodriguez,

We regret to inform you that your mother, Consuela Maria Rodriguez, was found dead over six weeks ago. She was listed as a Jane Doe until dental records could be located to confirm her identity. We still request, however, that her body be identified by a family member. Enclosed is the certified letter that was found on her person. It is addressed to the attorney of Mrs. Talinda Travis. We are sorry for your loss and our prayers are with you.

Sincerely,

Atlanta Coroner's Office

Talinda fought back tears as she approached Raymond. She wondered just how much a young man could handle. She was about to inform him that he has lost yet another parent. She decided that whatever was in the envelope from the lawyer's office should be first opened and read by him. Raymond had just put the last suitcase down in the living room when he turned and saw his mother approaching him. The look on her face told him all that something was terribly wrong.

"What is it mom?" Raymond inquired. He looked down and saw that his mother had opened the certified letter that he had signed for a few days earlier. He assumed the worst. For him the worst thing that he had imagined was that the adoption had not gone through. "I'm not going to be a Travis, am I?" He said as he waited for her to affirm his declaration.

"Oh on the contrary, sweetheart. The adoption is final. You're officially my baby, and we just have to go to the office to sign everything. Your name change is already approved as well because we submitted it all the same time," Talinda replied. She realized this may be a harder blow than she thought for him. The thought of something

124

happening to his mother had not entered his mind. She had silently hoped that that was what he would refer too. It would have made the next statement out of her mouth easier.

"WOW! REALLY? You mean its official...I mean, I really am a Travis! I am your son for real mom!" Raymond replied as he jumped in delight.

"Yes Raymond you're officially my baby," she said and she could no longer hold the tears.

"Great! Let's go now mom and sign the paper. I want to go by the DMV and get my new license that say Raymond Travis," he exclaimed as he jumped once again in delight. He looked into his mother's eyes and realized that was not all there was to be told. "Mom, what's wrong?" He now asked in a nervous voice.

"It's...it's your mom Raymond. I'm sorry, baby, but the letter was also to inform us that she passed away," Talinda replied as she placed her hand on his shoulder. He nonchalantly stepped away from her and turned his back. "Do you need a few minutes alone sweetheart?"

"No mom," he replied as he turned back to face her. "I'll be fine in a few minutes," he said in a shaky voice.

Talinda walked over to him and placed her hand on his shoulder. "Hey sweetheart, it's okay to cry. You don't have to be strong...you don't' have to hold it in."

At those words Raymond broke and cried in his mother's arms. "I pray she didn't die alone and lonely mom. She was always so very sad. Drugs were her escape...but...she did love me. She always wanted me no matter that...she always wanted me. She did a lot of ungodly things to keep food on the table for me. She really appreciated you and dad when you took me in. She said she no longer had to worry about me but wanted me to remember she was still momma. I don't know mom...I mean I don't think she was..."

"Oh honey, only God knows. All we can do is trust him," Talinda replied. She continued to hold Raymond in her arms. After he regained his composure and they released their embrace Talinda handed him the other envelope. It was addressed to Raymond and the letter from the attorney stated that it was still in her hand when she was found.

His hands shook as he opened the envelope and unfolded the letter and began to read the contents. Talinda watched patiently and searched his face for early indication of what the letter may hold.

Tears fell from his eyes as he began to read his mother's final words to him:

My Dearest Raymond,

First of all, make no mistake about it, I love you dearly. I always have. I am so sorry that I couldn't provide the type of life for you that you deserve. Part of the reason that I kept saying no to the Travis' adopting you was because I was jealous of the life they offered you. I know that sounds crazy...you would think I would finally be happy you were getting a better life. But I was sad because I wasn't the one who was able to give it to you. But I have since then changed my thoughts on it. I have sent a certified letter to Mrs. Travis' attorney stating my desire that she adopt you. I relinquished my parental rights of you to her. She is good for you and she needs you right now. So be strong for her and take good care of her the same way you took care of me son.

I am so proud of you. I was so happy when you were off the streets and back into school. You were always so smart and now I know that you will probably go to college and be a very important person. I will be going back to Puerto Rico soon to try to get myself together. I hope that someday in the future we will be able to have a true mother-son relationship. I will keep in touch with you Raymond Travis...I like the sound of that. It's a name of promise and of prophecy.

For whatever reason, God still loves me. He has given me a second chance to set things right. I dedicated what was left of my life to him and I'm going back to where it all began to pick up the pieces. I didn't want to take you away from what you have always known as home so I am placing you in the permanent care of Mrs. Travis. Tell her that I am greatly in her debt for caring for my baby boy for me. I'll write to you once I am settled so you will have a working address for me. Raymond, never doubt that I love you son. I am not giving you up and am placing you in her care. You will always be my little Papi.

I love you so much,

Momma

He smiled as he thought of all the happy times they shared when he was her little Papi. He also had such relief that his mother had indicated she was once again right with God. That was all that mattered to him at this point. He had feared it would be a suicide note accompanied by a drug overdose. He now wondered what had happened and prayed that she had not suffered at the hands of some crazed mad man or organized gang.

126

"Mom I would like to know what the police have found out concerning her death and what they have called it," Raymond said as he wiped tears from his eyes."

"Sure baby," Talinda replied. "We will go by the police department after we leave the attorney's office. Sweetheart, we also have to go by the morgue. Since they have found next of kin they are asking for family identification. Then they will release the body so we can bury her properly."

"Mom you don't have to..." Raymond started to say. Talinda interrupted.

"Shhhh...son we are going to take good care of her...okay," Talinda said as she stroked his head.

"Okay mom," Raymond said barely above a whisper as he buried his head in his mother's chest. He felt so much pain for his mother. Her life had been so painful and empty.

After they left the attorney's office Raymond was more upbeat. He walked out of the office a Travis and they called Bernard to give him all the news of the day. He was happy about the adoption and gave Raymond words of encouragement about his biological mother. He teasingly chastised Talinda because she had not called him the minute she touched down.

Raymond wanted to go to the DMV to update his license before going to identify his mother's body. Talinda allowed him to take his time in getting there. She understood all too well the overwhelming grief that accompanied that task.

Raymond fought back tears as he identified his mother and declined when Talinda asked him if he wanted a moment alone with her. They buried her in high fashion. Raymond declared that she would have loved all the fuss being made about her. Talinda spared no expense and got the best of everything for her. Raymond was grateful to Talinda at she had cared about his mother so greatly. The police ruled her death a homicide. The case was still under investigation, but they had run into brick walls on every side thus far.

~Chapter Thirteen~

Talinda was finally able to make the appointment for her ultrasound a week after she returned from Germany. She had decided to wait until after they had buried Raymond's mother and both Helen and Valletta were present. She was now just at five months pregnant.

They anxiously waited for the technician as she prepared Talinda for the ultra sound. Ooo's and ahhh's were heard in the room as the technician discovered the bundles of joy wrapped up inside of Talinda. There they were just as Brandon had declared in his final words to Talinda, a boy and a girl. They of course knew the boy would be named Brandon Frazier Travis, Jr. She and Bernard decided to keep the girl's name a secret until the day of delivery.

Talinda had her laptop, so they were able to have Bernard on video chat so he could see the babies. Dr. Harrell did however still supply them with plenty of pictures and videos of the babies for the parents and grandparents to share.

"All is well and they are developing fine and on schedule, Mr. and Mrs. Travis. They are just the right size for how far along you are and being twins of course. There are no foreseeable problems. The heart beats are nice and strong and everything appeared normal," Dr. Harrell explained to Talinda and Bernard, who was still connected on video chat. Talinda remembered to get the statement from Dr. Harrell giving her permission to fly back to Germany because she would be close to her sixth month when they flew out at the end of the month. Dr. Harrell teased her that she would not approve any extensions this time. She did not want her flying coming up on her seventh month of pregnancy because she is still being considered high risk. Talinda assured her she wouldn't call for an extension because she had nine teen agers with her and two weeks with them in a foreign country would be enough.

≈

The anticipation of the trip to Germany helped to keep Raymond's mind off his mothers' death. The next Sunday in church the junior and senior youth members along with Talinda began to plan their trip. They had all asked and received permission from their parents and the excitement mounted for everyone. They all had passports because before Brandon died they had a missionary trip planned for the end of the year to go to Africa.

Talinda and Bernard decided to treat them and pay for the entire trip to Germany. They were to take money only if they wanted to for souvenirs and the ones who couldn't afford it Talinda and Bernard would provide for them. They would leave the week following the last day of school which was only two weeks away. The girls were excited to know that now they would be able to go as well. Originally the trip was set for the four older boys of the youth group only. They were all on pins and needles with excitement and could hardly focus on the end of term exams. With graduation being the last day of school Jessica and Jonathan the two graduating seniors of the group were excited the trip to Germany wouldn't interfere with the ceremony.

Talinda was eager to see her husband again. She longed to be in his arms to feel the security and comfort from the strength of his embrace. She missed the masculine but sweet smell of his cologne and gentleness of his kiss. She closed her eyes and took a deep breath as she sighed. He thought of the powerful love that they shared. She said out loud, "I'm coming baby...I'm on my way."

They were all present and accounted for and decided to spend the night before the trip at Talinda's house to make the transition easier the following morning. Veronica camped out with her as an additional chaperone. Sarah now lived with her pending the adoption going through. With her being seventeen they didn't foresee any problems. There were five girls and four boys going: Jessica, Michelle, Lisa, Sarah, LaNiesha, Raymond, Troy, Reginald and Jonathan. LaNiesha had a secret crush on Raymond. She was very excited to be able to go to Germany with Raymond and hoped that she would finally get enough nerve to share her feelings with him. Unknowingly to her, he had feelings for her as well and had discussed it with his mother and Brandon when he was still alive.

"Alright guys, let's go over some of the ground rules for tonight and the trip," Talinda said as they settled down for the night. "The girls would be upstairs in the guest bedrooms and the boys would camp out down here in the basement. "First off, Veronica and I will not stay up all night watching over you. You are young adults who have been taught well and I trust that once we turn in for the night, the girls will stay on the upper level in the bedrooms and the boys will remain in the basement, without incident." She looked around the room as she spoke and made eye contact with everyone. The girls of course had the usual school girl grins on their faces, while the boys tried to maintain a macho not interested at all look. "Bernard has informed me that when we get there tomorrow he will stay in the town house there with the boys with our friends Jaison and Terry. And the girls will stay with me at Tasha and Jaison's house accompanied by Stacy. So we better get some sleep because although our flight leaves at 4:00 in the afternoon when we get there it will be 8:00 am the next day and we will have felt like we've been up for more than a day. Trust me the jet lag catches up with you fast. So don't stay up too long tonight talking."

Raymond started to gather the glasses and plates they used for snacks to take them upstairs. As he moved around the room he said, "Don't worry mom...you know we are all going to do the right thing."

"I know you are son," Talinda replied. "Hey girls, let's get the plates and take them with us as we go upstairs to save the boys a trip."

"Okay, Pastor Travis," LaNiesha replied as she walked over to Raymond to get the tray he had in his hand. Their eyes met and she looked away quickly and walked up the stairs. Talinda smiled and shook her head at Raymond as she followed. He gave her a knowing look and dropped his head to hide the uncontrollable smile on his face. The rest of the girls and Veronica gathered up the rest of the dishes and followed. They said goodnight to the boys as they left.

"Talinda, girl, are you sure? I can sleep in one of the other bedrooms you know. This is you and Bernard's master suite," Veronica said as they sit down on the bed in school girl fashion.

"Girl, please, neither Bernard nor Brandon has slept in this bed. When I came back from Germany last month I got rid of the old mattress and bought a new one. I just couldn't bring myself to make love in a bed with Bernard that I have made love in with Brandon. It was a kind of creepy feeling you know what I mean? Besides, the girls will be in the other two bedrooms up here."

"Okay, if you say so," Veronica replied. "You and I haven't really had time to talk since you've been back from Germany. So how was it girl...I mean give me the skinny. How romantic was Bernard and Paris?"

"Oh Veronica, it was a mid-summers night dream experience," she said as she fell back on the bed and clutched a pillow. "He is so romantic and sensual." She sat back up as she said, "Girl he is nothing like Brandon. He is so much more aggressive and erotic. Brandon was very reserved...even in the bedroom but Bernard was over the top girl!"

Veronica "Oooo....girl stop....mmmm it is getting hot up in here!" She said as she fanned herself. "Me and Jeff need a little of that spice girl. After ten years of marriage I have to admit we're getting a little...boring." At that comment they both laugh and then continue on in conversation.

"Girl we'd better go to bed," suggested Talinda after an hour or so passed. They were so caught up in conversation they hadn't noticed the time. "We're doing exactly what we told the teens not to do...stay up all night talking."

"I know girl," Veronica said. "I missed talking to you the last few months. We got close really fast when I met you after Brandon's death. It's been a long time since I had a girlfriend I could relate to or confide in. I missed our girl talk sessions. But hey you need your sleep little momma."

"Yeah," Talinda said as she yawned. They lay down and Talinda is out before her head hits the pillow good. Veronica decided to take a stroll through the house to make sure everyone is where they are supposed to be. To her surprise all the youth were fast asleep. She and Talinda were the last two to go to bed. She went back upstairs and lay down and was soon in dreamland herself.

No one had to be dragged out of bed the next day. By the time Talinda was dressed and downstairs the teens were all in the kitchen cooking breakfast with Veronica. She had to admit she was overly excited to be reunited with her newlywed husband. She tried not to show just how excited she was. She attempted to maintain her calm, cool, and collected image she had with the teens. But of course as soon as they touched down and Bernard came into the picture they would soon see a side of their leader they had never seen before.

"Wow, if this is what it takes to get Raymond up and going in the morning without three or four wake-up calls, we should plan trips more often," Talinda said as she smiled and mushed Raymond's hair.

Everyone laughed as Raymond replied, "Mom."

"I love you, sweetheart," Talinda replied as she kissed Raymond on the cheek and went to the refrigerator to get more juice out.

"I love you too, mom," Raymond replied as he walked up behind her and gave her a bear hug. She patted his hands and leaned back into him to receive his hug. The girls all go, "Ahhhh" as they shot LaNiesha a quick glance. "We'll see how much you love me when it's time to change the twin's diapers in the middle of the night," Talinda joked. She grabbed the juice as Raymond still hung on to her.

He kissed her on the cheek as he took the juice out of her hand and poured it for her. As he handed her the glass he said, "Don't worry, I got you mom."

Veronica looked at all the other young men and said, "You see that guys, now that's the way you take care of your mother and your wife." She then turned to the girls and said, "Any man that respects and loves his mother will respect and love you. If you want to know how good a man will treat you just watch him with his mother."

"I was taught by the best," Raymond said. He winked at his mother who smiled and shook her head as she took her seat. Once again all the girls smiled and cleared their throats as they gave LaNiesha a 'girls only club' look. She tried to look away and busied herself. She walked over to the stove to see if she could help Veronica with anything. Veronica could only smile and looked down as she continued to prepare breakfast.

They shared more conversation and laughter as they finished. They all check their bags after breakfast to make sure they had repacked everything they used the night before. They sat down in the basement and talked while they were waited to go to the airport.

Their flight wasn't scheduled to leave until 4pm. But because they would start to board at 3pm and check in was a couple of hours before that, not to mention it was so many of them, they decided to get to the airport early for check-in. That would give them time to have lunch there in the airport food court. Pastor Tills was there to pick them up in the church van around 11:30am. They said their goodbyes to Veronica as they pulled out of the driveway. Talinda left her with a key so she could check on the house for them for the two weeks they would be gone.

The kids enjoyed the flight over. They were amazed that they were so high in the air that the curvature of the earth could be seen. They thought it was cool to fly from day to night back to day.

They touched down in Germany at 8am European time. This time Talinda was prepared. She had added the international feature to her phone and told Bernard they would meet them right as you exit the secured area before going to get their luggage.

Tasha, Jaison, Stacy and Terry all accompanied Bernard to the airport to help transport the teens. They actually only lived a few houses down from each other so decided to just keep the youth at their houses instead of booking the guest house on post. Bernard had anxiously awaited the arrival of his wife.

"Don't worry Travis, she'll be here shortly," Tasha teased.

"Oh, cut it out. You guys are just as excited to see her as I am," Bernard replied.

"Oh, I doubt that," Terry said in an attempt to block Bernard's view of the passengers who has just off loaded and rounded the corner toward customs.

"Come on man, quit playing and move out of my view," Bernard said, as he playfully pushed Terry to the side. Just then his phone rang and it was Talinda. She said they had finally stepped off the plane and they should be able to see them coming through the gate as they spoke.

"Hey I see Talinda. There they are," Tasha said.

"Yeah I see you," Bernard replied as he hung the phone up. He practically ran to her. "Hey baby," he said. Before she could respond he pulled her into his arms and laid a passionate kiss on her. The youth were stunned and just looked at each other and then like it was previously rehearsed, all looked at Raymond for his response. He didn't notice them because he had watched at his parents with an uncontrollable grin on his face.

"Wow, I never remember seeing her kiss Pastor Travis like that in front of us before," Jonathan declared.

"Tell me about it," Jessica replied. "First she gets a new haircut and now this. He may look like Pastor Travis, but he sure doesn't act like Pastor Travis." The girls looked at each other with a knowing look and giggle. They realized they could now ask Talinda questions they had always wanted to ask her.

As they released their kiss Bernard said, "I love you sweetheart...I missed you so much."

"I missed you too baby," Talinda replied and they share another quick kiss.

"Uhmm...uhmm minors are present here guys," Tasha said as she playfully got in between Talinda and Bernard.

Talinda hugged Tasha and said with a sarcastic twist, "I miss you too, Tasha."

As she, Tasha and Stacy engaged in conversation, Bernard made his way to Raymond and gave him a big hug. "I see you took good care of my wife," he teased.

"Hey, she was my mom first," Raymond replied.

"Fair enough son," Bernard said as they both laugh. He turned to the youth and said, "Good to see all of you guys again."

Talinda introduced the youth to everyone while Bernard and Raymond were engaged in conversation. The girls give Talinda a 'wait until we get you alone we got a ton of questions for you look' which made her smile. After all the introductions had been made they retrieved their luggage. They all drove their SUV's and got sitters for the babies because they weren't sure how much room they would need.

Stacy suggested that she and Tasha take the girls and Terry and Jaison take the boys. So the newlyweds could transport the luggage and have some alone time on the way back to K-Town.

"You guys are just feeding this aren't you," Bernard said as he shook his head and laughed.

"Oh, you know we're going to talk about y'all on the way back to K-town...right girls?" Tasha said as she turned toward the girls with a sly wink and a nod of the head. The girls just smiled as they pick up their luggage and headed out to the door.

After they put all of the luggage in Bernard's SUV and the teens in the other two SUV's they were ready to go. Bernard escorted Talinda to the car and opened the door. Before she climbed up into the car he said, "Hey." When she turned around to answer him he kissed her and played in her hair. "I missed you so much baby. I am so glad you're back in my arms."

"Oh sweetheart, I missed you too," Talinda said as she initiated a kiss of her own. The youth in the meantime were amazed at their youth pastor's actions. They noticed that she was different when she returned from Germany but this was a whole new Talinda Travis and they were quite surprised. Suddenly Bernard's phone rang. He shook his head and smiled after he noticed who the caller was because he knew what was about to happen.

"Ok, Travis. Get a room already," Tasha said hardly able to keep her composure. "Look boy get that girl in the car we need to leave we got 80 miles to travel to get home."

"How did I know you were about to go there Tasha?" Bernard said in a joking manner.

"Well glad I didn't disappoint you. You ruining Mrs. Travis' youth pastor image you know," Tasha said. At that comment the girls all burst out laughing. "Now let's get going you got all night to make love to your wife."

"Tasha you got kids in that car with you!" Bernard exclaimed. He couldn't believe she had said what she did.

"What...please...who are all juniors and seniors in high school from the inner city. Trust me, they know what married couples do. Now get in the car Travis," Tasha said with an 'I got your number' tone.

Bernard shook his head as he helped Talinda up into the car and they get ready to drive off.

After they arrived they get the girls settled in at Tasha and Jaison's house. They decided instead to put the boys at Terry and Stacy's to give Talinda and Bernard some alone time in their townhouse the two weeks they would be here.

They tell the youth to eat and take a nap and then after lunch they would start moving. That way they would recover from jet lag a little easier. As excited as they were, as soon as their bellies were full jet lag sat in and none of them was resistant to nap time.

Bernard tried to get Talinda to go to sleep as well but she wanted to spend some quality time with her husband. Bernard said to her in between her kisses, "Baby, you'll be exhausted. Wait until tonight when you can sleep all night." But she did not cooperate with him. She has sincerely missed her husband and wanted to share her love with him right at that moment.

So he called Jaison and said, "Hey man, I'm gonna spend some time with Talinda. When the kids wake up, take them around base for a bit. I'm trying to get Talinda to go to sleep, but she is not hearing it... if you know what I mean."

Jaison laughed and said, "Man, I know you're excited to see your wife, but give that girl a break."

Bernard laughed, "Hey, it's not me man, it's her. She is not taking no for an answer."

"Oh, I feel so sorry for you, man...she's leaving you no choice and bending your arm," Jaison said sarcastically.

"Come on, man. Give us a break. We're newlyweds," Bernard replied in laughter. "Hey, get the kids up around two and text me when y'all are on the way out."

"Ok man," Jaison said. He laughed and shook his head.

Tasha read his expression and said with a smile, "So much for the perfect youth pastor image huh?" They laughed as they finished getting everyone settled.

A few hours later they gathered the youth and decided to ride around K-town instead of going on base. They would wait on Bernard and Talinda and tour the base the next day.

Raymond didn't inquire after his parents. He understood their need to spend time together. The youth all seemed to follow suit with Raymond. They had lunch at the market place. Bernard had already given Raymond enough funds to take care of everyone for lunch.

Later that night after Talinda finally woke up everyone had gathered over Bernard and Talinda's to decide what the game plan would be for the next few days. Talinda ate a salad and everybody relaxed in the living room in the downstairs area of the split level style townhouse.

She, Tasha and Stacy were in the kitchen and Stacy said, "Girl we thought you were going to sleep all night and into the morning. You slept through lunch and dinner. We were about to come check if you were still breathing. You slept the whole day away girl. Travis put you down for the count."

Talinda replied, "What are you talking about girl. It's just jet lag."

"Uhnn huh...more like Travis lag," Tasha replied

They all burst out laughing. "Tasha...Stacy y'all are wrong...stop it."

Stacy replied, "You know she's right. Travis knocked you out."

They laugh as Bernard entered and said, "What's so funny?"

"Nothing," Talinda replied. She rolled her eyes as she looked at Tasha and Stacy with a sarcastic smile.

"I came in to see what was taking you ladies so long we're waiting on y'all," Bernard replied.

"We're coming, we're just feeding your wife since she slept through lunch and dinner," Tasha said sarcastically with a smile as she looked at Talinda.

"Tasha, stop!" Talinda interjected. She flipped her hand at her with a 'whatever' gesture, trying not to laugh.

Bernard shook his head. "Something tells me I shouldn't be in here right now so, ahh...I think I'm just gonna leave."

"Yeah, you do that," Stacy said with a dotting the "i" finger gesture to get her sarcastic point across. "We'll be right out."

But as he left the girls walked in and they sat around in the kitchen instead. Jessica one of the teens said, "Can we ask all you guys a question?"

Talinda, Tasha, and Stacy all replied, "Sure."

"What's it like being married to military men?" LaNiesha asked.

Tasha said, "Well I'm military too so it's probably a little easier for me than it is for Stacy and Talinda."

"I'm so new at it I don't really think I'm qualified to answer the question," Talinda said a she looked at Stacy.

So, Stacy took a deep breath and said, "Let's see. Well, let me start by saying that it can be very trying and scary. You definitely have to know and trust God. War is real and people are dying there."

Talinda silently thanked God that she would never know that side of the house. She was instantly relieved that Bernard had planned to exit from the Air Force.

Stacy continued, "It's also a very exciting and adventurous life. Military men tend to be very romantic, spontaneous and aggressive. They tend to not take the love of their wives for granted because they never know when they will be gone for months sometimes years at a time. They do miss a lot of events. Terry missed our son being born and that crushed him. You definitely find out what you're made of. You also realize that you're stronger than you think. You have a husband that you are very proud of and terrified for at the same time. You learn to put your trust...your total trust in God because you have nothing else and you develop a strong relationship with him. The comfort of his Holy Spirit is the only thing that keeps you sane."

"Wow," said LaNiesha. "I don't know if I could do that."

"Yeah, I thought the same thing when Terry first asked me to marry him," Stacy replied. "And out of fear I almost said no. But my love for him overrode my fear and I just jumped in with both feet."

The girls all eyed Talinda. They wanted so desperately to ask her questions about Bernard but decided it wasn't time yet so they all just continued in small talk about military men and their lives with them. Talinda learned as well from the conversation. She silently thought how relieved she was that Bernard would soon be exiting from the military and the life they described she would have the privilege of escaping from.

~Chapter Fourteen~

They spent the next few days touring sites, visited castles and got a personal tour of the Air Base. On day four they were scheduled to visit Paris. Since Paris was known to be a city of romance they decided to have a "What's the big deal about sex" girl and guy talk session with the youth that night. The girls were in one hotel family style suite and the boys in another down the hallway. The ladies would have the babies with them of course. So they each ordered take out and all sat around on the floor and beds in a very informal setting.

The girls were now more eager to talk to their leader on a more personal level.

"Okay, girls," Talinda said with a look of discernment and an 'I have a secret' smile. "Go ahead...I know you're all dying to ask me some questions about Bernard."

They all smiled as Lisa broke the ice. She said to her, "Okay Pastor Travis...ahh...I've known you for a long time. I have never seen you as open intimately with Pastor Brandon as you are with Mr. Bernard."

"Yeah," Jessica said, "What gives with that?"

Talinda smiled and took a deep breath as she responded, "Well...I must say I have been waiting on this question for the last three days. The answer is simple...it's not so much that I'm different but the two men are very different. Brandon was reserved and private and Bernard is spontaneous and outgoing. Both are powerful men of God but with totally different personalities. I mean the only things they have in common are they look almost exactly alike and they both have a heartbeat for the youth."

"Ahhhh...excuse me Pastor Travis," LaNiesha replied. "I may not have known you as long as Michelle and the rest of the teens, but I would definitely say that YOU are different, too."

Tasha laughed and said to LaNiesha, "Okay, I like you." She turned to Talinda and said, "Come clean girl. They got your number."

Talinda smiled and sighed. "Okay...I guess it would be safe to say I'm different with Bernard. He, along with Tasha and Stacy here, taught me to relax. It wasn't that I was so much against showing affection with Brandon but he was against it. He didn't want the youth to lose respect for us. I thought we should have shown more affection especially since we had several intimate talks with you guys. I always argued that we didn't appear normal in front of you. Like I said, Brandon was very conservative when it came to openly expressing intimacy. Bernard sort of brought me out of my shell so to speak."

"What," Stacy said as she rolled her eyes in a sister girl fashion. "Brought you out? Girl, he broke your shell."

"More like crushed," Tasha added. They all laughed at that comment. The girls were excited that they had the opportunity to get to know their youth pastor on a more personal level.

"Okay," Sarah said. I have another question for you Pastor Travis. If you had to choose between Pastor Brandon and Mr. Bernard who would you choose to be with?"

That question completely threw Talinda because she never thought they would have enough nerve to ask it. Truly they were taking full advantage of the moment. Tasha and Stacy both simultaneously looked at each other first then rested their chins on the backs of their hands and looked at Talinda with a smirky grin on their faces. They waited to see what her answer would be.

Talinda pondered her thoughts. This was a question that she did not want to answer because of practicality, sexuality and completeness Bernard would probably win the battle. But spiritually and prophetically Brandon would win. So she decided to take the bailout route and replied, "Wow...ahhmmm...okay ladies I would have to say that I am glad to have the best of both and even more glad I don't have to choose."

"Oh you bailed out on that one, Talinda," Tasha said as she gave her a playful shove with one of the pillows off the couch.

"That's my story and I'm sticking to it," Talinda said as they all shared in laughter.

They continued to ask more questions of Talinda, Tasha and Stacy. They were careful not to get too personal, about their love lives. Finally, Lisa nudged LaNiesha and said, "What are you waiting for girl, now is the time to talk to her about Raymond."

Talinda turned and gave LaNiesha a mother's inquisitive smile as she rested her chin on the back of her hand. Tasha and Stacy leaned back with a slight strain of the neck. They tilted their heads down slightly as though they had looked over the tops of their eye glasses.

"Uhmm...," Tasha said with a hint of sarcasm. "I guess we had you figured right huh, little momma?"

LaNiesha dropped her head and smiled.

Tasha continued, "Lisa is right. You might as well get it out girl because everybody knows now anyway."

138

LaNiesha took a deep breath and looked at Talinda. "Pastor Travis…ahhmmm…okay…" She paused placed her hand over her face. She tried hard to control the huge smile of embarrassment that had developed. "Okay…I really like Raymond. I've liked him since my family first came to Grace. I was always so afraid to approach him because his parents were the youth pastors and I didn't know how you felt about dating. I mean Pastor Brandon was really nice but I always was so afraid of you. Not that you were mean or anything because you're not. I just thought you would tell me to get away from your son. And I'm equally afraid of Raymond as much as I like him. Uhmm…ahh I'm not making any sense."

Talinda smiled. "So, in a nut shell, I guess what you're saying, dear, is you want to get my permission to approach my son to tell him that you like him and see what his reaction will be."

"Ye…ye…Yeah," she said very nervously. "Ahhmmm…yes, ma'am that would be correct."

"I see…uhmm…oookaaay," Talinda said serious face as though she thoroughly pondered the thought.

"Oh, Talinda. Let that poor girl off the hook," Stacy said.

Talinda smiled. "I have always known that you had an interest in Raymond, and I actually thought that you would have already approached each other by now. LaNiesha I think you are a very nice young lady and you have been the topic of discussion at the Travis house many nights. Sweetie, Raymond is just as nervous around you as you are around him. He has talked to his father about you and no doubt will probably talk to Bernard tonight as well. I would say if he doesn't approach you soon you may have to approach him or you two may never start dating."

LaNiesha gave her a big smile and expelled a huge sigh of relief.

"I told you girl," said Lisa. "See…and you were scared to talk to her about Raymond."

LaNiesha just smiled and looked around the room again. She looked down, still just a little embarrassed. Stacy returned, changed TJ and fed him as the conversation continued.

Just then Bernard called to see if Talinda remembered to bring the book about the power behind the spiritual man. They were going to talk to the guys about some intimate issues.

"Yes," Talinda replied. "I'm sorry. I meant to give it to you before we separated for the night." He told her that he was on the way down the hall to get it.

"Okay, we'll crack the door so you can just come on in, sweetheart," Talinda replied. They hung up the phone and Bernard headed down the hall. He opened the door and was about to let the girls know he was there when he heard them talking. He paused because the subject caught his attention.

139

Jessica was sexually active with her boyfriend Jonathan. But they decided a few weeks ago they would attempt to refrain from each other.

Michelle is a virgin. She dates Troy who pressured her on a regular basis on the subject. The adults started to minister to them about sex and waiting. Michelle said as she had to fight back tears, "Guys I am running out of excuses with Troy about why we shouldn't have sex."

"Love shouldn't have to make excuses," Jessica said with tears in her eyes. "I wish I had known Pastor Travis before I met Jonathan. We probably would not be together. If Troy really loved you he would respect that you want to stay a virgin considering what you guys have been taught at Grace Tabernacle church for years. Believe me when I say I wish I were still a virgin. I see the honor in that now. If he's pushing you knowing what you guys have been taught, something is seriously wrong and you may want to check if the relationship is worth it Michelle. Please don't do it. It may feel good for the moment if he knows what he is doing but the price is too high. I wish on my wedding night I could be like Pastor Travis was and be nervous and excited knowing that I belonged to just my husband. Please Michelle, wait...don't do it...don't give in...please..."

Tasha replied, "Wow...we couldn't have said it better ourselves, Michelle. Jessica has hit the nail on the head. If he is pressuring you, sweetie, knowing what you guys say you have been taught then something IS wrong. Listen, ladies, unlike Talinda, I wasn't a virgin when I met Jaison. I was, however, a Christian by then and we vowed we wouldn't touch each other before marriage. Now there were a couple of times that we thought we wouldn't make it, but we prayed our way through. Those of you who are not virgins don't beat yourselves up about it. Just pray and rededicate yourself to God and move forward in purity. God will still bless you and reward you with a man that is willing to wait."

Michelle then said, "I don't know if what I feel for Troy is real love and I don't want to have sex with him on the chance that we might get married. He may get to college and then decide that he doesn't want to be with me. Then what...I've given myself to a man that is not going to be my husband and I can't get it back. For that matter he could decide tomorrow he doesn't want to be with me anymore. I don't want to be sitting in church every week knowing that I am sinning against God. I want to be able to look Pastor Travis in the eyes when I talk to her and not feel ashamed."

Talinda quietly sat allowing the girls to openly discuss everything as Tasha and Stacy ministered to them. They were so used to hearing her perspective this was an excellent opportunity for a different point of view. She too was learning things about them that they had not previously shared with her. On some aspects she could now see that she wasn't approachable because she was being viewed as perfect and pure and couldn't relate to them. This was proving to be an educational and eye opening experience for everyone.

"Yeah, that's the same mistake I made with Jonathan" said Jessica.

Just then Bernard interrupted. "Knock knock," he said as he entered the room to get the book from Talinda. "Okay baby. Thanks," he said as he leaned over to give her a kiss before he left.

"You need to hurry up and leave Travis because we're talking about you," Tasha said sarcastically with a smile.

He looked at Tasha and smiled. He then glanced back at Talinda and said, "All good, I hope."

She smiled and said, "Oh it's good, baby."

"I try to be," he said as he winked at Talinda.

They all replied with a school girl "oooooo." He smiled and left.

Stacy continued the discussion. "Getting back to you, Michelle... if he is not willing to wait then maybe he isn't the man for you. Unlike Tasha and Talinda, I wasn't a Christian or a virgin when I met Terry. I got saved in the midst of our relationship. He had recently got saved and was trying to honor me but I didn't understand because I didn't honor myself. A man can only resist a woman for so long. I put him to the test and eventually wore him down. His life wasn't stellar before he met me but he was trying to change his image and do the right thing. Immediately I wished that I wouldn't have because it was like our relationship lost something. While the guys were deployed the first time Tasha was rear detachment and didn't go. She started to work on me. I gave my life to God and she started ministering to me about how precious I was. She said you know what...a man has to have a license to fish and even a dog comes with papers...a dog girl and you're giving yourself free of charge. I remember feeling so cheap after she said that. She didn't say it to hurt me she said it to wake me up. She said it to make me realize my worth to God. I didn't respect myself, so keeping myself until marriage didn't have any value to me. That was just what the "older generation" used to do. I wanted to know beforehand if a man is good in bed and if he can satisfy me. I was foolish and unlearned until Tasha got ahold of me. So ladies please those of you who are virgins please stay virgins. Those that aren't make a decision to abstain from this point. And if your boyfriends can't handle it, then it's time for a new boyfriend."

There was a silence in the room. Stacy's words had penetrated deep and you could see that the girls had pondered her every word. Talinda was very grateful because she realized that there was no way she would ever have been able to convey that message or minister to them on that level. She had no knowledge of how Stacy or Tasha felt. "Truly," she thought. "God can and will use everything you have encountered in life for ministry. No matter how dirty you think you may be you are still useable by God."

Tasha interrupted the quiet atmosphere. "Hey, judging by the fact that Travis came to get the book, Michelle you may not have a problem after tonight because Travis, Jaison and Terry will lay it on the line for those boys. Military men experience a lot and they're going to tell it to them like it is. But hey ladies look we need to pray."

They all gathered in a circle and held hands as Stacy prayed:

Father,

> *We come before you in the name of Jesus. God, I would first like to thank you for bringing these young ladies into our life and allowing us to minister and impart into their lives. Truly we have learned just as much from them as they have learned from us. We have all exchanged our most intimate thoughts and issues with each other on today God, and have found that there are some serious issues and pressures going on in these young ladies' lives. Father, we pray that you will give them the wisdom and will power to resist temptation. We pray that you will give them the revelation of just how precious they are to you. They belong to you, God. They are not their own. Help them realize how precious the jewel of virginity is that lies within them.*

> *And Father, as the men are gathered together right now, we pray that they are being ministered to as well. Help them to understand the stress and heaviness of the pressure they've placed on these young ladies. Lord, as LaNiesha and Raymond possibly begin a journey into a relationship, we pray that you will be with them to lead and guide them that they may remain pure and blameless before you. God, even as adults we thank you for giving us wisdom in ministering to them.*

> *God, we must always be honest and open with them and be willing to share with them the true meaning of real intimacy. Lord, our desire is that our lights shine so bright in front of them that it will give them a hunger for You. Not only that, but a hunger to be in a pure relationship free from fornication. We have shared our mistakes and our triumphs. Lord, we pray that You will allow them to recall only that which You deem necessary in their lives. Father, we thank You for the bond that we have formed with each other, and we will be here for each other and available*

at any time for counsel. Thank you Lord, for the love
you have toward us that we share with each other.

In the name of Jesus we pray,

Amen.

Meanwhile, the guys were engaged deep in the realm of sexuality as well. Bernard returned with the book and began to talk very frankly with the young teen males.

"Okay guys. The girls are already deep into the conversation that we are about to enter into," Bernard said as he placed the book on the table. "Although I think I was one of the topics of discussion, the looks on some of the young ladies faces told me that some things are going on that they desperately wanted to discuss with our wives. Look I overheard a few things before they knew I was there. Which one of you is Michelle's boyfriend?" Troy uneasily raised his hand. "And who is Jessica's boyfriend?" Jonathan raised his hand. He looked at Raymond and smiled which eased the boys just a bit.

Bernard continued, "We may or may not get to this book about the power in the spiritual man. But let me start by saying this, you see us all standing here and our lives as fighter jet pilots in the United States Air Force is probably very intriguing to you. Listen guys, before I decided to settle down and get married I was wild...I was out there. When you have certain jobs women are abundant and you don't have to worry about having a fruitful sex life. Let me warn you, I'm very straight forward. I don't evade or sugarcoat the issues. I know you guys have had countless conversations with my cousin, Brandon, about sex and relationships. But I know my cousin. He would only go so far and say so much. But I'm not reserved in the least. We're going to go all the way with you guys. We are cleared for takeoff and we are about to engage the enemy.

The young men over here have a greater temptation than you do in the states. You think the pressure of living in the inner city is something. But I know you noticed in the last few days that there is almost every nationality in the word present right here in Germany. And some of these women from these different cultures are real aggressive and they will take you there sexually and drop you off. You will literally be lost trying to find your way back to reality after spending just one night in bed with them. They will turn a young teenager out over here," he said and paused to read their reaction.

This comment took the boys by surprise and they all just sort of looked at each other like "whoa, he knows us and he is going to go there".

Bernard continued, "So we can't afford to take the low road when it comes to teenagers and sexuality over here. Being from the city you guys probably already know exactly where we are going with this. With that being said one of you guys...Troy to be more exact...you are pressuring your girlfriend to go all the way. She's a virgin and she doesn't want to. She is over there bawling her eyes out because she is running out of excuses to keep you off her. But then Jessica...your girlfriend Jonathan, said something very profound to her. She said love shouldn't have to make excuses. This is what one teen age girl is ministering to another. Then I made myself known in the room so they would stop talking. Let me tell you something Troy and I'm speaking from experience son because I know Brandon has taught you better than to pressure this girl about sex. I know that the pressure is out there among guys to not be a virgin. I don't know if you're a virgin or not and that's none of my business. That's not what I'm here to try to figure out. Let me tell you something Troy and I'm talking to all four of you now. Do not open Pandora's' box because once you open her up it is almost virtually impossible to close it back down."

Jonathan dropped his head. He realized how true that statement was considering where he and Jessica were at in their relationship. Jaison and Terry watched the boys' reaction to what Bernard had said so they will know how to minister when it was their turn to speak.

Bernard continued, "Let me tell you something. God created man and woman to become intimate and to become one. You become one when you engage in sexual intimacy. The marriage becomes legal at the time of consummation not just because you have a piece of paper. Intimacy is the most perfect union between a man and woman because it is at that point that you become spiritually connected. You make a blood covenant with her when you have sex with her. In biblical times the groom would have to show the sheets of the marriage bed to prove that his wife in deed was a virgin. Because when the hymen is broken blood is spilled. That is why a marriage is a blood covenant and very sacred to God. So don't just go around having sex with females because you are making a blood covenant with them. You're transferring DNA...you're transferring spirits.

If you win the battle and have sex with Michelle, it is an intimate relationship that you will crave and you will not be able to do without it once you start. Physical and emotional intimacy is the glue that holds both a marriage together and our relationship with God. That's how important intimacy is. God gave man and woman the most powerful weapon on earth...love, and physical love is a force to be reckoned with. That is why he desires that we do not enter into it unless we have made a vow to be there forever. Because once you become one with her Troy...listen...look at me. Once you become one with her, you are not going to be able to resist her. There is always going to be something there that you are going to have to deal with when you are in her presence. You can move on with your life, get married to someone else, and not see her for years, but when you encounter her

144

again something in your manhood will rise up. You will have to battle the thoughts in our mind, because you have a soul tie with her. That is the reason that God has limited physical love to the bounds of holy matrimony. Sex outside marriage is wrong no matter how you try to justify it. Regretfully neither of us was a virgin when we got married."

Terry interjected. "Let me tell you young men something about sex and women. We all went to the academy together and we all did some pretty crazy stuff with some of the female cadets there. I used to be the 'who's the flavor of the week' kind of person. Nationality was never an issue; my motto was "whosoever will". Let me tell you something, some women are very willing to be your sex partners. Sex outside marriage has the potential to ruin you. There is a scripture that said a whorish woman will reduce the price of a man to the cost of a loaf of bread."

"Wow," Raymond replied and the rest of the boys were speechless on that comment.

Terry continued. "Listen guys, I almost made a career ending mistake. There was this one girl who would just take me there. She wanted to have sex in the cockpit of my F-16. Now you guys know we couldn't get y'all inside the airfield on short notice right. That's a classified piece of equipment. Well, I was so tempted to sneak her in one night. I wasn't saved then but I thank God I didn't do it. The night I was going to sneak her in there was a surprise inspection from the squadron commander of the base. I would have been in my F-16 having sex with a woman when my colonel walked in. I would have gone to jail. Who knows the real reason why she was there...spies come in all shapes and sizes. I didn't do it but I was so tempted to. That's what happens when you open Pandora's Box, it will take you places that you don't want to go, keep you longer than you want to stay, and cost you more than you want to pay. So you guys may think you are men. Real men don't pressure their girlfriends to have sex when they want to wait. Real men will honor and respect the fact that she respects herself. Real men will say let me find out what husband material really is because my thoughts are telling me that I have a lot to learn. I'm not trying to beat you up Troy but my mission is to drive a strong message home."

Jaison jumped in and said, "Listen, guys. Just like Terry and Bernard have said, we were all out there before we came to Christ and we all have done some crazy stuff. Not every woman out there knows God and you're going to run across some women who are going to tempt you. I'm not going to sit here and lie to you like others and say oh you're not missing anything, or it doesn't feel good. Oh you're missing a lot because sex is good when the woman on the other end knows how to work and move with you... its good. So I'm not going to try to deter you by saying it's not all of that because it is. It's like a high, but it's an expensive high and the price is too steep when it's outside marriage. And anything that can happen will happen when you commit sexual sin. God killed more people at one time because of sexual sin than any other sin in the bible. What was it Travis you taught in Sunday school a few weeks ago, twenty-four thousand people?" he said as he looked as Bernard who nodded in affirmation.

Jaison continued. "Yeah, God is just that serious about sexual sins because sexual sin is a direct sin against your own body. It's also a sin against God because you belong to him.

There is so much, but for the grace of God, that could have happened to us three while we were out there slinging it like we thought we knew how. The only reason we survived babies and disease is because we were at least smart enough to protect ourselves. When I met my wife I had to learn how to make love. I knew how to have sex but I didn't know how to make love. I was selfish and it was all about me in bed. I didn't have any desire or even remotely care if the woman was ever getting satisfied."

Bernard jumped back in on that comment. "It wasn't until Brandon came to visit me that I began the journey into a righteous life. I have been pure for the last two years. It took God two years to get my ex-girlfriend, Hayes, and all the other women out of my mind, spirit...and out of my loins. I wasn't ready to be a husband because I didn't know what real love was. I wasn't serious about God or anything else. I didn't understand it then, why Brandon was so adamant about me living a holy life. He followed my life after that and personally nurtured me. Now I know why...he was setting me up to take his place. He knew I loved God but I wasn't sold out like he was. But as I submitted I began to grow quickly in God. The closer I got to God the more I was able to withstand and resist the temptation to go back out there. These guys were already married so they had already gotten on track sexually, but I was still very much out there. I'm telling you guys what I know for a fact, intimacy between a man and woman is a connection that is not easily broken. Thank God for Talinda...a real wife. I thank God for purging and cleansing me these last two years to be her husband. I love my wife and there is nothing and nobody that is in my heart or my loins now but her."

"Dad, I am so glad you chose to follow God," Raymond said. "Dad would never have left you in charge of mom if you hadn't and I would be without a father right now." Bernard smiled and gave Raymond a one arm hug and nodded his head in agreement to what Raymond had said.

Terry said, "Listen Troy real love is described in chapter thirteen of 1Corinthians. If you can't put your name in the blank concerning Michelle then you don't love her. If you're pressuring her to have sex for whatever reason, then you don't love her."

"But I do love her," Troy exclaimed in an attempt to sound sincere.

146

"No, you don't," Terry replied. "You don't because you're pressuring her to have sex and you know her desire to remain a virgin. She is over there crying her eyes out Travis said because she doesn't want to have sex, and she running out of excuses to tell you."

Jonathan dropped his head at these words. He said, "You know what Troy, they're right. I did the same thing to Jessica. She was a virgin when she met me. I told her if you love me you will, and it worked. We weren't going to Grace Tabernacle so we hadn't learned what you guys had learned. We didn't know anything because our church didn't talk about sex with the teenagers. I said all the right things to her Troy. I said if you love me baby you will. Come on it's me I will always love you no matter what. I'm you're first love, don't you want to give it to your first love? Don't you want to give it to me verses some guy out there who don't even care anything about you? I might be the man you marry and if I'm not at least you gave it to a man that cares about you. That really loves you, but I didn't love her. At least not the way I was supposed to. I loved having sex with her, but not her."

Raymond now joined in, "You guys all know how I met my dad and where my life was headed. Dad had a way of just making you want to do the right thing no matter how dirty you were." Bernard smiled and shook his head fully understanding Raymond's words. "The more I learned from him, the more ashamed I was of the life I had chosen. I had sex with girls because it was a gang initiation. I never knew what it was like to have a real girlfriend. We had to have sex with five girls and produce evidence that we actually had sex for it to count. My dad Pastor Brandon gave us a milder version of what they just shared. My dad was a virgin just like mom when he met her. He didn't have the experience they had but never the less he was effective. But listening to them, its hitting home a little harder because they know where we're at and we can't hide it from them."

Reginald had sat back and listened for most of the conversation, but decided to join in. He was still a virgin and had taken much slack at school for not being afraid to say he was. He was very handsome and well-proportioned as a star athlete and had shied away from many aggressive girls and temptation. Although he had not come out of his outer clothing he had on many occasions like Joseph...ran to get away from some pretty hot situations.

He cleared his throat. "We're on fire young men. We're rare. People think it's crazy the way I think. We live in the city where it's okay to be sexually active. Where it's cool to be a man and have many notches in your belt to show how many girls you've been with. Guys are considered strange to want to be virgins, or abstain from sex until they're married. That's what girls want to do, it's okay for them to want to be virgins but it's supposed to be our job to make sure they don't. We all grew up hearing that and sadly my father is one of the ones who is trying to persuade me to get out there. He doesn't go to church with me and my mom. He actually thinks I'm gay because I have chosen to remain a virgin until I marry. But rest assured...I think about girls and sex all the time. It's not easy and I struggle, but after today I feel a little stronger. I'm going to be honest with you Troy. I watched you and Michelle one day and I overheard you talking to her about sex. I said to myself, God why couldn't she have chosen me for a boyfriend...I wouldn't have pressured her. I yearn for a virgin girlfriend but they are few and far between these days so I'm just single. But she's out there. I know she is. I just have to wait on God and he will bring her right to me. Stop pressuring her Troy...let her keep herself."

Troy finally spoke up, "Man, you guys are all right. I am pressuring her for sex. But it's not because of what you think. It's not because I'm a virgin...it's because I'm not. I opened Pandora's Box a long time ago and like Minister Travis said, I can't close it. I'm craving it and I can't deal with the desire. My last girlfriend moved away so I was looking for somebody else I can take to the next level. You're right, she is trying to keep herself for her husband and I'm trying to talk her out of it. I have to admit now that I don't love her, at least not the way I'm supposed to. I just need you guys to pray with me." He dropped his head in his hands.

Bernard took a deep breath. He was thankful that the conversation went in the direction that it had. He had taken a very bold and aggressively direct move with his approach toward Troy and Jonathan today. It could have just as easily back fired, and they could have shut down. But he knew he felt in his spirit that God wanted him to challenge these young men right where they were.

He went over to Troy and placed his hand on his shoulder. "You know, Troy, the lust a man has for a woman is very hard to overcome. Now I'm not going to tell you that you're not going to struggle after this day. You have to make yourself accountable to someone and make a decision that you're going to fight this thing. You guys are all juniors and have your senior year together other than Jessica and Jonathan who graduated this year, so be accountable to each other. Draw strength from one another. Don't go out on single dates with your girl if you don't trust how you're feeling that day. Date in groups. If you feel yourself falling say, hey man I'm struggling tonight and me and Michelle don't need to be alone. I had to get to the point that I told Hayes look, uhn uhn girl, we can't even be in the same room together because I knew where I was. I knew when Brandon started introducing me to what a real wife was that Hayes wasn't wife material. She was just somebody I was having sex with. I knew then, there was no reason to keep leading her on because she was not going to be Mrs. Travis. So I broke it off with her. I had no idea it would be Talinda and he was grooming me to take his place. And when I made that declaration and cried out to God to remove her from my loins, my appetite for her started to diminish, because before that it was strong. I'm not going to lie. I felt threatened when Talinda encountered her when she was over here the first time, but Tasha and Stacy had my back. Hayes is very aggressive and anything is liable to come out of her mouth. I kept reassuring Talinda she was a non-issue and when I see her now there is nothing there. Because for a time after I started my journey, I would see her and would be tempted to say hey girl lets go for a ride. I'm not flying this weekend lets go to Switzerland or Italy somewhere and do this thing. I'm not talking about your everyday average run of the mill sex. I'm talking about when a girl rocks your world in bed. When she knows all the right buttons to push to get you there okay...that's what I'm talking about. But I fought through and made myself accountable to Terry and Jaison. That's how strong a hold, the spirit of lust has. You can't afford to play with it because it plays for keeps. So wait on your wives, young men. Wait on them because a real woman of God will rock your world in a godly way, and that's a high you don't have to come down from. So get yourselves under control young men."

Troy fell to his knees and cried out, "God, I'm sorry. Will you all please pray for me?"

They all gathered around as Bernard prayed:

Father,

We come before You in the matchless name of Jesus. God, we all have struggled in the area of self-control. Troy is coming before You, Lord. He understands that he needs to get his loins under control. He is calling out to You in Your son, Jesus' name. Meet him at the crossroad where he stands today, Lord. As we lay our hands on him, we bind the unclean spirit and we lay hold of the spirit of lust. God, we pray that You will create in him a clean heart and renew a right spirit in him. Father, as these young men cry out to You for Your forgiveness we know that Your word said You are faithful and just to forgive when we confess our faults one to another.

God, I pray that as Jonathan and Jessica continue in their relationship, You will keep them. Help them to make themselves accountable in their relationship. Give them the strength to withstand in the moments that they feel weak in their flesh. Father, I pray for their minds, that You will clothe them in Your glory. Lord, I thank You for Reginald, and I pray that You will bring to him a chaste young lady who has kept herself as well. Continue to use him to minister to his peers,

*Lord. As Raymond continues to seek Your face,
continue to guide him. Give him wisdom in his future
relationships that he will walk in restraint. God, these
young men are mighty men of valor that the enemy
would love to sift as wheat. But just as You prayed for
Peter, we pray for them- that their faith will not fail
them, and that they will draw nigh unto You and walk
in Your grace.
In Jesus' name we pray,*

Amen

Troy and Jonathan cried out to God, and they all joined in and praised and thanked Him because today He had brought them a hard truth to them. A truth they needed to be confronted with. They continued to lay hands on the boys and spoke into their lives. Suddenly Troy looked at Bernard and said that he needed to talk to Michelle because he owed her an apology. He wanted to apologize publically so the he would accountable to everyone there.

Bernard smiled and patted him his back. "Okay if that's what you want to do. I'll call Talinda to let her know we are all on the way over."

Chapter Fifteen~

Talinda hung up the phone and looked at the girls. "Okay, ladies. The guys are finished and on their way down the hall."

Tasha and Stacy glanced at her to get a read on why the guys had decided to come over because that wasn't in the original plan. The guys soon knocked and entered the front door. Jonathan and Troy walk over and stood beside Jessica and Michelle. The girls were all silent and immediately Michelle's heart started to race because she could see that Troy had been crying and was very nervous about something.

Troy took Michelle by the hand and looked her in the eyes. "Michelle," he said, as his voice shook. "I owe you an apology. I haven't been a man of integrity or honor with you. We have been taught by our youth pastors about the value of keeping ourselves until marriage and I have been pressuring you to go all the way. I'm not a virgin, but I knew you were. My intentions with you were not honorable and I'm ashamed of that now. I know I don't deserve to have you as a girlfriend. You deserve a guy that is going to honor and respect you. Michelle, I'm sorry for pushing and pressuring you. Will you please give me a chance to show you I can be an honorable boyfriend? I promise I won't be alone with you when I'm feeling like I can't control myself. I'm making myself and our relationship accountable to everybody here and I want all you guys to help us...help me...stay on track with Michelle. I really do care a lot for you and I like spending time with you. I want to develop real feelings for you and not lustful ones. Michelle, will you be my girlfriend...my real girlfriend?"

All Michelle could do was cry and hug Troy. She shook her head to tell him "yes". Every girl in the room to include, the adult women were in tears. Jonathan turned to Jessica. "Jessica, Troy took all of my words." Everyone responded in laughter at that statement. He smiled and continued, he still looked Jessica in the eyes, "It's like he was inside my head. He said almost everything I was going to say to you. Although neither of us is a virgin because we have already crossed that threshold, I would like for our relationship to remain pure from this day forward. I'm sorry I didn't value or honor you enough to refrain from you. Tonight Ministers Travis, Thomas and Stallworth taught me a lot about myself. They read me like front page news and everything ugly about me was exposed. By the time I got through praying and crying out to God I realized I do care a lot about you. I have often said to you that I love you but that was mostly driven by lust to get what I wanted from you. Jessica I want to develop agape love for you. We are on our way to college in the fall and I'm glad that we're both going to Georgia State. That way we both stay at home and we can still be accountable to everyone with our relationship. Will you give me a chance to show you I can be a real boyfriend? Will you let me learn how to be a real man with you? A man that's full of honor, integrity and respect?" Jessica just like Michelle was at a loss for words. She just hugged Jonathan and buried her head in his chest.

"Wow," said Tasha. "You guys' discussion was definitely a whole lot deeper than ours."

Bernard replied, "Well, it was sparked by what I overheard when I walked over here. You guys were pretty intense yourself."

Bernard noticed that Raymond and LaNiesha made eye contact as they all stood in a circle and held hands. He prepared to bring the session to a close in prayer. He looked at Talinda, smiled and started to pray:

Father,

> *We come before You in the name of Jesus our Lord. God, we thank You for loving us enough to expose our faults and shortcomings. As these young people have confessed and professed to You and each other on tonight we know that You will honor their confession and the vow that they have made to You and each other. Those of us that have been charged with the accountability of these young relationships stand ready to serve and mentor them. We ask You to hold us accountable in our ministry to them.*
>
> *Father, we pray that any other relationships that the other youth embark upon will join with the same high standards that have been set here tonight between Jonathan, Jessica, Michelle and Troy. We thank you for a group of young people who have the mind and desire to serve You with a whole heart. Father, their lives will never be the same and they have grown to a new level in You tonight. Truly, Lord, You have created in them a clean heart and renewed*

in them a right spirit. To whom much is given, much is required. That holds true to everyone under the sound of my voice. Lord, we thank You for the love You gave and give to us.

We thank You for this time that we have had together to share and we pray that if anything has been said that You did not ordain or do not agree with that You will bless us and remove the error from our thoughts. God, we love You and stand always ready to serve.

In Jesus' name,

Amen

They remained in Paris a few days before they returned to K-town the following Wednesday. Bright and early on Thursday, they prepared for the Saturday night revival with the local youth. They planned on ministering in Word, drama and dance. While the ladies worked on their dance routine the guys all decided to challenge the old guys to basketball. So they took the boys to the gym on base to get them out of the girls' hair.

As they go ready to leave Bernard received a call from the orderly room. The commander needed to see him before the day was out because he had some news about his compassionate reassignment. They would stop by his unit in route to the gym. The boys embarked in a game of pool with Terry and Jaison in the day room while Bernard went in to see the commander.

"Sir, you wanted to see me?" Bernard asked as he entered the commander's office.

"Yes, Major Travis. Please come in," he replied. "Have a seat. I have good and bad news about your compassionate reassignment."

Bernard took a deep breath as he replied, "Okay. I don't know which I want first because they both probably have the potential to cause a major change in my life."

"That would be a correct assessment Major Travis," the commander replied. He paused and took a deep breath, which put Bernard on alert.

"Okay sir," Bernard replied. He prepared himself for the bad portion of the news about his compassionate reassignment. At this point the only bad news he could imagine would be that he had been denied and would have to finish his time out in Germany. He was totally unprepared for what his commander was about to say to him.

The commander cleared his throat and began, "The good news is when your unit heard they had gained one of the top pilots in Europe, they wanted you right away. They just built a new air strip and need seasoned pilots and air traffic controllers to oversee the final adjustments to the flight line. I know your leave is not up until next Wednesday but I will need you to report Monday morning to start processing."

"Wow, Sir. There is nothing bad about that," Bernard said. He was about to give God praise as his commander put a hand up to halt him.

"Wait, Major Travis. That's the good news," he said. He had Bernard's full attention again. "The bad news is, they are on their last two months of deployment in Afghanistan, and you are scheduled to be there anywhere from seven to ten days from now. So unfortunately..."

"Sir, please...," Bernard cut him off.

"I know, Major Travis," his commander continued. "Believe me I don't like this anymore than you do, but what can we do...duty calls. With that being said you need to report in uniform Monday morning to start processing. I know your leave is not up until Thursday so go ahead and sign back in off leave today to save your days for when your wife delivers. I will only require you to be here for processing. That way you can still spend as much time as you can with your family and take them back to the airport when it's time for them to leave. In all probability by this time next week you will probably be on your way down range."

Bernard stood there with his head down then looked up to the sky as though he searched diligently to God for answers. He took a deep breath and started to speak, "Sir you don't understand...my wife...you know I will not and have never backed down from deployment...but this time it's not just about me. I have a major responsibility that I have been entrusted with." He paused to take another deep breath and fought back tears he continued. He no longer talked to his commander but now had a conversation with his Lord. "I promised him...I promised him Lord...that I would not put her in this situation...Brandon...God please forgive me...this is beyond my control." He took a seat and buried his head in his hands and said in a desperate tone barely above a whisper, "God."

"Son, listen," his commander said. He no longer talked to Major Travis. But now spoke directly to Bernard. He walked over to him and placed his hand on Bernard's shoulder in an attempt to comfort him. "You are a man of integrity, you always have been. You don't know that this is not God's design. Don't you think that God knows the promise you made to Him concerning your wife and to the memory of your cousin? Don't you realize that He understands what is at stake here? Don't forget his power son and don't forget His sovereignty. God controls all things, even situations that we feel are out of control. Don't stop trusting God now."

Those words penetrated into Bernard's spirit. There is much that he did not know about his commander. He was surprised to say the

154

least at his insight into God's word and his promises. He stood and shook his commander's hand and stated that he would be in uniform Monday morning ready to begin processing. He then turned to exit the office when his commander stopped him.

"Here, Major Travis," he said as he hands him a folder. "Here is the gaining units support group information that your wife will need. The First Sergeant's wife's name is Gloria Thomas and your wife should get in touch with her upon returning to the United States. She will keep her informed on the unit's status and answer any questions she may have after you have deployed."

"Thank you, sir," was all Bernard could manage to say as he exited the office headed toward the day room where everyone waited for him. As he rounded the corner Jaison and Terry could read his face and both assumed the same as he had, that his compassionate reassignment had been denied. As he approached them they both hunched their shoulders in a 'what gives' posture.

He shook his head back and forth as he proceeded to fill them in on what had just transpired in the commander's office.

"Awe man, tell me you are kidding," said Jaison. "You're kidding, right?"

"I wish I were," Bernard replied with a sigh.

Jaison shook his head. "Talinda is going to flip. Are you going to tell her now or wait until you get ready to leave?"

"Wait?" Bernard asked. "I start clearing on Monday. How am I going to explain why they are calling me back in? I can't wait. I have to tell her now. This is going to crush her. I'm concerned about her stress level with the babies. I promised God that same night we read the letters that if she chose me I would get out. I promised God and Brandon I would never put her through deployment." He shook his head and wiped his hand over his face in disbelief.

Raymond watched them. Their demeanor told him that something had gone wrong. They gathered everyone together and jumped back into Jaison's SUV and headed to the gym. Bernard sat quietly.

As they exited the car to head inside Raymond turned to him and said, "Wait, dad. Can I talk to you for a minute?"

"Sure son. What is it?" Bernard replied. He knew exactly what Raymond wanted to talk about. He couldn't hide the frustration that he knew showed on his face.

"Is something wrong?" Raymond asked. "When you came back into the room where we were and you talked to Mr. Jaison and Mr. Terry, you had a real concerned look on your face...like something was really wrong. Are they not going to let you come home to me and mom?"

Bernard marveled at the fact they all thought the same way about how his meeting had transpired with the commander. No one thought in their wildest dreams that it could be anything else but that. Bernard cleared his throat and filled Raymond in on the events that would take place in the next week and a half.

Raymond eyes instantly filled with tears and he responded to his dad's statements with a shaky and stuttering voice. "B-B-But dad...people die over there. I-I-I don't think we could..."

"Raymond, I'm going to be alright son. I have deployed several times before and God has always been faithful," he said as he reassured Raymond. "I have to tell your mom today. I want to tell her while she has Tasha and Stacy to lean on and ask questions. There are things they can help her with that she won't ask me for fear that I won't be honest about it. Besides I couldn't keep it from her if I wanted to because I had to sign back in off leave today and report Monday morning to start processing."

Raymond looked in his father's eyes and said, "Dad, no...I can't lose another dad! I can't!" He could no longer hold back the tears as he leaned into his dad's chest for comfort.

"That's okay son. You don't have to be strong. Just let it out. I want to cry too, but I just can't. I don't have any control over this Raymond...I don't have any control," he said as he pulled Raymond closer into his bosom.

"I'm scared dad," Raymond said through his tears. "I'm scared. When I lost dad it was terrible for me. That was the worst weekend in my life. I didn't know whether I was coming or going...I was lost. He died...he died because of me and I struggled. Then you helped me and I knew we were going to be together...I knew we were going to be close and you were going to be my dad. And now I might lose you too..."

"You're not going to lose me Raymond. I have deployed several times and God has my back. It's going to be okay," Bernard declared in no uncertain terms as he pulled Raymond back in his arms because he had lost himself in his tears. "I got you son...I got you," he said unable to hold his tears back any longer. He whispered to God as he still embraced Raymond, "Oh God please help me. This is going to be so hard."

They gathered themselves and Raymond wiped his tears as they joined the others inside. They had already chosen teams and Raymond and Bernard both attempted to play a normal game of basketball but the guys all knew something was wrong. Raymond's eyes told the story and he was a little out of it during the game. He was a very good basketball player and was definitely not on top of his game today. No one felt comfortable enough to ask what the problem was because it appeared to be personal family business.

As left the gym Bernard talked to Jaison and Terry. "Hey, guys. I'm going to need some alone time with Talinda today. As soon as we get back she is going to read Raymond. Then she will look at me and read me. So let's keep the girls inside your house until we all get back and showered. That way Raymond has a little time to get it together before his mom sees him. Call Tasha and tell her to keep Talinda and the girls inside the house and away from the windows so they won't notice that we are back."

"Sure Bernard," Jaison replied. He called Tasha and asked her to step away from everyone so her reaction couldn't be read before he filled her in. She gasped in disappointment and said that she would keep everyone inside and wait for Jaison's call that they were ready.

Jaison and the other adults would take the youth out to lunch at a castle or something and then they would possibly meet Bernard and Talinda for dinner after he had time to talk to her about everything. They stopped off at the ATM for Bernard to get enough money for Raymond to take care of the youth for the day in case plans changed.

After they were all showered the guys all messed around outside the house and the girls now realized they were out there. The women came out to join them and Raymond sat on the step with his back to his mother and pretended that he was still had to put on and lace up his shoes.

"Okay, everyone," Bernard said as they gathered outside Jaison and Tasha's house. "This is the plan. You will all go have lunch and tour some of the castles with Jaison, Terry, Tasha and Stacy. We will all meet at the officers club on base for dinner..."

He was interrupted by Talinda who asked, "Sweetheart, what are we going to do? I mean why are we not going with everyone else?"

He mustered up a smile and answered her, "Well, we have some things we need to take care of before you leave." She had eyed him with must curiosity, but decided not to inquire further at the moment.

LaNiesha approached Raymond. He sat on the step as he still tied the same shoe. He desperately attempted to avoid his mother's eyes. She sat down beside him. "Are you okay?" She asked.

"Yes, LaNiesha. I'm fine," he replied but never stopped to look at her. "Why would you ask me that?"

"Well," she said with hesitation and noted the irritation in his tone. "It seems like you are avoiding the group a little bit. It just kind of looks like there is something on your mind."

He breathed in deeply and softened his tone, "I'm sorry. I'm just a little upset right now. My dad has some bad news for my mom, and it's going to crush her."

She paused for a moment and considered if she should ask him any further about it. She knew by his demeanor that it was personal family business. But she decided that she would just go ahead and ask anyway. She sighed and asked, "You wanna talk about it?"

"Not really," Raymond replied as he still tied the same shoe.

She noticed that he had tied that same shoe for a few several minutes. She realized that the news must have been pretty bad and pretty personal. She wondered if it was the right time to tell him how she felt about him. She decided to continue in conversation and express how she felt about him. "Hey, Raymond," she nervously said. Can I say something to you?"

"Sure," Raymond replied. He still had not looked in her direction but no longer played with his shoe. He looked down at his feet and his arms rested on his knees.

She took a deep breath and proceeded. "I like you. I've liked you ever since my family first came to the church. I was so afraid of your mom and dad. I didn't know if I should approach you because your parents were the youth pastors and your mom always taught us that we shouldn't pursue guys they should pursue us. So I didn't dare let on that I wanted to talk to you and you never seemed interested. So I felt like I was stuck. But while we were in Paris, I finally got enough nerve to talk to your mom and was surprised that she already knew I liked you. I guess I wasn't as good at hiding it as I thought I was." She paused and waited for his response hoping it would be positive.

"Wow. I don't know what to say," Raymond said in a somewhat nervous tone. As outgoing as he appeared to be, he was extremely shy when it came to one-on-one relationships with females. In a group setting or ministry related arena he flowed, but he was somewhat intimidated by intimate relationships. His experience in the gang was simply just about sex. But the thought of a serious and spiritually intimate driven relationship was new to him. "You always seemed disinterested in me...I mean you would practically ignore me. I liked you and even talked to my mom and dad about you but I never thought you liked me. You never even looked twice at me...or so I thought," he said with a slight smile.

LaNiesha smiled and replied, "Wow. Now I feel like we've wasted eight months being afraid of each other. All this time you could have been my boyfriend."

"Nah, I don't think it was wasted," Raymond responded. "Who knows? Maybe we weren't ready to be in a relationship. We've learned a lot in the last eight months. We may have made some major and unchangeable mistakes. My dad, Mr. Terry and Mr. Jaison laid it out pretty strong and I had to admit my thoughts about girls were not in the right place. Even with what my dad had taught us before he died, it was just different here in Germany. My dad was conservative but Bernard is just a in your face kind of guy and they made us really search ourselves you know."

"Yea, our session was pretty intense as well," LaNiesha said as she took another deep breath. After they shared an awkward moment, LaNiesha broke the silence. "So what do...I mean knowing what we know, where do we go from here? I mean... are you going to ask me?"

"Ask you what?" Raymond replied nervously. He had hoped that they were actually thinking the same thing.

She chuckled slightly. "Ask me out, silly."

"Yeah, I guess that would be in order, huh?" Raymond said. He still had not looked up at her.

She replied with a shy, "bite your nails" response. "Yeah," she said, biting her bottom lip as she waited for the question to come out of his mouth.

He finally looked up at her, took a deep breath and said, "LaNiesha will you go with me...I mean, would you be my girlfriend?"

She smiled and replied, "I would love too." She sort of nudged the side of his leg which made him smile.

"I guess I better not try to kiss you right now," Raymond said. "My mom and dad along with everyone else are probably watching us."

"Yeah, all the girls knew I was coming to sit beside you to finally tell you how I felt. But maybe before the day is over we'll have a moment alone and I can get my first kiss from my boyfriend," she said. She couldn't control the smile that took over her face.

"Yeah, I hope so," Raymond replied. "I know my dad is probably going to talk to me about how I had better be treating you and stuff before he..." The reality that his dad had to deploy overtook his thoughts again.

LaNiesha sensed his mood change and asked, "Before what Raymond?"

"Before he goes to Afghanistan," Raymond replied. He took a deep breath in an effort to fight back tears. "That's what he is getting ready to tell my mom. That's why they are not going out with us today and we cut the practices for the rest of the day."

"Oh, Raymond..." she replied, unsure what to say to him.

"I know," Raymond replied. He let her off the hook for a response. "There's not really much to say...I mean what do you say? I mean..." he just shook his head looked back down. "I'm scared LaNiesha...what if..."

"Don't say it, Raymond," LaNiesha interrupted. "Don't even think it...just believe God that he will protect him and bring him home safe."

Raymond wiped the tears that had formed as he said, "You're going to be good for me. You know you're my first real girlfriend don't you?"

"What?!" LaNiesha replied. She was totally surprised. She knew that Raymond wasn't a virgin, so she assumed he had had several girlfriends before her.

Raymond looked back at her again. "I never really had a real girlfriend. The last girl I dated was like a Knight initiation thing. It wasn't a real relationship. It was a gang relationship. You're my first outside the gang girlfriend."

She smiled in disbelief, "Wow I would have never thought that. You're so outgoing and sure of yourself."

"Yeah, when it comes to ministry I am," he replied. "But with girls one on one that's another story. It will probably be different with you because we were friends first so I'm somewhat comfortable with you, even though I've secretly liked you all these months."

"Wow," she said as she leaned into him. She bumped him in a 'you're kidding type fashion' which made him smile.

Bernard had observed the interaction between them. He touched Talinda and pointed at Raymond and LaNiesha. "Hey I think we have a little romance starting here."

Talinda smiled and replied, "Yeah, she has been crazy about him for the last eight months and he has been just as crazy about her. He talks about her all the time so it's kind of good to see them finally decide to talk to each other. I mean on more than a friendship status."

Bernard shook his head and said, "Hmmm...I guess I better have a little talk with him tonight."

"Oh, honey he already knows all of that...rest assured he and Brandon have talked extensively about it," Talinda replied. She smiled as she remembered how shy Raymond had been about that day. He had asked Brandon to tell her to leave the room.

"No sweetheart, I mean the do's and don'ts of dating in my house," Bernard declared. He realized he indeed was a father now and marveled at how he welcomed the responsibility and looked forward to the task. He did not, however, look forward to the task of informing his wife he would be deployed the following week.

"Wow," Talinda replied. She was warm inside at the fact that they indeed had become a family. "I guess you do need to talk about that before we leave to go back home. I mean assuming that they are actually dating now of course."

"Oh, baby. I think they are, or in the very near future, will be," Bernard replied. Unexplainable fatherly pride entered his heart. "Wow, I have a teen-aged son...this is awesome!"

Talinda only smiled and marveled at how easily he transitioned into his newly attained instant family. They continued to talk about the events of the day as Raymond and LaNiesha rejoined the group. Raymond now felt he was ready to face his mother. He felt his preoccupation with LaNiesha would be the perfect cover up for him. LaNiesha walked over to the girls and Talinda kind of followed to give Raymond and Bernard a moment.

"So, Raymond," Bernard said with a sly smile on his face as he stood beside him with a nod of the head in LaNiesha's direction, "Is that you now?"

A huge grin appeared on Raymond's face as he replied, "Yeah dad, that's me."

Bernard with a half shake of the head and a slight chuckle replied, "Alright Raymond...she's a beautiful girl. You know we're going to have to all talk about this a little later on tonight...and you be good this afternoon son."

160

"I knew you were going to say that...and you know I will dad," Raymond responded with a smile. Bernard patted him on the back and they joined the rest of the group.

They loaded up in the cars and Talinda and Bernard waved bye to them as they pulled away. She had begun to get an uneasy feeling. When her eyes met Raymond's she thought she sensed something but didn't press it.

Bernard grabbed Talinda's hand and they walked back over to their townhouse. Once inside Talinda turned to Bernard and said, "Okay, baby, why do I feel like you have something to tell me that I'm not going to like. Raymond practically avoided eye contact with me and I could feel the tension coming off of you."

Bernard mustered a smile and shook his head. He knew that he would never be able to hide anything from her. He pulled her into his arms and kissed her. In a reassuring tone said, "Now why can't I just want to spend the afternoon with my beautiful wife?"

She tilted her head back with a look said 'spill your guts Mr. Travis' and replied, "Well, for one thing sweetheart we were supposed to spend today and tomorrow preparing for the youth rally at your church Saturday. Now you've sent everyone away to tour the country side for the rest of today so we can spend the afternoon together. Not to mention earlier Tasha's whole mood changed after she received a phone call from Jaison. She also started avoiding eye contact with me. So talk to me baby...what is it?"

Bernard sighed as he responded, "I am not going to ever be able to hide anything from you am I?" He turned and walked into the bedroom as Talinda followed.

"No...you're not," she said as she moved closer to him. "So talk to me...what is it Bernard?"

He took a deep breath and shook his head. He ran his hands from the top of his face down and then placed them on his hips with an 'I give up' posture.

Talinda breathed heavy and replied before he could answer. "Why do I get the feeling you are about to tell me the Air Force denied your request to come home to us early? You're going to have to stay here for your last year aren't you?"

He replied barely above a whisper as he once again rubbed his hand across and down his face. "I wish it were that easy." He then replied loud enough for her to hear. "No, baby, that's not it."

"Okay," she replied as she swallowed hard. She had no idea whatsoever what is about to be said to her.

Unsure as to how to proceed, Bernard just started to talk. "No, it's not that. My compassionate reassignment is approved. I actually start to clear Germany on Monday and scheduled to leave country in about seven to ten days. That's why my commander called me in today. I had to sign in off leave but he is still going to give me this weekend with you and time to take you guys back to the airport next week. Baby when my gaining unit realized I was coming they wanted me right away. They didn't want to wait forty-five days because they are just completing a new airstrip and wanted some seasoned pilots to oversee the final training. It appears they have a lot of young pilots and want to make sure they are properly trained on emergency and short take offs and landings. I guess this is one of those times that it doesn't pay to be the best."

Talinda, in an excited voice declared, "Bernard what's so hard about that? You're going to be home in ten days or less..."

"No, sweetheart," he said as he cut her off. "I'm going to leave Germany, but I have to go to where they are building the strip and train with them for the next three to five weeks."

"Okay," she replied, still unsure what the problem is. "Looks like I'm still not going to see you for about forty-five days maybe but Bernard that's not off from the original plan...I mean what's so bad about that?"

He realized that there was just no easy way around this. He looked up and took a deep breath as he let out a sarcastic half chuckle. "Give me the words God...please."

She stood there in silence and watched him struggle with what he would say next. Deployment to Afghanistan was the furthest thing from her mind.

He closed his eyes monetarily as he took another deep breath. He opened his eyes. "Talinda...baby, the unit I will be assigned to at Robins Air force base in Warner Robins, GA is currently deployed to Afghanistan."

"NOOO! BERNARD...NOOO!" she screamed. He attempted to grab her, but she stepped back out of his reach. "You promised me Bernard! No! Please...don't! I can't...do this!"

Bernard attempted to move toward her again, but she pushed him away. She cried and was unable to speak. She stepped further away from him as he made up the distance she had put between them. "Sweetheart, I'm sorry but I don't..." he closed his eyes momentarily to fight off his own tears then continued, "...I don't have any control over this. I don't have a choice baby...I have to go...as long as I wear this uniform, I have to go where they send me."

He reached down and picked up the folder off the night stand and walked toward her again, "Here is a folder with all the information you'll need," he said as he attempted to hand her folder. She pushed the folder to the side as she turned her back to him and walked away still unable to speak.

"Baby, you're going to need this. Please take it," he said unable to hold his tears back any longer.

162

She suddenly screamed at the top of her lungs, "PEOPLE ARE DYING OVER THERE BERNARD!" she totally lost it and started to collapse.

He rushed over to catch her before she fell. "Oh my God! TALINDA! I got you, baby! I got you." He sat her down on the bed and held her in his arms.

She cried an inconsolable cry. Fear gripped her as her mind raced back to the night Brandon died. "God, please...no," she repeated over and over.

As Bernard held her, no words came to his mind that could ever come close to console her. He prayed over her and asked God to give her peace.

She appeared to regain control and just laid in his arms silent for about ten minutes. She sat up and started to have a conversation with God. "What am I supposed to do? How am I supposed to feel? My husband is about to deploy to Afghanistan and I'm scheduled to deliver our babies in three months. He may or may not return in time, or alive. God I don't understand and I don't know what to do."

"Baby," he said. "I've deployed several times before and God has always brought me home safe. Baby just trust God and I promise I'll..."

"No!" she said to cut him off. She placed her hands over her ears as she stood and walked away from him. "Don't you promise me...don't you dare make a promise to me that you are not sure you can keep. It's not just up to you Bernard...I watch the news and there is so much going on over there. So many uncontrollable factors..." she finished in a whisper, "So don't you promise me." She dropped her head in dismay.

He just sat and watched her; unsure as to how to respond to her and realized all too well she had a fair assessment of the gravity of the situation. The next series of words out of her mouth both startled and send him into a panic.

She turned her back to him and said just above a whisper but audible enough to clearly be heard, "Brandon...I just lost Brandon...I can't do this so soon. This was a mistake. I don't want to have to worry about you...I hate that I love you." Her shoulders dropped in despair she began to sob again.

"Baby...Talinda what are you saying!" He said as he rose from the bed and pulled her into his arms. Tears flowed from his eyes and he feared what she would say next. "Baby please...don't...don't...I need you...I...I...I...oh God...Talinda baby please...don't...baby don't hate our love...don't regret us...oh God baby please..."

"I'm sorry," she replied through her tears from deep inside of his embrace. "I'm just scared Bernard...I don't know what to do with this."

"Honey, I'm going to be okay," he said. He held her as tight and close as her stomach would allow, half afraid to let her go. "God will protect me sweetheart, he always does...you can bank on that...I promise..."

"DON'T," she yelled as she pulled away from him. "I SAID DON'T PROMISE ME BERNARD, BECAUSE YOU DON'T KNOW. YOU CANNOT BE ONE HUNDRED PERCENT SURE, SO YOU CAN'T PROMISE ME THAT YOU'LL BE HOME SAFE. DON'T SPEAK EMPTY WORDS TO ME IN AN ATTEMPT TO MAKE ME FEEL GOOD ABOUT WHERE YOU ARE GOING. DON'T PATRONIZE ME!" She paused then plopped back down on the bed. She held her head in one hand and had the other on her stomach. She gathered herself and said, "Oh God baby I'm sorry...I'm so sorry. I'm not yelling at you sweetheart. I'm yelling at the situation...oh Bernard!"

"I know baby," he said as he sat back down on the bed beside her. He pulled her back into his arms again. "It's hard to deal with. If it's any consolation sweetheart, I'm struggling just as much as you are with this. I'm afraid of the stress this will place on you and the babies. Today is the first day in my military career that I've ever even remotely considered disobeying an order. But look at the bright side sweetheart. They are only supposed to be there for about three to four more weeks. Unless they get delayed I could be home as early as twenty-one days instead of forty-five."

Talinda lie in his arms replied, "Bernard one day is too long for you to be there. Something happens over there every day. One day is one day too many...I'm sorry...I'm not being very strong or understanding right now. It's just," she paused as her tears consumed her again.

"Go ahead and cry baby...just cry sweetheart...just...just cry," he said as he tightened his grip and secured her in his arms to comfort her. He began to parade her with light kisses as he continued to speak words of comfort over her. She realized that what her husband needed at the moment was comfort himself. She put aside her fears and began to return his kisses. They soon found themselves caught up in a desperate and passionate love that consumed the heaviness in the atmosphere of the room.

He loved her as though it would be the last time he would ever hold her in his arms. She found comfort in the completeness she felt as he made love to her. His passion for her chased away her fears and she lost herself inside the love he shared with her.

But as she lie in his arms afterwards silent tears yet again began to flow down her face and unto his chest.

"Come on, baby. I need to get you something to eat, sweetheart. It's well past lunch," Bernard said as he kissed her tears away.

"I'm not hungry," she replied still cuddled up in his arms. She was unwilling to move from her present position.

He attempted to mover her as he said again. "Baby, come on. You need to...."

"I'm not hungry, Bernard," Talinda replied again as she secured her arms half under him and pulled herself deeper into his chest. Her hot tears still rolling down her face and hit his chest like heavy raindrops.

"Okay, baby," he whispered. He held her tighter and kissed her forehead. "Okay." They drifted off into a much needed and sleep. They were both emotionally exhausted. Bernard was awakened about an hour later as his phone vibrated and started to ring. Talinda readjusted in his arms as he reached over to the night stand to retrieve his phone.

"Hey Bernard, how is it going?" Jaison asked. "I was trying to wait on your call but looking at the concern in Raymond's face that neither one of you had contacted us, I decided to call to ease his mind."

Bernard took a deep breath and replied, "Jaison, it was an emotional rollercoaster. Obviously we missed lunch, so I'm thinking maybe we can have dinner over to you and Tasha's tonight instead of going to the officer's club. I haven't been able to get her to eat. Give Tasha and Stacy the heads up that I need them to minister to her."

"Okay my brother, will do," Jaison replied. "Get back to Talinda. We got the kids."

"Thanks, Jaison," Bernard replied, feeling the emotions build up once again. They said their goodbyes and hung up. He set his alarm and drifted back off to sleep with an undisturbed Talinda still in his arms.

Jaison turned to the other adults with him and explained the situation and the plan for the evening. They all agreed and said a quick prayer for Bernard and Talinda.

The alarm went off around 5:30pm and Bernard paraded Talinda with light kisses to wake her out of her slumber. "Come on baby we need to shower and head to Jaison and Tasha's for dinner. The youth are preparing dinner for us and..."

"I'm not hungry, Bernard," Talinda replied. She had interrupted him in mid-sentence.

"Okay, listen, Mrs. Travis," Bernard paused and smiled at the knowledge that she indeed was his Mrs. Travis. "It's not about you being hungry," he said in a stern but loving tone. "You have two beautiful babies growing inside of you that I vowed to take care of. Now sweetheart, nourishment is part of that vow. You may not be hungry Talinda Travis, but it's not just about you, sweetheart. It's 5:45 pm and you haven't eaten since breakfast. Baby...you're going to have to eat and that's all there is to it. So come on sweetheart. Let's get changed and get to dinner."

Talinda took a deep breath, mustered a smile and responded, "Okay."

Bernard breathed a sigh of relief, thankful that she had at least agreed to go to dinner. He looked forward to when he could pass her off to Tasha and Stacy. He had exhausted everything he knew to say to bring her comfort. But Stacy knew firsthand how she felt and so in wisdom he decided to leave it to the experts.

Not only did they get Talinda to eat, but they also prayed with her and were able to give her words of strength and encouragement. They also filled her in on statistics of war which reassured her greatly. She still felt a little gut punched but started to come around and get back involved with the youth and assisted them in preparing for the one day revival set for Saturday afternoon at 1pm at the base chapel. They spent Friday and finalized everything and were prepared for Saturday. They had all pre-voted on Raymond to bring the word. Talinda and Bernard asked him if he was still up to it given the circumstances that had been thrust upon them.

He simply replied, "Mom...ministry is always required." Talinda fought back tears. Being reminded of Brandon's motto had touched her deeply. The youth would also minister in dance and have several ice breaker activities and praise and worship planned. They also had a lot of door prizes and a pizza party planned for the evening at the base skating rink.

~Chapter Sixteen~

The youth were all pumped up. The ice breakers were a big hit. They talked and communicated like they had known each other all of their lives. The chaplain marveled at how the youth were so involved in the praise and worship.

Talinda stood at the podium to prepare them for the word and introduce the speaker. She looked at Raymond and smiled as she prepared to speak, "*GLORY TO THE LAMB OF GOD WHO SITS ON THE THRONE! HE IS WORTHY OF OUR PRAISE!*" With that being said the youth, still pumped up, all jumped to their feet and shouted and gave God praise. She continued to exalt for a minute or two then proceeded to introduce Raymond.

"Well, we have praised God, danced and shouted, played games and received prizes but now it's time for the word to come forth. Right before my son Raymond comes to the podium the youth have prepared a praise dance to introduce the word of the day. I was going to introduce him by telling his story but I have since learned that his testimony is part of his message. So I will just say to him that I love him and am so very proud of the man of God he has become. And in the famous words of Pastor Travis... *'give it the way God gave it...and don't apologize for it'*. I present to you Radical Disciples dance ministry. The next voice you hear will be that of Brother Raymond Travis."

Raymond smiled as he heard the name Travis attached to his. Bernard gave him a reassuring pat on the shoulder as the dance team was took their place to minister. Talinda, along with the youth ministers and chaplain, sat behind Raymond in the pulpit. As the song came to a close and the youth were once again on their feet praising God and applauding, Raymond took his place at the podium. He was somewhat edgy and had been known to jump right in with both feet to overshadow his nervousness. But today was different. He smiled, looked up to heaven, pointed to God and whispered, "Thank you, dad." He cleared his throat and began to speak.

Let us pray,

Father, we come before You in the name of Jesus Christ...a name that is above all names and at that name every knee shall bow and every tongue shall confess that He is Lord. Father we release You to change us. I pray that we won't leave the same way we came. I thank You God for the fire that You have lit in us and we don't take our assignments lightly. Father, You said in Your word let no man despise your youth. So Jesus, we will go forth in You with boldness like never before.

We will minister to our peers and we will compel them to live in righteousness. Father our goal is heaven and our mission is clear. We must make disciples. We love You and we are not ashamed of the gospel. We will deliver Your word to Your people, and we will rejoice in Christ Jesus. Let every heart be open to Your instruction this afternoon. We will praise You God for we are fearfully and wonderfully made. Marvelous are thy works and my soul knoweth right well.

We will bless you, Lord, at all times and your praise will forever and continually be in our mouths! OH, BLESS THE LORD WITH ME AND LET US EXALT HIS NAME TOGETHER. FOR HE HAS DONE GREAT THINGS AND HE IS FAITHFUL, JUST AND TRUE. HE IS THE WONDERFUL COUNSELOR, THE SAVIOR, AND THE RULER OVER ALL. THE PRINCE OF PEACE, MY ROCK AND MY SALVATION AND IT'S IN HIM THAT I TRUST....SOMEBODY OUGHT TO STAND TO THEIR FEET AND PRAISE THE LORD WITH ME! LET'S PRAISE THE NAME OF THE LORD IN THIS PLACE, AMEN!!!

The youth and congregation erupted in praise. The chaplain and the ministers all marveled at the anointing of God that was on this young seventeen year old.

Jaison leaned over to Bernard as they praised and declared, "Oh my God...wow talk about a powerful anointing. How about I'm feeling just a little bit intimidated."

Bernard chuckled and replied, "I know tell me about it...I told you these youth were special."

As everyone quieted down and took their seats Raymond began to speak:

"I studied and studied on what I thought the Lord...my mother and father the late Pastor Travis would want me to say. I gathered notes and had scriptures ready. I was prepared to talk about all the people in the bible who served God in their youth and pump you up to go forward and serve God with all you have. But if you have no root in the knowledge of the blood of Jesus in and on your lives it won't last you past the weekend. So I could hear God say this morning when I was in prayer to just speak from my heart and give my testimony. It may not be what you were expecting but it's what God told me to do.

A bunch of scripture and scripted words is not what you need today. The bible said in the book of Revelation that they overcame him...Satan...by the blood of the lamb and the word of their testimony.

On Thursday a lot of things changed for me. We received a bit of bad news...news that you all have grown to live by and understand. But news that caught my mom and me quite off guard and thrust us both into an unsure reality and future. The phrase 'tomorrow is not promised' took a new meaning to me the night my father died protecting my life almost six months ago. And now a few days ago it has taken on a deeper meaning to me.

My new dad Minister Bernard Travis has just informed us that he leaves headed for Afghanistan by the end of next week. This is new to me and mom and we didn't quite know how to respond. Just when you think you're strong God has a way of reminding you that you are still vulnerable and you still need him. I don't really know what I'm going to do if something happens to him over there..."

He paused to fight back tears. Talinda gestured to move toward him but Bernard touched her and kept her in her seat. "Let him get through it. He'll be okay," he said.

Talinda looked at him. "But, Bernard..."

"Shhh, Talinda," Bernard replied. "If he struggles too much I'll get him. Let's just see if he can make it through okay. Give him a chance first baby." Talinda swallowed hard and grasped Bernard's hands as she sat silently and prayed for her baby boy.

Raymond continued:

"Before my dad died, he said that Bernard would take care of us, that he was going to love us. If I lose him too, I don't know what I'm going to do..." Raymond dropped his head and lost his composure.

Talinda said to Bernard, "Baby, please go get him."

"Okay sweetheart," Bernard said as he got up and stood behind Raymond. He whispered in his hear, "Hey, man, it's going to be okay. I love you and I'm going to be alright. I told you I'm coming back okay. Come on Raymond...hey...I'm coming home...okay. I told you...I'm coming home...don't worry Raymond...God has me under his wing."

Bernard held him in his arms. "I love you dad," Raymond said.

Bernard replied, "I love you too. You take care of my wife."

"I got you dad," Raymond said. He smiled as he wiped his tears.

"You ready?" Bernard asked. "You got it?"

"Yeah dad," Raymond replied. He turned back toward the congregation. "I got it." He cleared his throat and continued his message for the day:

"When you grow up on the streets like I did, family is everything to you. I ran into my dad...my first dad, literally, in the park. I was about to go and kill myself. I wanted out of that gang so bad. I hadn't killed anybody and I didn't know if I was ever going to be able too. I had to rob people at gunpoint and have sex with five different women in 72 hours and bring proof just to get into the gang. It was full of sex, violence and death. I'm just thankful that I never had to actually kill anybody. I took the credit for killing this guy to stay in the gang. It was a gunfight and I never even drew my gun. People started shooting and this guy went down right beside me. I stood over him as one of the other gang members took the picture. I know it sounds crazy, but at that time they were the only family I knew so I wanted to remain a part of it. But I never shot anybody...I just couldn't make myself do that. When dad found me that night I was going to kill myself, because we were getting ready to go shoot people at random. Instead of meeting everybody else I ran. I just ran and ran.

I was going to kill myself in the park because I didn't want my biological mother to come home and find me dead in our apartment. She never knew what I was doing because she was strung out on drugs and would stay away from home weeks sometimes months at a time. So...I ran. I had to past a store before entering the park and that's where I ran right into dad as he was coming out of the store. He saw the gun in my pants and started chasing me. He caught up with me and stopped me. He started talking to me about God and he just wouldn't leave me alone. I even threatened to shoot him a couple of times."

This comment broke up the seriousness of the moment and some of the youth started to laugh at Raymond's last statement. LaNiesha prayed silently for Raymond. She had never heard his story spoken so bluntly. She was overwhelmed at the anointing that was on him as he spoke. She was very proud of him. But she also had another feeling arousing inside of her as she watched him, one that she struggled to control.

Raymond continued on in a chuckling but serious tone:

"He had said to me, 'I'm ready to die son, but you're not. So I'm going to stay here until you're ready'. He wouldn't leave me alone and then he took me to his house. All the way there I was thinking...what kind of love is this that this man has? Doesn't he know who I am? Doesn't he realize the danger of bringing a Knight home to his family? Doesn't he understand? This could be death for his family. When I walked into their home I could feel a presence. When Pastor Talinda came around the corner from the kitchen there was such an anointing on her. At the time I didn't know what anointing was but I could feel God and it was amazing. I couldn't even raise my head to look at her. I didn't know what to do I was just standing there shaking under the presence of God that filled their home. And when she walked up to me there was so much love...they had so much love and it was real. They took me in and I gave my life to God. They treated me like I was really their son.

Then a few months ago he died for me...he gave his life so that I could be standing right here. Recently the adoption was final and I finally became a Travis. The blood of Jesus is awesome! Don't...guys don't play church. Don't come to church and sit here just because your parents make you come. Don't come here and think that you have all this time because you don't, tomorrow is not promised to you. You may be in the wrong place at the wrong time and get killed by a gang member for the jacket or shoes that you have on. Most of them don't care about anything or anybody. So don't sit in church and just be here. Don't waste the blood of Jesus...it's too precious. If you're going to come to church you might as well be real. There is no sense in sitting here Sunday in and Sunday out and still die and go to hell. Just because your parents make you come to church doesn't make you saved. The bible said all have come short of the glory of God. It said in Romans 10:9–10 'That if thou shalt confess with thy mouth the Lord Jesus, and shalt believe in thine heart that God hath raised him from the dead, thou shalt be saved. For with the heart man believeth unto righteousness; and with the mouth confession is made unto salvation.'

Guys listen...you won't make it into heaven on default. You have to get on your knees and confess him for yourself. I thought it was bad growing up on the streets on the wrong side of town in the east end of Atlanta, Georgia. But you guys have all kind of temptation over here. There is every country and nationality...the women don't hardly wear any clothes and nude beaches are legal. I couldn't imagine being a young male teenager here. You young men need the blood of Jesus operating in your lives. We have been tempted on several occasions since we've been here. These girls here are off the chain...we thought they were wild at home...but here...man guys get the baptism of the Holy Spirit is all I can say. It makes us glad that we are with the girls that we are with. It also makes us appreciate and respect them all the more. We've had an awesome trip and I'm really sad that it's coming to a close. I'm even more sad that my dad has to go back to Afghanistan, but I'm trusting God to bring him home. Please pray for my mom and me because this is all new to us.

But don't waste this opportunity. Don't play with God...fall on your knees and confess God...give him your life for real. Don't waste the blood of Jesus. Be here because you love God, fall on your knees and ask him for his spirit. That day before my dad's funeral when we were all filled with the Holy Ghost helped us to be able to get through it. It was hard...he was our leader and we were conducting the service. It was hard to bury him...to say goodbye. But the power of the Lord fell on us and we all received the baptism on the Holy Spirit that day. I was worried about my mom and how she was going to be. I knew who Bernard was already when he showed up. I already knew who he was going to be...I knew before they all knew and I was happy for my mom. My dad made me promise not to say anything to her before everything happened. He knew he was going to die but what he didn't tell me was he would die saving my life."

He paused for a brief moment then continued through tears:

"When I met Minister Bernard Travis, he looked just like my dad. When he started to talk he even sounded like my dad. He ministered to me the very first day he met me. I teased him about staring at my mom during the basketball game at a youth barbeque at my grandmother's house in Athens the day after my father's funeral. I wanted to tell him so bad that he was going to be my dad. But I couldn't because I promised dad that I wouldn't say anything. So when mom was coming to Germany the first time to bring him the letter I knew why she was coming. I wanted to tell grandma and grandpa when she left but I was afraid they would call her and tell her. So I did what my dad told me to do, I didn't say anything until she called and said they were married. My dad was right. God told him he was going to die. He changed the will to take care of me and mom. He knew it...and he left a letter asking Bernard to marry my mom and take care of me. I have been blessed to have two moms and dads and six grandparents. And believe me I take full advantage of it. I never knew my real grandmother or family back in Puerto Rico and now it doesn't matter.

So, young people listen to me...don't play with Jesus. If you know in your heart of hearts that you really don't know him, then today is the day of salvation. Don't take a chance because tomorrow is not promised to you. You guys know firsthand that everybody doesn't come back from Afghanistan alive. Today is the day to really believe in Jesus in your heart. We're teenagers. We're going to make mistakes. I'm not saying you're going to live a perfect life from this day on. I'm going to probably make a mistake next week, tomorrow or even later

172

on today who knows. But I know that I can ask God to forgive me and I can repent and move forward.

A lot of kids and teens don't want to come to God because you're thinking my life is going to end. You're thinking that you won't have any more fun. Well that's just not the truth. We have a great time. We do what everybody else does. We go skating, to dances, and to parties. We go to prom, football, and basketball games. Most of us are on the boys and girls basketball and soccer teams. Jonathan plays football and is on the debate team. We are all over the place. We have youth rallies, concerts with live bands, and carnivals in the park. You don't have to give anything up that's not ungodly that you do. You just have to begin to do it for Christ. He has to be the center of all you do. We strive to be the best players on the team. We don't drink, smoke or do drugs. Most of us that came over here are couples. Some of us just started to date recently. We made a decision this week that we would have accountability with our girlfriends. We decided to date in groups to control fornication. So from now on when we are struggling with our hormones we just simply won't be alone with them.

Listen guys, I beg you...don't make an eternal mistake today. Don't sit in church all your life and never profess Jesus Christ as your Lord and Savior. Some of you know you're here just because your parents are making you come. You've never thought about God one way or another. Today is the day to come to God...make that choice. My mom, my dad, the ministers, they will pray for you. They will lead you to God...all the youth that came with me know how to lead you to God and they will pray with you as well."

He turned and looked back at his friends who sat to the right of him on the platform. He motioned for Jonathan, Troy, Michelle, LaNiesha, Sarah, Jessica, Lisa and Reginald to come down to the altar.

"They know how to pray with you. They are all filled with the Holy Spirit and they know how to get you to Jesus. We've been taught well. If you know you've been playing church...you know who you are, don't let another day go by without knowing who Jesus Christ really is. Come find one of these youth to pray with you...come right now don't wait come right now!"

The altar flooded with youth that day. Talinda beckoned for the adults to stand still. "Let's just see how they handle it. If it gets to be too much and they seemed overwhelmed, we will help them. But let the youth minister to the youth." They all agreed and began to pray for the youth as they ministered. Some of the kids were filled with the Holy Spirit and spoke in tongues.

About two hours later Raymond finally returned to the pulpit to end the service. "Okay, we are going to leave you in the hands of your youth ministers. They are such good people so please take advantage of what you have here. They have imparted so much in our lives these last nine days that we have been here. From what I understand they have reserved the skating rink for us tonight and we will have a pizza party. It's all free so please come out and join us. We have asked them to leave it open for the public because we want the unsaved youth to come in. We want to show them that Christians have more fun. Everybody clapped and cheered and a couple of girls yelled out, "We love you Raymond!"

Raymond smiled and replied, "We love you guys, too. We'll pray for you and you pray for us. We'll see you tonight."

With that being, said he stepped down from the pulpit. The chaplain gave out instructions about the skate party for later that afternoon before he closed out the service. "I know you guys probably have a ton of one on one questions for them but write them down and ask them tonight. We need to let them get back to their rooms to rest. Ministry takes a lot out of you."

Lisa turned to LaNiesha and said, "I bet little Miss Spanish what's-her-name who yelled out a minute ago, would love to have some "one-on-one" with Raymond."

The girls laughed as LaNiesha replied, "I know, right? You know I'm gonna make sure that doesn't happen."

"Oh, we'll be watching her," Jessica Replied. "We got your back, girl." They laughed as they exited the church to the cars.

The youth went into their perspective houses and were soon out like a light. No one had to persuade them to take a nap. They knew all too well how ministry flat drained you when people pulled on the anointing on your life. The adults settled in at the Travis' townhouse to talk about the service and fellowship.

After a much needed rest, they piled into the SUV's and headed to the skating rink. They sorted through their CD's along the way and pray that God will be with them as they continued to minister to the youth.

The K-town youth were surprised with how up to date the Christian music was. They half expected the hymns of their parent's era. Most everyone was on the floor skating other than a few groups who sat and conversed here and there. Jennifer and Maria sat in a corner and whispered about Raymond. Maria was attracted to and very much hoped that Raymond was available. After a couple of rounds on the floor, some of the girls gathered at a table with Talinda, Tasha and Stacy to have some girl time.

Maria sighed as Jennifer said, "I think he is dating that LaNiesha girl. You see how they are with each other. So you need to back off and leave him alone." She eyed her friend because she had a mischievous look on her face. "Don't you even start with him, Maria.

Besides, they will be leaving the country in a day or two. Hey look, look, look...they're holding hands. See...I told you."

"Dang!" Maria exclaimed. "I sure was going to try to get him. He is a cutie pie...oo-kaay."

"No, you weren't," Jennifer shot back at her. "He's not like the guys over here. These guys from Grace are saved for real. You saw how they were today. They are powerful. They respect their girlfriends. They're different. They are doing things for God and they don't care who sees them or talks about it. They made me realize that I was not at all serious about God. I was one of the ones just going to church. But not anymore, it's all or nothing with God for me, from now on."

"Yeah, I hear you," Maria replied. "Come on, some of the girls are talking with Minister's Stallworth and Thomas over there. Let's go join them."

They join the conversation at the table just as Tasha asked Michelle about her and Troy's relationship since Paris. They sat down just as Tasha said, "So, Michelle, how are you and Troy?"

"Oh Mrs. Tasha, it's so awesome. Ever since we had the "what's the big deal about sex talk" in Paris, he has been so different," Michelle replied all smiles.

Tasha smiled and gave her a playful tap as she said, "Yeah, I saw you guys sitting out on the deck for a long time the other night."

"Yes. He wasn't all touchy feely like he usually is," Michelle beamed. "He is so respectful now. We discussed everything. He apologized to me again. It was just great."

Michelle turned toward Jennifer and Maria and said, "You guys are so blessed to have them here with you. They are so open. You can just ask them anything. It's not very many adults who are going to be that open with you about sensitive issues. They are willing to share their mistakes with y'all and everything. Don't get me wrong, Pastor Talinda is very open with us, but she led a very different life from them. So, we hadn't been able to go that deep with her, because she really couldn't relate." She turned toward Talinda and said, "I mean, no offense Pastor Travis."

"None taken, sweetie. I understand completely and you're right. I was a virgin when I met my first husband. The things Tasha and Stacy discussed with you girls, I had no experience in," Talinda replied and touched her shoulder for reassurance that she hadn't offended her.

Jessica commented, "Yeah, they helped us with some serious and sensitive issues in our lives. I am really going to miss them when it's time to go home. Take advantage of them while y'all have them here with you."

Maria looked somewhat surprised as she said to Tasha, "Minister Thomas, you never had this type of discussion with us. What gives with that?"

"Well," Tasha replied. "You guys never really showed much interest in us being in your lives. We tried to open up to you young ladies and have girl talk sessions at several of the youth services. But y'all thought we were just trying to be nosey and get in your business."

"Y'all are really missing out by not taking advantage of them in your lives," Lisa said. "But also let me say this. They shared a lot of intimate things with us in Paris. Pastor Travis talks with us about intimate issues all the time. She shares things with us about her marriage that the younger girls didn't get a chance to hear. And we knew if it got out then someone in the senior teen group had to share it. So you have to been young ladies of integrity, because they are sharing things about their marriage that they probably shouldn't. So y'all are going to have to keep their secrets." Jessica and Michelle both nodded their heads in agreement.

"Wow," Jennifer sighed. "I guess we have been missing out, huh. I could have really used your input before I lost my virginity a month ago, and may..."

Maria cut her off. She grabbed her by the hand and said, "Jennifer, I thought you said you weren't going to do it. What happened?"

"He kept pressuring me...and...it just happened," Jennifer dropped her head almost in tears. "Now he hardly even looks at me. He's been avoiding me the last two weeks, after I told him I might be pregnant."

"Jennifer!" Maria exclaimed. "Did I not teach you anything?! Why didn't you tell me?"

"Because, Maria!" Jennifer said as she looked up in desperation. "You're sexually active and you're always saying, if you are going to do it...protect yourself, protect yourself...PROTECT YOURSELF! I wasn't about to tell you I was to too stupid and didn't." She dropped her head in her hands. Maria put her arm around her for emotional support.

Stacy placed her hand under her chin and forced Jennifer to look at her. "Jennifer, sweetheart, have you taken a pregnancy test to be sure?"

"No ma'am," Jennifer replied as she wiped her tears. "But it's been six weeks since Cedric and I had sex and I haven't had my cycle.

"Well, you just answered my next question," Stacy replied. "I was about to ask who the father was."

Michelle sighed as she thought how thankful she was that the adults had intervened in her life. She knew how easily that could have been her and Troy, had it not been for the Paris trip.

On the other side of the skating rink, a new romance kindled between two other youth of Grace Tabernacle Ministry. Sarah and Reginald had been spent quite a bit of friendly time together since Paris. They chit-chatted smiled at each other as they skated along.

As they rounded the corner into the straightway Reginald shifted their general conversation to a different topic. "Hey, that was a pretty intense session we had in Paris."

"Yeah, ours was very emotional and to the point," Sarah replied. "When Michelle broke down crying talking about Troy, it sort took our conversation in a different direction. But then Jessica gave like, the perfect advice."

"Well, Minister Travis and the rest of them jumped all over us," Reginald said as he remembered the moment. "I mean, I just sat back listened at first. I was the only guy over there that was actually a virgin. Most of the discussion didn't apply to me. I have run from quite a few girls in my life. It's just hard, because there are just not as many girls who are virgins to date anymore. Plus, I'm considered weird. People get it when a girl says she is keeping herself for her husband. But those same people look at you like you're gay, when it's the guy that's doing it, or trying to anyway. It gets harder and harder every day."

"Yeah, I know you mean," Sarah replied.

Reginald looked at her somewhat surprised. But for the first time, he really, looked at her. They skated off the floor and sat down at a table.

She continued on, not really sure she understood the nature of his countenance. "I have had a few boyfriends but nothing really serious. I mean, only one of them lasted past a few months. That probably doesn't count, because we were both fourteen going on fifteen. I probably shouldn't have been dating anyway, but my foster parents allowed it. Sometimes they are reluctant to set any real family boundaries for foster kids, you know. Anyway, when he realized he wasn't going to get off first base, much less hit a home run with me, he dumped me for a girl who would. When it came time to have sex, I shut down because I was too afraid. Since then, I haven't really had what you would call a serious boyfriend. A lot of guys don't stay with you long, when they find out you're not going to put out. Not even the Christians ones...unfortunately."

"Virgin...you?" Reginald asked in disbelief.

"Wow, here my past is catching up with me again. Why do you find that so hard to believe?" Sarah replied in a non-offended but defensive tone.

"No it's not that," Reginald said. He had a heavy apologetic tone to his voice. "It's just that...I just remember you telling a little of your testimony at Pastor Travis' funeral and one of the youth meetings. Because your dad molested you when you were eight, I just assumed that meant he had sex with you. That he probably..."

"Penetrated me vaginally," she said, which finished his sentence.

"Yes," Reginald replied. He felt instantly judgmental.

"No, he didn't," Sarah added. "But he may as well have. I mean, he did everything but that. He put his mouth all over me and forced me to do the same. Then he rubbed himself on me until he was satisfied. I remember it just like it was yesterday. He did it more than once before I got up enough nerve to say something to my mom. I thought she was going to say, what were you doing? This man was my father. Your daddy is not supposed to hurt you, you know."

"Yeah...that's crazy," Reginald replied. He had such a newfound respect for Sarah. "Wow, I didn't know you were a virgin. I mean, it's not like I go around asking girls. I can't imagine being you. To have your trust totally destroyed by a parent, who crossed the line with you sexually."

Sarah looked at him for a brief moment before she continued. Reginald was only the second male she had ever felt comfortable enough with to talk about her past. Pastor Brandon Travis had been the first.

She hunched her shoulders slightly and continued, "To tell you the truth Reginald, I'm just really afraid to have sex. I'm afraid that...all I'm going to do is think about what my father did. Whenever a guy really even attempts to get close to me like that, I have to talk to myself so I don't freak out on him. I mean as long as he doesn't touch me suddenly, or hug me to long, I'm okay. Like when the guys in the church hug me its different, because they are not trying to be my boyfriends. Y'all are all like big brothers to me. Most guys that are interested in me I usually run off, because I'm too tense with them. I wonder sometimes, if I'm going to be able to be normal with my husband. If I ever get one, that is."

"Wow," Reginald replied for the lack of a better word.

"Predators don't realize the damage they do to their victims," Sarah replied in a desperately attempt to keep her tone normal. Her insides had begun to shake. "They don't realize how it makes them so abnormal when it comes to intimacy. They don't realize the damage they do. Damage not only to their bodies, but to their minds and souls as well. How they wound their spirits. You feel so used up, you know. You think to yourself, nobody is going to want me. I mean really...I was molested by my father. You think everyone is thinking what did you do at eight years old to make your father desire you? You little seductive...you know. There are so many stigmas for the victims. That's why people keep quiet about it. They don't say anything. Our justice system has been known to be cruel to the victims, by justifying the predators. Like I said, it's hard because people have said to me, what did you do at eight years old to make your daddy want to have sex with you? Nothing...I was being an eight year old. The predator never gets exposed about having a lust spirit. They always end up looking like the victim because of some little "fast tail girl" as they call us. Recently, when Sister Lindsay Armstrong told her testimony at the youth meeting, about her pastor that molested her and the baby she was forced to abort, I felt so connected to her. Finally, someone knew my side of the story, you know. I told my aunt that I needed to talk with her. Lindsay and I went to lunch and I felt so much better after talking and praying with her. Sometimes you think you are completely over something because you grow up. But all you are is that little eight year old trapped in a seventeen year olds body, terrified and accusing of any man that looks at you the wrong way. Finally, I knew that I wasn't dirty. It wasn't my fault. I wasn't doing anything to make him want to have sex with me."

Reginald just sat and listened. He had absolutely no idea what to say. Then it donned on him...she just needed someone to listen.

"These last few months I have been so free. You go through stuff and you think, why me? But I'm learning that sometimes you go through trials for the next person that may not be strong enough, to get through their issue without your testimony to give them hope. Now, I know it wasn't me. I guess when I get my next serious boyfriend, I'll really be able to gauge my true deliverance," she paused for a moment to smile at that thought before continuing.

"I want to go see my mom. I haven't seen her since it happened. In foster care, I was never allowed to go see her. Now that I'm with my aunt she has scheduled a visit. She was supposed to be paroled a few years ago, but ended up in an altercation a few days before her parole and was placed in solitary confinement. But she is up again soon and we are praying she will get released. I really want to see her. She believed me. From the first time I said it, she believe me. She went to jail protecting me. She gave up her freedom for the chance for me to have mine. So a few weeks after we get back from Germany, I will see her for the first time in eight years. I'm a little nervous. I mean, what if she doesn't understand why I never came to visit?"

"Oh, I seriously doubt she will think that. She will be too happy to see you," Reginald interjected. "Wow, I'm amazed. You just never know about people. All this time I'm thinking, you're probably promiscuous because of what happened and you are just the opposite. I sort of thought you were probably just doing our own thing."

"No," she replied. "I was ashamed. That is until I talked with Ms. Lindsay about it. Now I realize the shame is all on my daddy, not me."

"Sarah, I owe you an apology," Reginald said. He was about to touch her hand but remembered that maybe that wouldn't be such a good idea. "I misjudged you big time...and...over looked you too." He voice was soft towards her. She noticed it, but unsure what to do or say she just played it off.

"It's okay," she replied. "I'm used to getting misjudged and overlooked.

"Nah, it's not okay," Reginald replied unable to hide his inner feelings that seemed oozed out of his eyes as he looked into hers. "You're very pretty."

Sarah began to get a little nervous as she replied, "Thanks."

"No, I mean it," Reginald replied. He realized she thought he was just being nice to her. "You're...very pretty."

"Well, I've always thought you are very handsome too, if that makes you feel better about misjudging me," she said in an attempt to break up the serious and tense atmosphere that was just created by his declaration to her. They both smile, but neither broke out into a full laughter at the comment.

"I mean, I knew you were a virgin because you have said it before," Sarah said to break the two second silence that seemed to last a lifetime.

Reginald smiled and replied, "I've been asking God for a virgin girlfriend for a long time. There's been one in my face and I never even saw her, until now. I assumed because of your past, you were damaged goods. Boy was I wrong." He cleared his throat and took a deep breath before he asked her, "Sarah, I would love to...I mean, I would love to take you to the movies or something when we get back home."

"You're asking me out on a date?" Sarah replied in an unbelievable tone.

"Well," Reginald answered. "I guess I'm trying to do a little more than that. But, I think I need to talk to your aunt first to see if it's okay. If you're able to date and have a boyfriend."

Sarah chuckled as she replied, "I don't need permission from my aunt to date or have a boyfriend."

"Oh but you do," Reginald stated in no uncertain terms. "You are living under her roof...you kinda do. What she said goes in your life right now, because she has custody of you. It's is not like foster care because she's family, so it's different."

"Wow," Sarah replied. "I guess you're right. This is all new to me. I am used to being able to do what I want, when I want. But you're right Reginald."

"Yeah, you're not in foster care anymore. You have to give your aunt the respect of being your legal guardian," Reginald added.

"You're right," Sarah said. "I hadn't thought of it that way. I think maybe her guilt of not adopting me when I was eight has sort of swayed her leniency with me. But with that being said, you "really" want to go out with me?" She replied in a 'please don't change your mind' tone.

"Yeah...yes, I do," Reginald replied. He was still not sure if he should attempt to make any physical contact with her. "I want to do more than that. I want to be your man...I mean..." he dropped his head and smiled.

"Okay," Sarah replied in a childlike tone.

"With all you have gone through, I could probably learn a lot from you. You are probably way more mature than me at this point," he replied.

"Don't be so sure about that Reginald. I was about to say the same thing about you," Sarah said with a smile.

180

"Okay, I guess it's safe to say we will learn from each other," Reginald replied. "The one thing you don't have to worry about is me pressuring you for sex. Because I am really, really, really trying to stay a virgin until I get married. I don't know if I'm going to succeed, but that's my plan."

"Well, with my mindset about it right now, you plan will succeed. I still have a ways to go to feel normal about sex with a man. So it will be great to have a boyfriend that is not going to pressure me about it," Sarah declared with much relief in her voice.

"Then its official?" Reginald asked. "I mean, after I talk to your aunt. You'll officially be my girlfriend?"

Sarah smiled and shook her head and she answered, "I would love too. If you're sure that's what you want. Being my boyfriend may prove to be to..."

"Don't," Reginald said. His declaration stopped her in mid-sentence. "Don't say what you were about to say. I wouldn't have asked if I didn't want to. Sarah this isn't a charity case. I'm not "throwing a dog a bone", so to speak. I really like you."

"Wow...o-okay," Sarah replied. She couldn't hide the fact that she beamed with delight. She couldn't recall the last time she had felt so warm and complete on the inside.

At the moment she felt she would no longer be able to contain the utter joy she felt inside, the boys came by the table and grabbed Reginald. "Come on man, its all guys on the floor for this song. We can't get Raymond away for LaNiesha. She got him whipped already." They laughed and he winked at Sarah as he skated off with them. She smiled and then noticed the girl's engaged in a conversation that looked pretty intense on the other end of the food court area and went over to join them. As she approached the table she noticed that Jennifer, one of the girls from the Germany youth group, crying and the others gathered around and consoled her.

Tasha said to Jennifer, "Okay, are you sure that it's Cedric? Are you positively sure that the father couldn't be anyone other than him? Before we make any moves or decisions, we need to be concrete on everything sweetheart."

"Yes Ma'am, I understand," Jennifer replied. "I'm sure. I was a virgin when I slept with him. I haven't had sex with anyone since and I was not on birth control."

"Well, the first thing we have to do is inform your parents and his," Talinda interjected. "Then your mother can make you an appointment for an official pregnancy test. Because sweetie, if you are indeed pregnant, you're missing out on critical prenatal care right now."

Jennifer sat and shook her head in disbelief. She looked up at Stacy who sat directly across from her. "I don't want to be a mommy. I mean...I just want to be sixteen." She paused then repeated the same thing again, "I just want to be sixteen. I'm so stupid...I feel so stupid." She buried her head in her hands and wept.

"No you're not," Maria replied. "If anybody is stupid it's me. Here I am telling you to protect yourself, protect yourself. But a real friend I would have been saying not to do it at all. Because I was sexually active, I was so focused on you protecting yourself. I didn't see the value in staying a virgin. I wasn't trying to convince you to stay one, probably, because I wasn't. I gave in to pressure at fourteen and I've been sexually active since then. But the truth is it's not really all that anyway. I mean, I'm still trying to figure out what's so great about it. I just do it now because guys expect me too. I liked being the girl that all the boys wanted to go out with. But now all of a sudden it just seems meaningless. So, I'm the one who is stupid, Jennifer, not you." Maria continued to hug her and rest her head on Jennifer's shoulder area. Silent tears ran down her face.

"None of you are stupid," Talinda replied. "What you are is taken advantage of. The devil comes at the young mind early, to try to persuade you to make a decision about sex that you are not ready to make. He comes when you're not maturely enough to make a logical, or biblical, decision about intimacy yet. Your hormones are raging when you're way too young to weigh the cost and the devil takes full advantage of that. Parents usually put discussing sex with their children on the back burner for far too long. The devil doesn't mind talking to them about it. He is eager to give them his version. That's why it's so important to be a part of a good youth ministry. We as women, have to develop relationships with young girls in our churches. So they can come to us openly a freely to discuss any issues or pressures they are having about sex."

"I will from now on," Jennifer replied still lost in her tears of disappointment and discouragement. "I'm not going to keep anything from my mom or you guys from now on Minister Thomas and Minister Stallworth."

"I'll be here for you. If he doesn't want anything to do with you, then that's his lose. Even in the delivery room I'll be there," Maria said. She still had her head on Jennifer's shoulder and continued to wipe her tears.

Tasha stood and said, "Well, I'm going to go over here and talk to the men. I know for a fact that Cedric's mom is single and here in Germany without his father. She is a pretty no non-sense kind of mother with him. His fear of telling her is probably why he is ignoring you. He is definitely going to need the men right now."

"Okay Tasha," Stacy replied. "Now, Jennifer, look at me sweetie. I know you may not be ready to be a mom. But you are about to be. Know this, like Maria said, we are going to be here for you and help you in any way we can, okay."

182

Jennifer shook her head. Through her tears she asked, "Will you be with me when I tell my parents? I don't want to face them alone. My daddy will be so disappointed in me. Ughhh...so much for being his little princess?"

"Jennifer, parents are more understanding than you think. They are not angry at you for making the mistake. They are angrier with themselves for not helping you to prevent making it. They are going to be disappointed. But that has nothing to do with their love for you, that's not going to change. You're still going to be his princess," Talinda said.

Jennifer continued to wipe her tears and the others consoled her. They told her it's wasn't the end of the world and the situation would work out. Stacy asked Talinda would she accompany them to inform the kids' parents of the situation.

The conversation with the men left them very discontented and they all shook their heads. They were angry at themselves that they had allowed the young men to shut them out of their lives and not pried their way in uninvited.

Out on the floor the guys all knew something was up. Cedric noticed Jennifer's tears and feared that his secret was probably out.

"Hey, I wonder what's up with the girls over there," Troy said.

"Yeah, it almost looks like somebody died," Jonathan added.

"Someone is about too," Cedric said. "And I'm pretty sure that it's me."

"What do you mean," Matthew, one of the youth stationed there inquired.

Cedric's remark got Mark's attention. He waited for his friend's response.

"Well about a month or so ago she finally gave into me," Cedric answered.

"Whaaat! We thought the way you were avoiding her that she turned you down flat. Man you didn't tell us you got that," Matthew added in a manly 'you the man' gesture.

"No, I didn't tell you guys because my victory was short lived. A couple of weeks after that, she told me that she might be pregnant," Cedric replied and waited for the fireworks from his friends to ignite all over him.

"What!" Mark exclaimed. "You mean to tell me you didn't use protection, Cedric."

"No, man I didn't. I figured she was on birth control," Cedric responded. For the first time he seriously pondered the fact that he was about to be a father. In frustration he declared again, "Look man, if she was giving it up, I figured she was on birth control."

Mark shook his head and said, "Man it has nothing to do with birth control. You could have caught something. Do the initials, S-T-D mean anything to you?"

"From a virgin, man?!" Cedric declared. He shook his head at the realization that he was about to be a father. "What was she going to give me?"

"Yeah, I guess you're right about that," Matthew added. He still did not see the seriousness of the situation.

Reginald then asked, "And so you've just been ignoring her?"

Cedric took a deep breath and replied, "Yeah, I told her it probably wasn't mine."

All of the guys at the same time as though it were rehearsed declared, "AWL, COME ON MAN...REALLY!"

"Okay, okay I know guys. I was scared okay," Cedric replied as he dropped his head. The shame and consequences of his actions had begun to fall down on his young shoulders like a ton of bricks. "I'm sixteen years old guys. The youngest in this group right here, including all you guys visiting from the states. I'm not ready to be a father, okay. I was scared...I panicked. You guys know my mom. She is going to kill me."

"I guess you had better get ready," Matthew replied. The revelation had finally set in.

"Yeah I guess so," Cedric said as he looked in the direction of the girls. "I can't believe I've been ignoring her."

"That's just foul, you know that right," Troy declared. "You can't run from your responsibility. Look, I was all over my girl before we came over here. I was trying to get her to give in to me. By the time Minister's Travis, Stallworth and Thomas got a hold of me in Paris, I went bawling to her apologizing. I can't believe Minister Travis let y'all get away with that. They were on us."

"Yeah," Jonathan added.

"We don't talk to them like that. I mean, they tried at first, but we just shut them down and out of our lives. We were supposed to have some new thing with them. This weekend with y'all was supposed to kick it off. But I guess its a few weeks to late though," Matthew answered.

Reginald said, "Man y'all been missing out. They tell you like it is. They make you want to keep your stuff in your pants. They're the real deal."

"Well, it looks like you secret is out over there too," Mark replied. He tapped Cedric on the shoulder and pointed to Bernard, Jaison and Terry. "Minister Bernard is signaling for you to come over there to them."

Cedric took another deep breath and said, "Y'all pray for me. The looks on their faces tell me I need to fear them more than my mom right now."

Cedric left to go talk with the male ministers while the women and teen girls prayed with Jennifer. They discussed the best course of action on how and when to inform both of the youth's parents. They

184

all agreed that they should tell them as soon as possible. They called the parents and changed the pick-up arrangements for Jennifer and Cedric. The ask them to come to Bernard's house to pick them up instead at the skating rink.

Before the left the rink the youth all exchanged numbers, found each other on the internet, and became friends on their social networks.

After the teens were all settled at Terry and Jaison house, the adults sat down with Cedric, Jennifer and their parents. They informed them of the situation. Cedric apologized to Jennifer for his behavior toward her the past few weeks. The parents, although disappointed, all agree that they both be responsible for their actions.

The trip to the airport was bitter sweet for the youth. They had thoroughly enjoyed their vacation to Germany and had much to tell their parents upon their return to the United States. Raymond rode mostly in silence. Although he enjoyed himself his mind was stuck on that fact that his dad would soon be in Afghanistan. Although he wanted to accompany his parents in Bernard's SUV he knew they needed some last minute moments and conversation together.

They all began to share their goodbye hugs as they prepared to go through security at the airport. Bernard hugged all of the youth and saved Raymond and Talinda for last. When he finally reached them everyone seemed to stand back a few feet and watch. He pulled them both into his arms and kissed their foreheads. He fought back tears as he whispered to them, "I love you both so much." Talinda was unable to speak. She just held on to him as the tears flowed down her cheeks. "Sweetheart, please...don't," Bernard continued. He struggled to keep his composure. "Baby, I am going to be okay. No matter what happens over there God is faithful and He will protect me like He always has."

He turned his attention toward Raymond and said, "You promise me that you will take care of my wife Raymond."

Raymond replied through his tears, "I promise dad...I promise. You promise me that you will come back alive."

Bernard was about to respond when Talinda interrupted the conversation, "Don't Bernard...don't you promise him that. You don't know...you can't promise that because you don't know...Bernard..."

"Shhhh...." He hushed Talinda as he lightly kissed her. "It's alright sweetheart." He turned his attention back to Raymond and said, "I promise that I will come home alive son."

"No, Bernard don't...you don't know...you're not sure so don't..." Talinda said before being cut off by Bernard again with a passionate kiss. She melted in his arms and tears flowed down her face as he kissed her. Raymond attempted to move out of Bernard's grasp but he tightened his grip on him and turned his attention back to him. "Son I promise I will come home alive."

"I'm going to hold you to that dad," Raymond replied.

"You do that son...you do that," Bernard replied as his voice cracked. He struggled with all his might not to cry.

Tasha and Stacy said their last goodbyes to all the girls as they moved into the line to go through to the gates. The boys all followed and left Talinda Raymond and Bernard still embraced.

"Oh God help me," Bernard whispered as he squeezed them even tighter in his arms. "I don't want to let y'all go. I love you both and I promise that I'm coming home."

"I love you too, dad," Raymond replied as he released his hold on Bernard to go through security. Bernard continued to hold Talinda in his arms and she cried.

"Why do I feel like I am never going to see you alive again?" Talinda said as she buried her head in his chest.

He placed his hand under her chin and forced her to look up at him. He mustered a smile as he declared, "Baby, listen to me. I have done this several times before. God is faithful...He's faithful Talinda. Come on sweetheart," he said. His voice started to crack again. "I really need you to be strong right now. Trust me baby...and trust God...I'm coming home, alright." He didn't wait for her to reply his just kissed her like he would never see her again.

She felt the desperation as his held on her and she looked into his eyes and said, "Bernard..."

He broke the gaze. He looked down then back up at her, "I'm alright, baby. It's going to be okay...it's going to be okay. Come on, Talinda. You have to go. You're going to miss your flight if you don't go now. The kids are waiting for you...come on sweetheart." He released her and walked her up to the secure area. He kissed her again and said goodbye. He watched as they round the corner out of sight. Talinda did not look back at him after going through security. Raymond yelled goodbye and I love you to his dad as he walked away with one arm around his mother for support.

Tasha and Stacy sensed that the Bernard may need a private moment with the guys, and prepared to walk away. Tasha touched Jaison on the shoulder and said, "Sweetheart you guys go take care of Bernard. We'll meet you at the car. His body language is saying that he is not okay."

"Yeah," Jaison replied. "This is his first time he has to leave a family behind. It's different than just going over there as single man."

Bernard turned toward Jaison and Terry as they walked up beside him. "This is so hard," he said in a shaky voice. "God, this is so hard. I don't know guys...I mean I'm not feeling this deployment. She could sense it...she could feel that I'm unsure."

186

"Come on man," Terry said. He placed his hand on Bernard's shoulder. "What do you mean you're unsure? God has been faithful to us time and time again. Come on, Bernard."

Bernard shook his head. "I don't know, Terry. There's just something different this time. I mean, I don't know these guys. I got a weird feeling we're going to get hit."

Jaison replied, "Oh, now Bernard, come on man. Don't you start talking like that. You're right, it is different. This is the first time that you are leaving a wife and children behind. It's not the same as leaving your mom and dad behind. It's a different level of your heart affected. It goes deep my brother. Don't worry...you're going to get back long before those babies are born. Come on why don't you let me drive you back. Terry can drive my truck."

Bernard shook his head. "No Jaison. I'll drive myself back. Thanks for being here for me guys, but I just want to spend some time alone with God."

"Alright man, if you're sure," Jaison said as he gave him a light pat on the back between his shoulder blades. They exited the airport and headed back to K-Town. The following week, Bernard left for Afghanistan.

~Chapter Seventeen~

Meanwhile, life with the Goodfellows' moved along peacefully. That is, until Suzette Timmons joined the church. Their son, Tre, is about five and a half years old and they now had an addition to their family, a daughter Callisha who has just turned 10 months old.

Suzette Timmons had a huge crush on Justice and had decided in her mind that she could do a better job at being his wife than Nevette. So, she designed a plan to play the victim role to get close to him. She conjured up an issue that most people would not question the validity of. She claimed to have been molested by an uncle most of her childhood. She had begun to talk to Derrick about her problems. Nevette wasn't buying it. When her uncle passed away as she claimed, and her family who "didn't believe her", she had cut all ties and moved to the south to get away. There was really no way to check out her story. At least no one was interested enough to look into it. Nevette warned Justice about her clingy advances toward him. But he didn't see it that way and all but chastised Nevette for not having compassion for Suzette. He accused Nevette of jealousy. This of course infuriated Nevette even the more.

Nevette and the other women of Victory Tabernacle Church all kept a close eye on her. She and Lindsay were out to lunch at a local restaurant one day when Suzette entered. Nevette was glad to be able to put a face to the woman she had been telling Lindsay about and shared her concerns with.

She sarcastically laughed as she commented to Lindsay during a phone conversation one day about how Justice hadn't wanted her on the Falcons therapist team to have close contact with all those men. He always thought her touch was arousing even if she hadn't intended for it to be. He often pointed out how anointed she was and how much attention she drew from the men in the church.

But he himself on this particular occasion was blinded by ministry when it came to Suzette Timmons. She began to let it be known to Nevette in subtle ways that she was in competition for Derrick's love;

188

a very bold move to say the least. But Nevette being very confident in both her marriage and her husband did not feel the least bit threatened by her at first.

Nevette was already extremely unhappy because she never wanted to join this particular church in the first place. She listened to the then favorable advice of others to allow her husband to choose a house of worship for the family. Derrick had been somewhat intimidated at times of Nevette's insight into the things of God. He had been licensed shortly after they had joined the church a few years ago. Nevette had cautioned him on allowing man to advance him before God had completely equipped him. Although she knew he was called to the ministry, she did not feel he was quite ready for the role that this particular pastor had placed upon him.

It soon became apparent to Nevette that this woman had the potential to be very dangerous and it wasn't long before Justice and Nevette begin to have arguments over Suzette. On this particular Sunday things seemed to not only escalate to a heated debate, but went much further than they both expected or were comfortable with.

"Why are you always protecting her Justice?" Nevette said slightly raising her voice. "She is not a victim Justice can't you see what she is trying to do?"

Justice looked up as if asking God for guidance and then said carefully, "I'm not protecting her Nevette. Sweetheart, she just needs friends. Just try being her friend and minister to her baby, then you'll see...,"

"She doesn't want to be my friend Justice, she wants to take my place," Nevette said cutting him off.

Justice said as he reached out to touch her, "Oh sweetheart, come on. That is not going to happen. Honey, I am not the least bit attracted to her."

"It's not about your attraction to her. It's about her attraction to you. Justice you need to take this seriously. She makes me nervous and I don't trust her. She wants me out of the way baby. She is different with me than she is with you. She does everything she can to be involved with everything you do in the church. Why can't you see it Justice?" Nevette said as desperation entered her voice.

"Why can't you see that she just needs friend's baby?" Justice replied.

"Okay, then, if she needs friends and help then she should be coming to the ladies. She has nothing to do with us. She always comes to you Justice can't you see? Baby please..." Nevette said before Justice interrupted her.

"The reason she doesn't come to the ladies of the church is because none of you show her any love and compassion baby," he said in a very sarcastic tone.

"Well, apparently Mr. Goodfellow, you're showing enough love for all of us," Nevette shot a sarcastic tone back at him.

"Come on, Naythia. You know better than that baby. I have no interest in that woman what so ever sweetheart. She needs help spiritually," Justice said in a calmer tone.

"More like mentally," Nevette replied.

"Nevette that's not fair baby," Justice said slightly elevating his voice again.

"What is it about her that makes you defend her Derrick?" Nevette asked in a very irritated tone.

"What is it about her that makes you attack her, Nevette? You're acting like a jealous wife!" Justice shot back at her.

"Derrick Justice Goodfellow, II. I can't believe you just said that to me," Nevette said, almost in tears.

She started to walk away from him. He grabbed her by the arm and said, "Wait, baby, listen to me."

"Let me go, Derrick. I'm not going to do this here at church. I'm not going to air our problems in front of everybody," she said as she pulled away from him.

"Problems? What problems? Nevette you're the only one that has a problem with this," Derrick said. He raised his tone again.

"Derrick!" Nevette said in a hurtful and frustrated tone. She shook her head as though she needed a moment to collect her thoughts and then said, "...ok you win. Go ahead...minister to her until the cows come home, I don't care!" She then turned to walk away from him again.

"Oh, now come on, Naythia," Derrick replied. He grabbed her by the arm again. He realized this argument was about to go too far.

"LET GO OF ME DERRICK! YOU WIN!" She yelled as she pulled away from him. She lowered her tone and fought back tears she continued, "Minister to her...do whatever you want, I'm done with it. But, I will say this. You better have her under control Derrick. Because if something happens to one of us, when she finally realizes that you don't want her and does something crazy, I will never forgive you Derrick. You have no idea what you're dealing with. She is not what you think she is."

"Nevette, what's going to happen? That woman is not interested in me like that baby," Derrick replied defensively.

"Derrick how can you be so dull, everyone sees it but you. Look...I'm outta here. Go ahead Minister Goodfellow, put your missionary hat back on and get to work. I'm taking our children home, so I guess I'll see you when you get back from your bi-weekly missionary trip," Nevette replied sarcastically as she turned to walk away. She headed down to children's church to gather Tre and Callisha and left the church as tears all but rolled down her face.

A few of the men walked up to Derrick and asked him was everything okay with him and Nevette. He replied everything was fine

190

that Nevette was just being a little jealous and unreasonable. Minister Darrin Jenson waited until the rest of the men left and asked if he could have a minute with Derrick.

"Sure, Minister Jenson what is it?" Derrick asked.

"Tread carefully with this, Derrick. A lot of times women see things that we men overlook. I've never seen your wife opposed to you ministering to anyone...I mean...just take that into consideration. You know Evangelist Goodfellow better than anyone in the church. So you are the only one that knows if she is out of character right now. Search yourself Derrick and make sure..." he replied unable to finish the last statement because Derrick interrupted.

"Okay Darrin, I hear you. But like I told Nevette...I am not the least bit interested in Suzette Timmons. She has been through a lot and it is our job to minister to her," Derrick said rather defensively.

"Yes, you are correct on that. But did you ever stop to ask yourself why the women are not taking care of her? I've never known them to turn away ministering to anyone. I mean...we have several women in this church who have been through molestation that could help her get to the other side of through. But instead of talking to the women she chooses you Derrick...just tread carefully my brother. Your first obligation is to love your wife as Christ loved the church. Your wife is clearly not happy with the situation. The church is only as healthy as the family units that make it up," he said as he shook Derrick's hand. He walked away without waiting for a response. As he stood there alone, Derrick pondered his and Nevette's statements as Suzette walked up to him. She had witnessed the conversation with him and Nevette. She was elated that he had defended and chose her over his wife.

"Today is the day that I will turn up the heat," she thought. "I really appreciate your staying to talk with me, Minister Goodfellow. I have really been down lately. I thought your wife was staying today?" she asked. She knew full well that the opposite was true.

"She needed to get the kids home," Derrick replied not wanting to expose his wife's disassociation with her.

"Ok, shall we begin then," she said in an almost seductive tone that he totally missed.

"Yeah, sure," he replied as they enter one of the prayer rooms. He is unsure why he decided to leave the door open for the session. He sat down on the couch as he said they should pray before they can get started.

She did not wait nor want to pray. She moved over to sit beside him, put her head in her hand and sighed, "Every time I think I'm past this, it just seems to take over my thoughts again."

She then leaned her head on Derrick's shoulder and pretended to weep. He was somewhat uncomfortable with the situation but didn't say anything. She wept as she talked about her situation and inched

191

in until she was almost in the center if his chest. She placed her hand on his chest and wiped her tears in a way that slightly caressed him as well as left evidence on his shirt that she was there. "I'm gonna get past this," she said softly as if recovering from the sorrow of her thoughts but did not remove her head from his chest. "I have to because it's controlling my life." Then without warning she leaned up and kissed his cheek and lips before he could respond to her. His reflex was somewhat slow because she had completely caught him off guard.

He pushed her away and stood up. He said, "Whoa...what are you doing, Sister Timmons?"

"Oh come on, Derrick. It was just a matter of time before this happened. I felt your attraction to me the first time we met. And how you took up for me with Nevette earlier...I knew today would be the day that we would share our first kiss," she said as she attempted to walk into his arms.

Derrick turned and took a few steps away from her. He felt absolutely dumbfounded as he realized that Nevette had discerned the situation correctly. He immediately felt guilty of everything he said to his wife earlier. He saw a big piece of humble pie coming with dinner tonight and he owed his wife a huge apology as well.

He turned back toward her and said, "Look Sister Timmons, you have greatly misunderstood my actions. I love my wife. I have no interest in you other than to minister to you. With that being said I don't think it's a good idea from me to continue counseling you. I will inform pastor to assign a female minister to you tomorrow. For now I think we need to close out this session and leave. My wife is waiting on me."

"You don't have to be ashamed of your feelings for me Derrick," she said as she walked dangerously close to him. "Don't worry. I won't tell your wife. I'm willing to share until you can break it to her."

"Break what to her?" Derrick replied. He felt the panic that had filled the air in the room.

"The divorce...what else?" she replied in no uncertain terms.

"Now I know you have the wrong impression Sister Timmons. I don't have any feelings for you other than on a professional and spiritual level," he replied. He felt he has lost control of the situation.

Before he could respond she walked up to him and placed her arms around his neck and came close to kissing him again. She missed her target and landed on the side of his face and hit his shirt collar as well. He grabbed her arms and pulled them from around his neck and pushed her away.

"Whoa, whoa, whoa, Sister Timmons. This is not going to happen!" He replied and stepped back from her yet again. "We had better leave...this session is over and I won't be able to see you anymore. I am positive I am ill equipped to minister to you about your situation."

192

"Oh you'll see me, Derrick...you'll see me or you'll be sorry," she said with a seductive but evil look as she walked by him. She touched his chest as she went by him and said, "It'll work out you'll see. We should keep us a secret for now." She winked at him as she exited the prayer room, seemingly in complete control of the situation.

He stood there momentarily after she left dumbfounded. "Derrick, how could you not see that coming?" He thought. He rubbed his hands over his head and terror hit him as he thought about her words, *"you'll see me or you'll be sorry."* He also remembered what Nevette had said just about a half hour before, *"if something happens to one of us when she finally realizes you don't want her and does something crazy, I will never forgive you Derrick."* He cried out, "Oh God! Please protect my family! Forgive my arrogance God...oh God please help me. I've erred Lord...I've erred."

He locked up and left the church. As he drove home, he replayed the scene in his head over and over again. He arrived at home but remained in the car for a few moments to ponder what he would say to his wife. Finally he exited the car and entered the house. He had not realized he had lipstick on his shirt or face. He walked into the kitchen not sure if he should mention any of this to Nevette. He was at the refrigerator getting a glass of juice when Nevette walked in. Tre and Callisha were with their grandparents. Nevette had stopped at Wal-Mart on the way home and run into them. Of course Callisha wanted to go with Nanna and Papa so she and Tre left with them. They were due to bring them home in a few hours.

Derrick took a deep breath as he turned toward Nevette. She walked up to him and asked how the session went. He decided that he wouldn't say anything about it and would just assign her a new counselor and let it go.

He answered as he took his jacket off, "It was okay but she needs more help than what I can give, so I'm gonna ask pastor to assign another minister to her."

She looked at him with both hurt and disgust on her face as she walked up to him. He reeked of Suzette's cheap perfume.

He took a defensive mode as he said to her, "What?" He had no idea why she looked at him like that. "I thought that would make you happy baby. You win...I'm not going to minister to her anymore."

"Derrick, you are so full of it," Nevette said. She grabbed his collar with one hand and rubbed the lip stick off his face with the other. She held up her finger so he could see it and all but yelled, "I don't know...it looks like you gave her a lot of help to me." Then she wiped the lipstick off her finger onto his shirt and walked away in tears.

He went behind her and grabbed her by the arm. He said, "Wait, baby, it's not what you think. Okay, you were right sweetheart. I was talking with her and all off a sudden she just kissed me and started talking crazy about me and her and letting you down easy...it was crazy! I didn't know what to do Nevette."

"Derrick, you have lipstick on your shirt and face! And you have her perfume all over your shoulders and chest. It doesn't exactly look like you were caught off guard to me. Derrick, you're 6'4" and 240 lbs. She is no bigger than me and you're not going to convince me that she man handled or strong armed you. She touched you more than once to get her perfume all over you," she said as she pulled from his grasp and walked away from him again.

"This is not happening to me," he thought as he followed Nevette to their bedroom. When he caught up to her he said, "Honey, look, it really wasn't like that. You have every reason to be upset about this. I know it looks suspicious but baby you have to trust me. I'm your husband..."

"Really Derrick? Because earlier I couldn't tell whose back you had or side you were on. I was a jealous wife and she was a helpless victim that your "non-understanding" wife refused to help. You stood there and accused me of attacking her and being compassionless! I mean...compassionless Derrick? She played you like a flute and now you walk in this door smelling like her with her lipstick all over you and I'm supposed to just be okay with it and trust you!" She let out a heavy sigh. She knocked his hand away as he attempted to grab her as she walked by him out of the bedroom back into the kitchen.

"Sweetheart...Nevette...please baby, let's not do this. Let's not fight over her because she is not worth it," he replied. He had failed miserably at disarming her.

She let out a sarcastic laugh as she replied, "Are you kidding me? Derrick, you are a real piece of work, you know that? A few hours ago she was not only worth fighting for she was worth defending and I was a jealous wife! So spare me Derrick...and excuse me if I don't feel "compassion" for you in your self-imposed dilemma."

As he stood there with his head down and his hands on his hips searching for an appropriate response, Nevette retreated down the hall to the office that doubled as her prayer room. She closed and locked the door behind her. He heard the door close and the lock click. As he stood there in the kitchen alone, he had a sinking feeling that he would spend many more days this way.

Up to this point he could not remember a time that he and Nevette had stood on opposite sides on anything let alone have a verbal fight about anything. He found himself in strange territory and without direction on to how to proceed.

He walked into the living room and knelt to pray. He could feel tears form and begin to fall as he cried out unto to the Lord:

Father,

God...please I need Your help. I'm desperate God. I find myself on unfamiliar ground and in need of Your counsel Lord. I first ask You to forgive me Father. In my arrogance and stupidity I have put enmity between me and my wife. I have allowed an outside source to bring division in my household. The hurt in my wife's eyes is something that I never thought I would see as a result of my actions. I'm afraid God...I'm afraid that this will get out of hand. Please God intervene in our lives and on our behalves.

Jesus, I have no idea what to do...please help me! This woman God...I don't know what to do about her. I don't know how to proceed...what do I say to her Lord...what do I do...how do I handle it Father? I have erred Lord and played the fool...help me God. All that You have entrusted me with is at stake. I stand to lose everything You have blessed me with if this situation takes a turn for the worse. I love my wife Lord. Please mend the wounds in her heart that have been inflicted by my hand in the course of this current situation.

Father, I pray for peace for my home. Lord I am in need of the comfort and guidance of the Holy Spirit. Lord here I am, kneeling and asking for Your mercy and grace in my dilemma...

The doorbell rang and interrupted his prayer session. He rose and wiped his tears as he answered the door. His knew it would be his mother bringing the children home. He put on the best face he could as he opened the door.

"Daddy," Callisha cried out as she held her hands out for her father to take her.

Tre was equally happy to see his father. His mother on the other hand read him and inquired of him was everything okay.

"Hey DJ. Is everything alright son?" She asked Derrick. Tre ran off down the hall to look for his mother.

"I don't know mom," he answered as he walked into the living room to sit down. She closed the door and followed him feeling somewhat alarmed.

He sat down on the couch as he said, "Oh God mom I have got myself in a situation I thought I would never be in."

"Let me guess...Suzette Timmons," she said. She placed her hand on his knee to comfort him.

He looked at his mother. He was both amazed and confused. "Mom how did you..."

She held a hand up to stop him. "Nevette shared her concerns with me about her a few weeks ago dear."

Before he could say another word Tre rushed into the room and asked, "Daddy, where is mommy?"

"She is in her prayer room, Tre," he answered as turned his attention to Tre. He turned back to his mom and said, "Wait a minute mom. Let me take the kids to Tre's room. Hey Tre come on son, you guys play in your room while I talk with Nanna for a bit." He stood and walked down the hall to Tre's room. Callisha felt her father's despair and was somewhat clingy as he attempted to put her down in the floor to play but reluctantly stayed and started to play with her big brother.

He returned to the living room and sat down beside his mother. "What happened son?" she asked.

Derrick proceeded to fill her in on the events of the last few months. She sat quietly and listened without interrupting him. Although she knew some of what he would say because of previous conversations with Nevette, she felt that he needed to hear himself say it out of his mouth to get the full gravity of the situation. Her theory proved correct because near the end of him narrating the events that led up to where they were that very moment, he dropped his head and fought back tears.

When he had finished she replied, "Well son I can't say that all this is new to me. Nevette and I, among others had been praying that God would open your eyes to the truth about this woman. I guess we should have prayed that it didn't come in a way that would threaten your relationship with Nevette and cause serious tension between you two. Listen Derrick, she is doing the right thing...she is praying. Trust the God in her to mend the rips she felt at this moment. Do you want me to take the kids back home with me tonight?"

"No mom, we should be okay," he replied. He tried to sound confident but was anything but. "Besides, if they aren't here I probably won't have anyone to talk too."

They share a laugh at that comment as she rose to leave. "Okay son well tell Nevette I said hello and I'll be praying for you two."

"Thanks mom," he said and kissed her goodbye.

He closed the door behind her, locked it and headed down the hall to check on the children. He listened as Tre shared about their afternoon with Nanna.

~Chapter Eighteen~

Nevette emerged from her prayer room an hour later. She proceeded to the kitchen to prepare dinner for her family. Tre heard his mom come out of the room and ran out to meet her. Derrick picked Lisha up and followed Tre out to the kitchen.

"Mommy, I thought you were going to stay in there all day. I missed you," Tre exclaimed as he hugged his mother.

"Oh Tre, mommy is sorry she stayed in there so long, but she had a lot to talk to God about," Nevette responded. She did not so much as glance up at Derrick who now stood beside her and Tre as she knelt to his level to talk to him.

Tre wiped tears from his mother's face and said, "Mommy, why are you crying?"

"Well Tre. You remember how mommy said that sometimes when you talk to God and he answers your prayer it gives you tears of joy," she said as she stood up to walk to the sink.

"But mommy, you have a sad face not a happy face," Tre said very observant to her facial expression. He was very smart and discerning for his age.

Nevette walked over to the refrigerator as she replied to Tre, "Oh mommy is okay, Tre. Really she is. Hey, do you want to help mommy prepare dinner?"

"Sure mommy. I'll help you," Tre exclaimed. He loved being mommy's little helper.

Lisha now squirmed to get out of her daddy's arms and get some attention from mommy as well. Derrick soon found himself on one side of the kitchen and his family on the other. He was not sure of what or if he should say anything to Nevette, so he decided to say nothing for now. Neither of them wanted to have the discussion in front of the children.

He stood and watched her and the children and a fear of separation overtook him. He had to leave the room because he was unable to control his emotions. The words Nevette said earlier rehearsed in his ears yet again, *"I'll never forgive you."* He announced that he was going to go take a shower before dinner. He desperately wanted to get Suzette's smell off of him. Nevette never even looked up or responded to him.

He felt much better after a cool refreshing shower. Nevette had been right about another thing; Suzettes' perfume was cheap, although he hadn't notice that he smelled like her until Nevette mentioned it. They were still busy preparing dinner and no one acknowledged him as he reentered the kitchen. Feeling very awkward he decided that he would go downstairs until dinner was ready. He took his clothes and jacket down with him to put in the washer. Nevette usually did laundry, but he didn't want her reminded of Suzette the following day. Nevette saw him pass by her with the small laundry basket in his hand and was grateful that she wouldn't have to smell Suzettes' cheap cologne the next day when she did laundry.

Nevette had not said five words to Derrick since she emerged from the prayer room and sent Tre downstairs to retrieve him for dinner. As they sat around the table he pondered in his mind what he would pray when he said the blessing over the meal. Nevette put her head down without even taking a second glance at him. Tre noticed that his mom and dad had not engaged in their normal amount of conversation. He asked his dad if he could pray.

Derrick happily obliged, and Tre started to pray:

Father God,

> *My mommy and daddy say we should thank you for everything, so we thank you for the food that me and mommy cooked. Oh, Lisha helped a little too. God, I thank You for mommy, daddy and my little sister Lisha. God, that's not her real name it's her short name. Her real name is Callisha Renee Goodfellow. My real name is Derrick Justice Goodfellow, III. That's the same name as my daddy and my Papa. They are number one and number two and I'm number three. Just like You, Your son and Your Holy Spirit. God please take care of us and protect us. Thank you God for making the food that me and mommy and Lisha cooked, good for us to eat. Jesus thank you for loving us and we promise that we will love each other too like You said in the Bible that we are supposed to do. Help my mommy and my daddy to remember to love God.*

In Jesus' name,

Amen

Nevette and Derrick's eyes met as they all said amen to Tre's prayer. "Truly," Derrick and Nevette both thought. "God had used this five-year old to bring exposure to his parents."

They attempted to have normal conversation through dinner for the sake of the children. Justice knew he quite possibly could have a long cold night ahead of him. He was eager to get alone with his wife so he could officially apologize for his actions earlier at church and afterwards at home.

As they cleared the dinner table Tre ran off to his room to get in some last minute play time and Nevette picked Lisha up out of her booster seat after she wiped her hands and face. She was about to head down the hall to change her when Derrick turned toward her and asked, "Okay baby. Do you want kitchen or tub duty?"

"It doesn't matter to me, Derrick. Choose whichever one you want and I'll take the other. I'm fine either way," she answered.

"Alright then I'll do the kitchen tonight, and if I finish before you do I'll be in to help you," he replied. Ha had hoped to get a smile out of her. But she simply said okay that would be fine. She had not given him the chance to say anything else as she headed down the hallway calling out to Tre that it was bath time.

With the kids safely tucked in bed and prayers said Nevette and Derrick head for the master suite.

As they entered the room he turned to Nevette and said, "Okay, we need to talk about today. Sweetheart, we are inside of a big misunderstanding here. I am so sorry for my actions today at church. My ego just jumped outside my head and took over my tongue. You were right with everything you said about Suzette. I missed it baby...I totally missed it."

She continued to move around the room as he talked and prepared what she needed for the next day. But mainly she just didn't want to sit in front of him and listen. She felt very awkward for some reason that she couldn't explain. She had to admit to herself that her feelings were very hurt by her husband at the church. She felt betrayed by him. He walked over to where she stood in front of the dresser. He turned her toward him and gently laid his hands on her shoulders.

He looked at her with all sincerity as he said, "Naythia, I need you to look at me, baby. Listen, the one and only good thing that I said to you today was this. I have absolutely no interest in her whatsoever. I am not the least bit attracted to her Naythia. She totally caught me off guard. She was weeping about her situation and then she just laid her head on my shoulders. That's probably why you smelled her on me. I was very uncomfortable with it Nevette but wanted to let her finish what she was saying before I asked her to move. The next thing I know she is caressing my chest and kissing on me. I was in such disbelief that my reaction to her was slow. She was on me before I could intercept her. Nevette I love you, look at me baby...I...love...you. Boy did I misjudge her character but baby please, you know you can trust me."

She looked straight in to his eyes and said, "Derrick, you weren't even going to tell me what happened today after I left church. If she wouldn't have left her calling card all over you, I would have been oblivious. You were going to lie to me Derrick, and now you say that I can trust you." She sighed and turned to walk into the bathroom to take a shower before going to bed.

Derrick stood there, not sure what to say because he knew that what Nevette had just exposed was the absolute truth. Had not Suzette left lipstick and her smell all over him he would not have shared the events of the day. But for the same reason that he was experiencing now. He did not want to fight about Suzette and he didn't want to admit that he was one hundred percent wrong about her. That he had no discernment whatsoever and lacked wisdom in the situation.

He walked into the bathroom ready to expose his thoughts to her. Nevette however was already in the shower. He decided he would just sit there and talk to her while she showered.

"Nevette," he said as he sat on an armed decorative bench just outside the shower. She did not reply, but he continued on as though she did. "I really am sorry sweetheart. I was arrogant, prideful, stubborn and very disrespectful to my wife. I can never remember a time when you have sided with someone else over me when I have requested something of you. I lacked wisdom and discernment in the situation. I should have known better. I was just on a testosterone high I guess. I sat and thought about some of the things that I said to you. Not only am I ashamed of what I said to my wife. I'm also ashamed of where I said it, in public, and in the house of God. Baby, please accept my apology."

Nevette did not respond. She stood in the shower in tears. She was in tears because, first and foremost, she was wounded by her husband's words and actions earlier that day. She had indeed felt betrayed by him. She was indeed jealous of the time that Justice had given to Suzette. She was also remorseful at how she handled the situation. She had disrespected him in front of other people. Something she prided herself in not doing. She was known for being very respectful and submissive to her husband. Today she was anything but that.

Justice waited patiently for a response from her and was about to turn and go back into the bedroom, when he heard her crying. Instead, he got undressed and walked into the shower. Before she could protest or say anything he pulled her into his arms and just held her.

"I got you, baby. I'm so sorry, sweetheart. I know I hurt you today, so just cry, baby. Just go ahead and cry because I got you...I got you," Justice whispered in her ear as he held her.

He began to parade her with kisses and you could feel the atmosphere in the shower shift from despair to love. A desperate love filled the room as they began to caress each other and were soon engulfed in each other's love as the steamy hot water rushed over their bodies. The water was both comforting and sensual as they shared a passionate love that transcended all barriers and broke all despair.

He kissed her again just before they emerge from the shower rejuvenated by the passionate love they had just shared. He dried off and walked into the room with the towel wrapped around his waist. She stayed behind and started to oil herself down. Justice looked over his shoulder into the bathroom after he noticed Nevette wasn't right behind him. He walked back into the bathroom and stood behind her He kissed her lightly on the neck as he wrapped his arms around her.

"Come on, baby, let me do that for you," he said in that sweet sexy voice that always intimidated her. He grabbed the oil and led her by the hand into the bedroom. He motioned for her to lay on the bed as he began to massage her body with oil.

Nevette moaned as she replied, "I think I'll have to get mad at you more often if I'm going to get an oil massage out if it."

He smiled and replied, "Baby you can get this anytime you want to. You know that I love putting my hands on you."

"You are so bad," she said as she shook her head laughing with such satisfaction in her voice.

"Yeah...and you love it," he replied as he began to kiss her across her shoulders and down her back.

She sighed a satisfying moan as she replied, "Mmmmm...you know it baby."

As they lay in bed, she cuddled in his arms, rested her head in his chest and gently caressed him. She sighed and began to speak of the day's events.

"Justice, I don't want to fight about her. I don't want to fight about anything. Sweetheart I'm sorry about so many things today. I disrespected you and you were right, I was jealous of the time that you were giving to Suzette. That was the main reason that I lashed out at you about her. I shouldn't have implied that you have no spiritual insight because you do baby. You may have missed it with her but I have always prided myself in treating my husband with the utmost respect no matter what. Today I failed miserably sweetheart. Truly you can be right and wrong at the same time. But listen Justice...," she said as she lightly kissed his chest. "...She does make me nervous and this has the potential to get out of hand. Promise me that you won't keep anything else from me concerning her. We need to be watchful of her Justice there is something very unnerving about her."

Justice agreed with his wife. He kissed her on the forehead and sighed within himself. He knew perfectly well that he had already broken that promise before it left his mouth. He had failed to mention that Suzette had delivered a verbal threat to him that he would be sorry if he didn't continue see her. Everything in him told him to tell Nevette but he decided against it and hoped that the decision wouldn't come back to haunt him.

They lay in bed and talked, caressed and loved on each other until they drifted off to sleep.

But Suzette was anything but backing down. Over the next six weeks she continuously sent Derrick a strong message that she meant exactly what she said and was very much capable of following through with her threat.

Panic hit Justice as he soon realized Suzette was spiraling out of control. His heart raced as he tucked the fifth letter away in his personal drawer on his way out to work that morning. He had not kept his word to his wife that he would not keep anything from her concerning Suzette. A promise he made to her six weeks earlier after they had a very passionate make up to an explosive day.

He had hoped the problem would go away if he just didn't address or acknowledge anything that she did. His shunning of her only escalated her fury and it became very apparent that this was not going to simply die down. Suzette had threatened Nevette's life in three of the five letters expressing that they could be together if she were "out of the way". But this last one sent even more terror through him because she now threatened his entire family.

He didn't want to show Nevette the letters because he had hoped he could diffuse Suzette's anxieties. He also did not want his wife to begin to walk in fear but he himself was tormented and became overly protective of her and the children which brought much suspicion. On several occasions Nevette asked him was everything okay and had Suzette done anything worth mentioning. He would hold his breath every time he answered his wife knowing full well the information he gave was insufficient and incorrect. To be honest it was an out and out bold faced lie and he knew it. He could feel his world slipping away when his worst nightmare began to unfold on that dreary Thursday morning.

Nevette was off that day and was on the phone with their investment company in an attempt to iron out a problem with their IRA's and needed the statements to prove their investments made to date. She opened the drawer in pure innocence and was terror stricken by what she found. Unable to focus she informed the voice on the other end of the phone that she would have to get back with them at a later time.

As she read the letters addressed to "My dearest Justice" she was both scared beyond imagination and furious at the same time...

≋

It had been just over six months since Brandon's home going service and the twins took up every ounce of space Talinda had inside of her. She was seven and a half months pregnant now and had entered the miserable stage of her pregnancy. For some strange reason the thoughts of the weeks following Brandon's death entered her mind. Talinda marveled at how she, although all her family was there to comfort her, still struggled with Brandon's death. How at times even though she was happily married to Bernard, she still found it difficult to enter their home. There were many things in her life that were a continuing ministry to her; the twins she carried in her womb; the love of Bernard, and the bitter sweet moments she had as she anxiously awaited their arrivals.

Because of the drudgery of having to relive the moment she had not looked forward to the emotions Brandon's trial which was set to begin in the next week would bring. She did, however, look forward to completing her first husband's mission that concerned Quavis. Everyone, especially Bernard, who had deployed, wanted her to forgo being there for the entire proceedings. She knew the trial would get her mind off her deployed husband who was due to return from Afghanistan in less than a month. Bernard, however, worried about the added stress the trial would bring on Talinda and the babies and desperately wanted her not to be a part of it. But she knew she was on a mission...a mandate from God. She knew she had to fight for Quavis because God had a plan for him, and she had promised God that she would "*forgive that his work would be complete.*" She had every intention on being a woman of her word.

"Oh Bernard," she thought out loud. I know it's only been just over a month, but I miss you so much, baby. Just two more weeks and you'll be home."

Raymond had mixed emotions and often questioned his mother if God really meant they should fight for Quavis to be free. He remembered how Quavis was affected by his father's love but still struggled with complete forgiveness toward him. But that wasn't the only reason Raymond was now apprehensive about Quavis' freedom. He had recently found out information that all but changed how he felt about his father's mandate that "*ministry was always required*". The news he had received stirred an emotion in him that he had not felt since his days on the streets with the Knights...anger. An anger that had him pondering revengeful thoughts.

He sat downstairs and played video games while his mom talked to Bernard via video chat. It was early in the afternoon on Saturday. He had missed his father's call the day before, so eagerly awaited the moment his mother would call him upstairs so he could chat with his dad.

Talinda sat in front of the screen. She smiled and talked to her loving husband as she reassured him that she would be alright during the trial. All of a sudden, she heard a loud, screeching sound. Bernard suddenly leaned back in his chair and yelled, "OH MY GOD!"

Talinda sat in horror as the loud explosion hit close beside and rocked the tent Bernard was in. She could see debris flying and Bernard was thrown from his chair as the computer screen went black.

"BERNAAARRRDDD! GOD NOOO! PLEASE GOD! YOU CAN'T DO THIS TO ME...PLEASE! BERNARD...BABY! PLEASE! OH GOD NO PLEASE DON'T DO THIS TO ME AGAIN! BERNARD...BERNARD! OH GOD NOOO.....PLEASE GOD NO! PLEASE OH GOD NO, BERNARD! BERNARD...OH GOD, OH GOD, OH GOD! OH GOD! HELP ME!" She screamed as she grabbed her stomach and doubled over in pain.

Raymond heard his mother scream and rushed into the room to see what was going on. "MOM! WHAT IS IT?!" He yelled as he helped her up and over to the bed. "Mom, I heard your scream all the way downstairs."

Unable to speak, all she could do was point to the computer screen. It was on the home screen page of the video chat. She was crying uncontrollably and held her stomach, still doubled over.

"MOM, THERE'S NOTHING THERE!" He said in a panic. WHAT IS IT MOM? MOM! I'm calling 911!" He dialed 911 for the ambulance. Then he dialed his grandmother in Athens. "Nanna, something is terribly wrong with mom. She was talking to dad on the video chat and all of a sudden she started screaming and now she's doubled over in pain. I called for an ambulance. I can't find out what's wrong. I'm scared something may be wrong with dad. And she looks like she may be getting ready to have the babies. Nanna, please come quickly! The ambulance is on the way to take her to the hospital!"

Stay tuned as the saga continues.....

Discussion questions:

1. Were you pleasantly surprised with the union of Talinda and Bernard or deeply disturbed? If so, tell us why?

2. Could you clearly see the direct relation to the book of Ruth in the bible with Brandon's request of Talinda and his cousin Bernard?

3. It what way(s) has the book aided you in ministering to the Lindsay's of the world?

4. Has the book given you the courage to stand up in the face of the enemy to expose the Mother Carver's and Pastor Miller's?

5. Which character did you relate to the most is this volume? Why?

6. Did the book encourage or drive home the need to pioneer or get involved with the youth groups in your local church?

7. How approachable would you say you are to the teens in your church? Has the book prompted you to get more involved?

8. How would you say the author was with assessment of today's youth and some of the challenges they face?

About the Author:

Minister Cynthia Harris is a native of Atlanta, GA. She and her husband of 26 years, Minister Kim Harris, are the co-founders of T.O.S.O.T. (The Other Side of Through) Ministries, LLC. She has dedicated years in her local church writing the plays for the Christmas and Easter programs. Her longtime friend and founder of Still Useable Ministries, Evangelist Susan Marshal, solicited her to write a stage play for an upcoming women's conference. From that stage play, the series "The Other Side of Through" was birthed. Many of the instances in her works are inspired by challenges, situations and tragedies that have occurred in her own life. She implements the power and process of how God brought her through when the pieces began to fall apart and unravel. She is passionate about writing and understands this is her mandate from God. She aspires to reach and minister to the hurt, confused and lost with her gift of imagination and knowledge of the Word of God, through romance and drama. She was born to write, for such a time as this.

~ Ministry is always......Required! ~

Other works by Author Cynthia Middlebrooks Harris:

"The Other Side of Through: All Things Work Together..." Book one: The series began with this introduction into the lives of Talinda and Nevette. It is available at www.tosotministries.org; CreateSpace.com; and Amazon.com.